MUSSOLINI'S CHEST

To Ed with best wishes

Graham Donnelly

MUSSOLINI'S
CHEST

Graham Donnelly

The Book Guild Ltd

First published in Great Britain in 2019 by
The Book Guild Ltd
9 Priory Business Park
Wistow Road, Kibworth
Leicestershire, LE8 0RX
Freephone: 0800 999 2982
www.bookguild.co.uk
Email: info@bookguild.co.uk
Twitter: @bookguild

Typeset in Garamond

Printed and bound in Great Britain by CPI Group (UK) Ltd, Croydon, CR0 4YY

ISBN 978 1912575 657

British Library Cataloguing in Publication Data.
A catalogue record for this book is available from the British Library.

To Carolyn

I

Even the tardiest of shopkeepers had finally taken down the boards and opened the door onto the first autumn chill as Luca Morenelli skipped down from a still-moving single-decker bus and turned, with something of a flourish, back up the High Street. As he walked the fifty yards or so towards his café he was noticed by half a dozen shopkeepers; some of them came out of their shops but he didn't look at any of them. His eyes, squinting in the bright sunshine, were fixed firmly on the café which bore his name on the facia. When he reached the café door he gripped the handle and stopped for just a moment or two before opening the door and walking in. He stopped to turn the sign on the door to 'CLOSED' and pulled the blind down before facing the six or seven customers.

"Please leave now. No charge for anything you have ordered," he said quietly. There was a pause as the customers stared, and then they all rose and, in relatively slow motion, did as they were asked. All that is except Bill Capstick, the barman at the Welsh Harp, who took a second to gather up his uneaten, and now free, bacon sandwich before heading for the door. Then, with the door closed and locked, Luca sat down at the same table as his wife, opposite the chair she had slumped into as soon as she'd seen him.

Luca, though Italian, had lived in England since 1925, when he'd come from his home in a small town in Umbria to work as a waiter in an Italian restaurant in London, an opening his cousin had found for him. His father, while not exactly poor, was from a humble background and had worked in a local vineyard. His mother, on the other hand, was the daughter of a silk merchant. This wealthy businessman had been disappointed with his daughter's choice, especially after his other daughter managed to win the heart of a member of the minor aristocracy and become a contessa, albeit not a very wealthy one.

There was never any chance that Luca would benefit from either his grandfather's or his aunt's connections. He had become both skilled and proficient as a waiter in Italy and he'd honed these skills once in London, so much so that he had had a promising career working in restaurants and hotels in the West End. In 1936, while at one large restaurant, he had met his future wife, Ellen, who was working there as a cashier.

Ellen was born in Devon, but in the 1930s the local job market had become very difficult and she and her sister had travelled to London to seek jobs. Now five years later, her sister had married and returned to Devon. And so it was that a number of circumstances conspired to bring Luca and Ellen together.

Luca was thirty-seven years old and felt ready to settle down. He was tired of living in staff accommodation, convenient though it was, and he had a hankering to run his own business. Ellen was pretty and he liked her naturally curly light brown hair and well-shaped legs. She was always dressed impeccably and looked professional; he admired that. As a cashier she understood business matters and he admired that too.

Ellen was thirty-one and lived alone in a bedsit now that her sister had returned to Devon. She was certainly attracted to Luca: he was good-looking, had charm and was ambitious; but perhaps most of all he offered the means of escape from her lonely, rather humdrum existence. There was no burning desire on either side but they felt suited to each other and that was that.

They had married the following year and taken the lease on the café they now sat in. The café had formerly been a tearoom, run for over twenty years by the previous proprietress. The lighting and equipment were powered by gas, and the place had an Edwardian feel about it, with its lace tablecloths and bone china cups. The closest things to a main meal on the menu were Welsh rarebit, beans on toast and eggs cooked in various ways. When Luca and Ellen took over the café they introduced cooked breakfasts and lunches, to attract a regular clientele from the local factories and small businesses. They spent quite a lot on installing electricity and new cooking and refrigerating equipment, and it paid off as business began to pick up. Luca saw this as a beginning and he hoped to go upmarket to a better class restaurant at a later date. On the first floor of the premises was a flat which had not been used for several years; once decorated, Ellen soon made it into a small but comfortable home. They had just got the business going their way when war broke out... and this meeting was the first in five years.

They sat in silence for what seemed an age to both of them, and they not too obviously examined one another. Ellen knew it was her husband but still could hardly believe it. As well as the shock of seeing him again, she found him very different to that day she'd watched him set off to the internment camp. Physically he was much the same: the long, well-shaped nose, the high forehead, the dark eyes under heavy brows and the slight smile in repose; but there were subtle changes: the thick black hair was a little greyer and well groomed, the clothes less Italian in style, most of all his former luxuriant walrus moustache had given way to a neat trimmed one. Overall, he reminded her of her husband but he had become someone else. The weird thing was that he spoke differently, as if his words were dubbed by somebody else. In short, he seemed more *English*.

He thought Ellen looked faded, and he could see her hands were trembling slightly. Of course, she wasn't as young as she'd been when he'd left, and she was wearing an apron, but he could see from the carefully applied make-up and shiny hair that she hadn't let herself go.

Luca looked around the café. It was almost exactly the same as he had last seen it: eight tables covered in vinyl red-check tablecloths with four bentwood chairs round each table; the high counter with a wooden front and marble top surmounted by glass cabinets containing cakes and filled rolls; behind this a sink and boiler for hot water, with kettles and other drinks and mixing equipment and a hatch leading to the small kitchen beyond. Looking through the hatch was a young woman of twenty or so whom Luca didn't recognise. She was presumably an assistant Ellen had taken on at some point after he went away. The woman caught his eyes looking at her and she looked away.

Before Luca could say anything, she called out to Ellen, "I'll just go and get the butcher's order and a couple of other bits, Mrs Morenelli. I'll be back in half an hour."

Luca heard a rustle of clothes and a clank of keys before the back door opened and slammed. So, his wife had not remarried.

Ellen broke the silence: "I thought you were dead," she said quietly. "Everyone did," she added.

Her husband fiddled with the components of the cruet set on the table. They were the same as when he had left: the salt and pepper pots, the Sarson's vinegar and the HP sauce bottle with its label written both in English and (rather exotically he always thought) French.

"It's a long story," he said eventually.

"You were declared lost at sea when the *Arandora Star* went down."

"It's a long story," he repeated.

"Tell me," she said, digging her nails into her palms and speaking calmly.

Luca had rehearsed this homecoming many times in his head and this was not how he'd thought it would play out. He had imagined that Ellen would be overwhelmed with joy to see him and

4

would run into his arms. Instead she had just sat down and stared at him.

Yet as they faced each other, Luca realised that it was meeting Ellen that had made him feel as much English as Italian. When they'd married he'd thought in Italian, spoken English of a competent but limited variety and cared almost solely for things that were Italian. With Ellen he had seen life through an English prism and he now thought in English. He enjoyed some of the things about life in England that were completely foreign to him before, like relaxing in a pub or talking incessantly about the weather and other things he couldn't identify but would miss if they weren't there; he had become accustomed to some people calling him Luke and sometimes he even introduced himself as such. He knew and could cook English breakfasts and English dishes and make decent English tea – most of this he had learned from Ellen. With all that had happened to him, and to Italy since he had left, his home country seemed distant in every way possible. If anything, what had happened to him since he'd last seen Ellen had made him even more English. This was now his home, this was where he had learned to feel at home, and this was why he had come home.

Ellen had last seen Luca in the early summer of 1940 when – after Italy entered the war on the side of Germany – the British government had given orders that all Italian men should be interned, even those who had lived in Britain for many years. She had barely got used to him being interned when the ship he'd sailed on was lost and she'd found herself widowed. At first she'd been devastated. He was for her the hub of their life together; he was the one who was strong in difficulties, decisive when choices had to be made and was always loyal and dependable. So she was at a loss in so many ways when he was interned, and his death had made that sense of loss permanent.

Then she had, like so many people in wartime, found inner resources she did not know she possessed and had kept things going, both the business and the home. She had done these things

5

at first as a testament to him. Even though she knew he would not return, her memory of him had acted as a spur to carry on and make him proud of her, in a metaphorical way. In practical terms this meant that she was as meticulous in her business dealings and in the way she managed things as she knew he would have been. She even produced a passable version of his popular Italian ice cream in the summer months to make the point. Ellen surprised others, and herself even more, by the way she was able to step out of a supporting backroom role to become an effective businesswoman.

Out of respect for her late husband Ellen also endeavoured to take as much care over his family's interests as he would have done, and in particular his aunt's property. In March 1940 Luca's aunt, the contessa, had foreseen that Italy might become involved in the war and had sent many of her family's most valuable items in a large chest over to England for safekeeping by Luca. Her reason for taking this step was a kind of each way bet on the outcome of the war. She calculated that if Germany and Italy won then Luca, as an Italian, would be spared confiscation of property by the occupying powers and her valuables would be safely protected. On the other hand, if Italy lost the war there was the risk that her property in Italy would be ransacked and her valuable possessions looted. She had not anticipated the Blitz and that her valuables might have been less at risk had she left them where they were.

They had not taken much notice when the chest had first arrived, brought there by a local haulage firm which had its garage a few hundred yards away. The chest had been heavily padlocked, and Luca had heaved a sigh of relief when the driver presented him with an envelope containing the keys. They had opened it only once to check inside and had found the contents quite overwhelming. The pervasive theme was the colour gold: gold fabrics, gold jewellery, gold coins, gold picture frames and on and on, gold. Almost all the items were antique, and though there were some pieces from earlier centuries the baroque period with rococo ornamentation and design, and other florid styles, dominated. After this they always jokingly referred to the chest as 'Mussolini's Chest', as Luca fancied that some of the gaudy things they had found in it might well have appealed to *Il Duce*.

The chest had been stored under the stairs at first, but after war was declared by Italy and Luca was taken away Ellen became increasingly concerned for its safety, especially once the bombing of London began. She felt she ought to try to store it in a place which could offer more protection in the air raids. In addition, there were other concerns. It would have been good, noble even, if criminals had spared their fellow citizens from fear of theft along with everything else during the war but Ellen knew the opposite was true. Only last week Mrs Brown, the newsagent and tobacconist, had been burgled and lost her entire stock of cigarettes.

Ellen did not want to leave the chest with a storage company because she was not sure that it was legal to have the assets of an enemy country's resident in her possession, so she looked to find an informal solution to her predicament. Some days she would see the chest and try to imagine places where it might be safer, but she couldn't move it on her own to try these different options. In any case, official advice was that under the stairs was probably the safest place in a building if a bomb fell so there was probably no better place available.

The shops in the High Street had been built in different periods and some had started out as houses and been converted to shops at a later date. Consequently, the layout of the buildings varied from one to another and one day Ellen suddenly remembered that several of the shops had cellars. So, she approached one of the shopkeepers with a view to storing the chest until the war was over. He raised concerns about insurance and responsibility and damage but eventually agreed and asked no further questions. She had no hesitation in leaving the keys with him as well and didn't give the chest another thought until after the end of the war.

II

Luca had left for internment without fanfare. None of his neighbours or friends had seen him off, apart from Cyril Johnson, the chemist in the High Street. Luca had been taken to an internment camp near Liverpool and he had assumed that he would be sent to the Isle of Man where many of the internees were held. Instead he was one of those selected to go to Canada as one of a group of Italian and German internees and German prisoners of war.

Internment was a dispiriting experience. As an internee a person was neither accused of nor had committed a crime but was effectively singled out purely by their origin as being a potential traitor. In consequence there grew round the structure of internment an illusion of criminality. The internees were detained in camps with few possessions, few rights and the deprivation of liberty. In effect they were treated as imprisoned criminals, and it was difficult for those who came into contact with them not to regard them as such. For those who were interned it was almost impossibly difficult not to resent being imprisoned without trial for a crime they had not committed, even if, in abstract, they understood that internment was necessary. For some of those interned it was often difficult not to think that they must have done something wrong to be treated like this.

Luca had resigned himself to internment intellectually and,

although he thought it unfair, was stoic enough to reflect that life was rarely fair. But Canada was different. He would be not just separated from all he knew but permanently cut off from it. What if Britain lost the war? How would he ever get back? He committed himself in a rather vague way to trying to escape before he got to the ship. He had hardly got to know any of his fellow internees and certainly did not know any well enough to discuss the possibilities of escape before the proposed move to Canada was initiated. Anyway, he knew that if he mentioned his idea with anyone it would become common knowledge in no time; a secret shared is a secret shared again.

Everything happened so quickly once plans were set in motion that he was unable to consider any kind of escape opportunity before he arrived at the docks. He found himself standing at the quay, watching his luggage and that of his fellow prisoners being loaded onto the ship. He was without a plan but still clung to the hope of making a run for it, however futile that turned out to be. As the internees and prisoners were being assembled on the quayside, he loitered toward the back of the Italians near one of the single-storey buildings, in the hope that something might turn up. Then he had a lucky break. Most of the Italians were fairly acquiescent with the process of embarkation and the guards tended to be more watchful of the Germans, especially the prisoners of war, and concentrated their resources on them. A few of the Italians were, however, nervous of the sea crossing and one of them became agitated and then hysterical. Some of the other Italians began pleading and arguing with the guards on behalf of their compatriot and for a second or two all the guards' attention was drawn to the commotion as they tried to calm things down and restore order.

Luca reached behind him to the handle of the door to the building and it opened. Within a second he had backed in and closed the door. He had no thought as to what to do next and expected the door to open again before he could think of anything. He could feel his heart pounding while he glanced around. The building was lit by a couple of windows and it was full of winching equipment, platforms, frames and other such items. Immediately he saw another door across the room and ran over to it.

Still no discovery and this door was unlocked too. He opened it slightly and could see that it gave access to an area which would not be visible to the guards. By the door there was a reefer jacket and he grabbed that as he headed out of the building. He listened for sounds and could hear nothing except the heated but indistinct altercation between the guards and the Italians. Perhaps they hadn't noticed his absence yet as it had only been a few seconds. He put the reefer jacket on over his own clothes, despite the warmth of the day, then skirted away from the quayside and, hiding from public gaze as much as he could, tried to assess his surroundings. He didn't understand the layout of the docks but he could see there were other ships. One in the distance was flying an Italian flag! How could that be, if Italy was at war with this country? But the arms of Savoy were missing from the centre of the flag and the red was faded; so, not Italian, but foreign at least. Using all the guile he could muster, Luca avoided areas of activity and surreptitiously approached the cargo ship at its mooring.

The ship was *The Graball Bay*, registered in Cork. Of course – an Irish flag! Ireland would be nearer than Canada. He walked towards the ship slowly but as if he belonged on it. There appeared to be nothing going on, no loading or unloading, nor anyone about, but the gangplank was in place; could he just walk on? Surely not. He looked around. It had only been a few minutes since he'd broken away from the guards but they would surely notice his absence soon. For lack of a better idea he walked up the gangplank, which was patched in places and rattled and wobbled as he moved. One, two, three paces and nothing happened. Four, five, six paces and noth…

"Hey you! What d'you want?" an Irish voice called out.

He carried on up to the ship and was confronted by a man in his forties looking down at him from the bridge. He had a cap pushed back off his forehead revealing dark curly hair and similar hair sprouted out of his collarless shirt. He rolled up his sleeves as he waited for an answer.

Luca said the first thing that came into his head: "I wondered if you needed a cook. I am very good."

The Irish sailor frowned. "You don't just wander around the docks looking for work. That's not how it's done. We don't need a cook in any case. You're not English. Where are you from?"

"Spain."

Just then Luca saw, out of the corner of his eye, two soldiers walking along the dock in the distance. The Irishman saw them too – he also saw the expression on Luca's face.

"They after you?"

Luca realised things might be turning hopeless, but the soldiers hadn't seen him yet so he fell on the man's mercy in a last desperate plea.

"I am Italian. I have lived in England for ten years but they want to send me to internment in Canada. Please help me."

Astonishingly, after barely a pause the sailor pulled him by the arm and led him below. He took him into a small storage space.

"Stay here," said the sailor and pulled a curtain across the opening. Luca heard him clamber up the ladder and then there was silence. Luca waited with a mix of hope and dread. The hiding place was dark and smelled of oil and yeast; it made him feel nauseous and quite claustrophobic. The hiding place had no other way out; it was a cage as well as a place of safety. He heard voices in the distance but couldn't make out what was being said.

Back on deck the sailor watched as the two soldiers sauntered along the quay, their rifles swung over their shoulders by webbing straps. Even from fifty yards he could see they were strolling rather than marching. They were chatting and looking at each other rather than around them. One of them started whistling and the sailor could feel his own tension ease as they got nearer. They looked up at him as they drew level.

"How's it going, boys?" he called out cheerily.

They smiled. "All right, mate" said one of them and he waved.

The other called out: "Got room for a couple of stowaways?" and all three of them laughed. Then they carried on towards a ship further down the quay.

The sailor went below again. "It's fine," he said. "They weren't looking for you." He pulled his cap off and ran his hand through his hair. "What do we do with you now?"

"Are you going to Ireland?" asked Luca.

"Later this morning; in a couple of hours." He looked at his watch. "The crew will be on board soon. We'll be in Dublin tonight. But what are we going to do with you?"

Luca smiled but said nothing.

The sailor was silent too. This was his ship. He was the captain and yet he had made a ridiculous and cavalier gesture to protect this man. He couldn't let him stay aboard. The crew might go along with it but what about the pilot? What about when they arrived in Dublin?

"What's your name?" he asked finally.

"Luca Morenelli."

"Look, Mr Morenelli. I'm in a bit of a quandary. I would like to help you but I can't afford to be caught taking Italian internees out of England. I think you'll have to get off the ship and try to make a run for it."

"Could I not hide away until we get to Ireland? If I get caught I will say you knew nothing of this."

"Have you any papers or identification?"

"Nothing. I ran away from the place where we were assembled and left my luggage behind." As he spoke he put his hands in the reefer jacket's pockets and felt something. He pulled out two pieces of paper.

"What are they?"

"I don't know. This is not my jacket."

The Irishman smiled. "A thief as well as an absconder, eh?" He took the papers and looked at them. One was a receipt from a chandler's and the other was a wage slip with the name 'Harold Baxter' on it. He thought for a second. "Your name is Harold from now on. To look like Harold you need to get rid of that ridiculous moustache. Come on." He took Luca to a washroom and found him scissors, a razor and some shaving soap. "Shave that off and make yourself look as English as possible and then come and see me in my cabin." He pointed towards the stern. "Meanwhile, I'll try to think things out."

Ten minutes or so later Luca knocked on the captain's door and went in. He had shaved off the moustache as instructed and had found some hair cream with which he had smoothed down his hair and given it a sharp parting.

The captain had now put on a collar and tie and was wearing a jacket with braiding. He nodded when he saw Luca.

"That's better. There's just one problem."

"I know – my top lip?"

The captain smiled, "Yes. Come on." He took Luca to the galley and mixed up a paste of olive oil and coffee which he applied to Luca's white upper lip. "That'll do. It's not perfect but I think it'll work," he said, as he finished blending it in with Luca's tanned complexion and rubbed off the excess mixture.

"I am very grateful. Why are you helping me so much?" asked Luca as he examined his new appearance in a mirror.

"Search me," he shrugged. "Let's just say we all need a break sometimes."

"Thank you. I do appreciate it," said Luca.

"Sit down." The captain motioned to a chair. "I have an idea. Now and again we take a passenger on board, and I think we could pass you off as a sailor who is on board to pick up a ship in Dublin. I'll give you some clothes to make you look like a sailor, but the problem is your accent so you had better not speak too much, or just say you're from Gibraltar or somewhere. Perhaps you could pretend you have a touch of laryngitis and you've lost your voice. Just don't raise suspicions… for both our sakes."

"What will I do when we get to Dublin?"

"There's not too much bother with an Irish ship. I'll get you out of the docks and then you're on your own."

Luca nodded. This was better than he could have dared hope.

"Come on. I'll get you some clothes and something to drink." The captain made Luca a mug of tea and then went off to find some overalls and a duffel bag for his own clothes.

The Graball Bay set sail later that day. Luca leant on the rail and watched as England slowly shrank and finally disappeared, as he went into exile from his adopted country. He felt nothing emotionally other than relief that he was free from the British authorities. His main concern was to avoid any difficulty when he got to Ireland.

His presence on the ship aroused no comment from among the crew, especially with his new appearance: clean-shaven and with reasonably well-fitting overalls. There was a sticky moment when he was introduced by the captain to the mate, who asked him what ship he was signed up for in Dublin, and he held his throat and coughed. The captain came to the rescue by saying that it was one of a couple operated by the same shipping company, but Luca (or rather 'Harold') wouldn't know which until he got to their office. The mate raised his eyebrows but merely nodded and went about his duties. Both Luca and the captain thought it better that he hide himself in clear sight rather than try to keep out of the way, and this seemed to work.

The crew gave him tea and a snack and soon got the message that he was unable to speak much apart from the odd word. Fortunately it was a smooth crossing so there was no need to worry about seasickness or being asked to perform any duties. He spent most of the time on deck, staring at the sea, watching the crew going about their tasks and, in boredom, counting the rusting rivets in various parts of the ship. He surmised that some of the crew might have thought his presence on board a rather odd situation but they didn't say anything of the sort to him.

The most nerve-wracking time had been during the couple of hours he was on the ship before it set sail. During this period he spent most of his time watching and waiting for any sign of the British authorities looking for him, but they never came. For whatever reason, and he never found out, he was not reported missing.

After the kerfuffle at the embarkation point the guards failed to notice that somebody had run off; perhaps they miscounted as the prisoners went aboard or possibly somebody answered to his name when there was a roll call. Whatever the reason, he was presumed to be aboard the *Arandora Star* when she left Liverpool for Canada. Luca assumed that his escape would eventually come to light but he hoped that he could find somewhere in Ireland where his trail would be hard to follow. In fact, his disappearance was never officially recorded, as the *Arandora Star* was torpedoed by a U-Boat seventy-five miles off the west coast of Ireland the next day, the second of July. A total of 805 people were lost, and the majority of the bodies were never recovered, so Luca was counted among those missing presumed dead.

When the ship arrived in Dublin the captain was true to his word. He gave Luca a receipt for his passage in the name of Harold Baxter and walked with him through the disembarkation area and customs without anyone paying much attention. To Luca the captain looked happy and carefree, and he found himself relaxing as the exit gate approached. His old swagger returned as the fear of detection receded and the frisson of getting safely into Ireland grew. The captain took Luca out of the docks, nodded to a couple of policemen chatting on the pavement and walked for a couple of minutes with him before they drifted down a side street to make their farewells.

"That was not as difficult as I thought it would be," said Luca, his pulse still racing after the brief encounter with the policemen.

The captain smiled. "It's all about looking like you belong and walking slowly. People see me here all the time so they wouldn't think anything of it. It's not as if you were dressed as a bear."

Luca laughed. "I don't know how to thank you."

The captain shrugged. "No need. Look, Italians are not interned here so you shouldn't have any trouble now, but the fact you have no identification papers might arouse suspicion so be on your guard." He looked at his watch. "Well, I have to get back to the ship, so I wish you good luck." He pulled out a wallet and gave Luca two pound notes. "Here's a couple of quid to tide you over while you sort yourself out. If you take that main road over there, East Road, and then turn right into Sheriff Street that will take you towards the centre of town."

"Thank you for everything. I don't even know your name."

The captain extended his hand: "Ned Flannery." He walked off without looking back.

Luca stood and watched Flannery walk away until he disappeared round the corner. He stood where he was for a minute or two. The euphoria of the escape and the flight from England seemed to have evaporated. It was as if he was a car that had had all its tyres let down at once. He felt like he had when he was a child and had lost his mother in a crowded department store. Then he looked at the two pounds in his hand. Two pounds: three days' pay from a man for whom he had done nothing. The Irishman had been very kind. He felt uplifted by this generosity and he also realised he was very hungry.

He walked along East Road, as he had been directed, and then followed his nose as he looked for somewhere to eat. As he walked he began to feel more as if he belonged in these new surroundings. He had never been to Ireland before but Dublin didn't seem that different to London. He was walking past Victorian terraced houses not dissimilar to those he was used to, and the cars drove on the same side of the road. He stopped when he saw a familiar post box with the letters 'GR' embossed on it below the crown, the only difference to ones in London being that it was painted green and not red. The contrasts were certainly not like the ones he had experienced when he'd arrived in England from Italy.

Eventually he came across a fish and chip shop on a street corner. So, they had those too. He went in and bought plaice and chips in an open newspaper wrapping and went and sat on a wall to eat them.

The birds were still singing and he felt uncomfortable in his jacket so he took it off and used it as a soft seat. The crick he had felt earlier in his neck and the slight headache behind his eyes seemed to have all but gone. While he ate he turned over the events of the last few hours and tried to formulate a plan of action. He considered he had been lucky, very lucky, and he found pleasure in going over the sequence of good fortune. People sometimes make the most careful and well-structured plans of action, then everything goes wrong, and yet he had made it! A sequence of chances had gone his way, from the docks in Liverpool to sitting here, and if any one of them had gone differently he would be on the ship for Canada. He would not make the mistake of assuming that his luck would hold indefinitely. He had to factor in that he was due a few unlucky throws of the dice and plan for what he did next.

Briefly he toyed with a romantic fantasy of escape to a rustic idyll where he could work (not too hard) on the land and commune with nature far from any fear of detection or disturbance. But he knew that would never work. For one thing he had never worked on the land in his life and for another this country was not Italy. This was a land where the grass is always green because it rains a lot, and the opportunities for lazy afternoons in the sun might be a little limited. He told himself to forget the romance; he needed a more prosaic plan of action. This meant that he should do what he knew best. He would stay in Dublin and work in a restaurant or a bar, and he would merge into the background so that he was inconspicuous.

He had been so deep in thought that he hadn't been aware of the fish and chips but he screwed up the empty papers before depositing them in a dustbin in the side alley of a closed shop. The salt and vinegar had made a beer and a smoke seem very attractive and he was tempted to seek out a bar. But he wanted to get on, so he decided he would wait until the right opportunity presented itself. In the meantime he walked into a tobacconist's to buy some cigarettes and matches. For the first time since arriving in Ireland he realised that he was a stranger as he was confronted by cigarette brands very different from those he was used to in England. Luca anxiously scanned the array of cigarette brands for one he recognised.

"Hello. What can I get you?" said the man behind the counter.

Luca looked blank for a moment... "Um, twenty Sweet Afton please," he said eventually, seizing on a name that he liked the sound of, "and a box of matches." He felt himself colour a little but the man didn't seem to notice.

With a cigarette between his lips Luca followed Sheriff Street until he reached Amiens Station; he then found himself on Talbot Street and surmised from the grander buildings that he was close to the city centre. Nearer the river the number of bars and pubs and restaurants increased and it was just a case of picking the right one. He was looking for a bigger bar that would employ more staff and, after crossing the river and walking around for a bit, he chose a pub called 'The Nag's Head' on Fleet Street and walked in. He followed in a couple of office workers on their way home and hung around while they were served. A youngish blonde woman was behind the bar polishing glasses. Then a man of about forty in an apron suddenly rose up from the cellar and started pulling off a few pints and pouring them away.

The barman held a newly pulled glass of beer up to the light and said, "What would you like, sir?" as Luca came up to the bar.

"A pint of mild and bitter, please," replied Luca. He leant on the bar. It was shiny over a patina of beer stains, glass ring-marks and cigarette burns. The décor probably hadn't changed much since Queen Victoria last visited Dublin, with its high, smoke-tanned ceiling, round wooden tables, and windows with obscured and etched glass.

The barman pulled the pint, first the half of mild and then the bitter and presented it to Luca. "That'll be eleven pence, please," he said.

Luca delved into his pocket and found the change from his cigarettes and matches. He looked through the coins and found one inscribed 'florin' and '2s' and gave it to the barman.

The barman gave him the change and smiled. "Been a nice day, hasn't it?"

"Yes," said Luca, too pre-occupied with his own thoughts to engage in conversation.

The barman wasn't sure if Luca wanted to chat and so moved away to attend to his other jobs.

Luca raised the glass and silently toasted the day. The beer was not too warm and gushed down his dry throat. He looked round and wondered if this was the sort of establishment where he would be happy working. He would prefer a restaurant but would he be suitable for an Irish restaurant or even a hotel? Come to that, would he be employable in an Irish pub? He had no experience of working in pubs in England, let alone Ireland. He looked around the place and his gaze met that of the barmaid's. She had finished polishing and putting away the glasses and was emptying and cleaning the ashtrays on the bar. She smiled with her eyes as well as her mouth.

"Did you come in off a ship?" she asked.

For a moment Luca wondered how she had guessed but he had forgotten he was still dressed in his reefer jacket over the marine overalls.

"Yes. I am a ship's cook but I am thinking of trying my hand at something else." He surprised himself by the speed of his response and hoped it sounded genuine.

The barmaid smiled again. Luca thought she was attractive. She wouldn't see forty again but she was not too old for him. She made him think of a doll with a roundish face, small nose and full lips. Her blonde hair was probably dyed, and she wore it at shoulder length in the style of Betty Grable. Her lipstick and nail varnish were of a matching shade of red. She was wearing a cream blouse and dark skirt over which was an apron. All in all he was impressed.

The barmaid emptied another ashtray into the bin under the counter and began cleaning it. "Where are you from?" she asked.

He hesitated but then remembered the captain had told him that he need not fear internment here. "Italy," he replied.

"You speak very good English."

"Thank you. I have worked with the English a lot on ships and so I have gradually picked it up." He was warming to his story-telling.

A customer had approached the bar. The barmaid glanced back at Luca as she turned to the customer.

"Evening, Jack. Usual for you and Mick?"

The man nodded, "Yes please, Nancy. How are you this evening?"

Luca supped his beer and wondered if he should take a seat. He really wanted to ask for some information about job opportunities in the area. The barman who had served him earlier had moved round to serve customers in the public bar, so he couldn't ask him. On the other hand he didn't want to appear too pushy with Nancy. He was about to move away from the bar when Nancy turned back to him after serving her customer.

"I know I'm being nosey," she said, "but are you passing through Dublin or have you got a job lined up here?"

He smiled. "I don't mind you asking. Actually, I thought I would see what's on offer in Dublin before I make any firm plans. Do you know if there is much work going in hotels or restaurants round here?"

"Are you thinking of an Italian restaurant?"

"Not necessarily. I can cook English," said Luca, "or Irish," he added.

Nancy grinned. "I am not an expert on cooking jobs. We do lunches here, and a lot of other pubs do too. I can only think of one Italian restaurant in Dublin – The Unicorn on Merrion Row. There are plenty of other restaurants and hotels; I don't think it would be too hard to find something. People come and go in this job – but you would know that yourself."

He nodded. He was sure that he would get something, but the situation was more pressing than Nancy realised. He had little money, few clothes and nowhere to live. He wanted a job which ideally came with accommodation and a uniform, such as at a hotel. But a hotel would want references and probably identification papers, so he would have to start somewhere that wasn't too fussy about background or paperwork. This could take a little time, and in the meantime he needed somewhere to stay which would allow him to eke out the little money he had. He finished his beer and offered the glass to Nancy. "Mild and bitter, please."

Nancy took the glass and filled it up as the barman had before.

"Can you recommend any reasonably priced hotels where I could stay for the next couple of nights?" asked Luca.

"Well, the landlord here does rooms if you want one," she said. "They're comfortable and clean and you'll get a good breakfast. Would you like me to ask him to speak to you?"

"Yes please. You have been very helpful, Nancy. Have a drink yourself." He gave her two shillings.

"Thanks very much. I'll have half of stout later." She gave him a sixpence in change and went off to fetch the landlord. A couple of minutes later a large man with a ruddy complexion and dark hair neatly parted in the centre, and wearing a dark grey suit which appeared to have shrunk a little, emerged from the room behind the bar.

"I believe you'd like a room for the night, sir?" he asked. "We have got one. It would be four and sixpence, including breakfast and your own towel, payable in advance." He rattled the sentence off without pausing, so that Luca couldn't tell whether paying in advance was always the case.

"That will be fine. Can I stay another night if I need to?"

"Yes, that'll be no problem, sir. Just make the same arrangements tomorrow evening if you wish to. What name is it?"

"Luca Morenelli," said Luca, worried about using his real name but then realising that he was unlikely to have even been reported missing by the authorities. He paid the man the four and six and noticed that his first pound was disappearing fairly quickly.

"Have you got your luggage there, Mr Morenelli?" the landlord enquired.

"No, just this duffel bag; I left the rest at the docks. I will collect it tomorrow."

The landlord laid a key on the counter. "The room is number 3. When you want to go upstairs just ask any member of staff and they'll show you the way. Breakfast is served between seven and nine." After an exchange of pleasantries, the landlord went back to his office.

Luca noticed that Nancy was busy so he took his drink and sat at one of the tables. A newspaper had been left on the seat and he skimmed through it while he enjoyed his second pint at a more leisurely pace than the first. By the time he'd finished this drink the clock over the bar showed eight o'clock and the bar was filling up with the evening's customers. In this, the saloon bar, there was a steady hubbub of sound from a dozen conversations, some animated, others full of laughter and a couple that were quiet and wholeheartedly serious. He could hear from the public bar the sound of a piano, much more laughter and a generally boisterous spirit. He realised it wouldn't be long before his table would need to be shared with others and, as he felt pretty shattered, he thought he wouldn't be up to any conviviality with talkative strangers, so he sought the solitude of his room.

He walked over to the bar, half hoping to see Nancy, but only the barman who had served him earlier in the evening was there. Luca asked if he could be shown to his room and the man lifted the counter to let him through and take him upstairs. The stale smells of the pub – beer and spirits, cigarettes and sweat –

followed him up the worn lino-covered stairs and all the way to his room.

The room itself was small with a single bed covered in a faded quilt and an elderly wardrobe and chest of drawers. On the chest was a matching jug of water and a large bowl, the glaze crazed in places. The floor was covered in a patterned lino and there was a small red rug near the bed, strategically placed over one of the worst patches of lino. A dark bedside cabinet with an ashtray on top completed the furniture. Luca walked over to the solitary sash window and opened it with difficulty. The noises of the street outside rushed in with the fresh, if humid, air, and a slight breeze relieved some of the stifling heat of the room.

He lay on the creaking bed and a broad grin slowly spread over his face. Objectively he knew that the room was poky and the bed not exactly comfortable but it was great to be there. The previous night he had slept in a dormitory at the internment camp, a cramped accommodation with the beds too close together and the most limited privacy. Such sleep as he was able to get had been punctuated by snores, coughs and a variety of other noises, some indefinable but all pretty awful. Tonight he was free. As long as he kept within the law he would be able to sit out the war here.

He smoked a cigarette and thought about a plan of attack for the next day. After breakfast he would go job-hunting and get his bearings. He thought he should go to the Italian consulate in case they could help him in some way, perhaps with new papers and a passport. He couldn't wait to get going in the morning. He put out his cigarette and was asleep almost immediately.

III

When he awoke Luca had absolutely no idea of the time. His watch had stopped at 4.30 and the fact that it was light told him nothing. He needed the lavatory and remembered that the barman had said there was one on his floor. He opened the door gently as he didn't want to wake people if it was very early, but he couldn't help the door creaking. He walked along the corridor and each of the floorboards seemed to creak too, but at the end of it he did find the lavatory.

After another creak-laden walk back to his room, the noise of the cistern crying in his ears, he washed in the cold water from his jug and saw the 'tan' from his upper lip dissolve in the bowl. He stared in the mirror; as the skin looked a bit less anaemic this morning and was covered by dark stubble he determined not to worry about it. Then he dressed, not in the overalls but in his own clothes which he had forgotten to unpack the night before from the duffel bag.

Wandering down the stairs to find out the time, he found his way behind the bars and into a large hall with a high ceiling and several rooms off it. On one wall a large pendulum clock made its presence felt with an insistent tick-tock. It showed six o'clock; so, not an ungodly hour but too early for breakfast. From his surroundings he could see that the pub had been built on a grand scale. Apart from the public and saloon bars he now found an entrance to the lounge bar which had a sign on the door reading 'Residents and Functions Only' and was decorated in faded fine burgundy flock wallpaper with comfortable rose-coloured armchairs and sofas. There was also a dining room where presumably lunches would be served and which he saw was presently laid for breakfast. He put his watch right by the clock in the hall and went into the lounge where he found some magazines to help while away the time.

There were old copies of *The Dublin Magazine* and English publications like *Picture Post* and *Country Life*. He picked up one of the *Picture Post* copies from November 1938 and flicked through an article about the Nazi treatment of prominent Jews. He was just reflecting that he had never met a Jew until he arrived in England and was wondering why the Germans thought they were so different, when he heard the back door of the pub being unlocked. He looked out into the hall to see a woman in her fifties glance in the mirror and touch her dark hair, her head tilted to one side. She was holding a shopping bag which she nearly dropped when Luca said, "Good morning".

The woman put her hand flamboyantly to her heart. "Jesus, Mary and Joseph! You made me jump. Where did you spring from?"

Luca smiled, "I beg your pardon. I was in the lounge. I woke early and was passing the time until breakfast."

The woman nodded then looked at the clock. "Well, I'll be getting the breakfast on soon. Would you like a cup of tea to be getting on with?"

"Yes please."

The woman, having identified herself as a cook, took her bag into the kitchen which bore a 'Staff Only' sign and took an apron off the hook on the back of the door.

"Sit in the lounge and I'll bring it in to you."

Luca did as he was told and listened to the cook filling up and putting the kettle on the stove and then getting some china out, noises he had heard a hundred times a day for most of his working life. Some minutes later the cook came in with a tray, on which was a brown teapot with cup and saucer, milk and sugar.

"Would you like a full breakfast? Egg and bacon, tomatoes, sausage and black pudding?"

"Yes please, and some toast?"

"Sure. What room number is it?"

Luca was aware that she was observing him rather closely as she waited for the kettle to boil. He looked down at his clothes and saw how creased they were after a night in the duffle bag. What with that and his unshaven appearance he wondered what she must think of him. Her manner had changed somewhat because now when she spoke it was louder and clearer, "Are you over here on business now?"

"You could say that. I am hoping to work in Dublin."

"I hope it goes well for you. I shall serve the breakfast in the dining room so perhaps you'd go through when you're ready."

She bustled off to cook the breakfast while Luca enjoyed his tea. He had come to love English tea, especially in the morning, and he was very pleased that Irish tea was pretty much exactly the same. He had also got used to eating a cooked breakfast in the mornings since he came to England, especially when he ran the café, as it enabled him to work through the busy lunchtime period without needing a break. He took his tray into the dining room and sat at one of only two tables set for breakfast. The cook brought in his breakfast several minutes before seven o'clock.

"You are very kind to cook my breakfast early for me. I hope I'm not a nuisance."

She threw her head back, "Oh, it's no trouble at all. I'll get you some more tea," and she walked off with a rise in her step.

He ate his breakfast slowly, savouring it. There was white pudding as well as black and the white was a first for him. It was a very good breakfast. While he ate he turned his mind back to his plans for the day. The first thing must be to find a job. He would decide what to do after that. As he finished his breakfast he heard newspapers thud on the floor in the hall. He rose from his chair and saw that they were being picked up by the cook. He took a sixpence from his pocket and handed it to her. She stared at it, an unexpected gift.

"That was a very good breakfast, thank you. May I see a newspaper?" he asked; "one with job vacancies?"

The cook looked through the papers and gave him two that she thought were the most suitable. "Just put them in the lounge when you've finished with them if you don't mind."

"Thanks," said Luca and went back into the lounge. He looked for the 'Situations Vacant' column in both papers. One of them had vacancies for cleaners and chambermaids in hotels but nothing for him. However, the other had two jobs which looked promising. In one advertisement a waiter was required for one of the grander hotels in the city and the other was for a wine waiter in a restaurant which described itself as being on the south side of the river. The hotel job came with accommodation, if required, while the restaurant job had a much higher hourly wage but was part-time. He figured he could do either but they were bound to want references – "*Merda*," he muttered to himself under his breath.

He decided to make a visit to the Italian consulate in the hope they could give him some advice. Finding a pencil on the desk in the lounge he copied out the details of both jobs on a postcard from the letter rack then returned to his room. He was conscious he needed to smarten himself up to go for an interview and decided his first requirement was a shave. He looked at his watch; it was nearly eight o'clock.

He descended the stairs and asked the cook how he could get back into the hotel if he went out. She replied that he could ring the doorbell on the back door and someone would let him in; however, he was supposed to vacate his room by ten unless he was staying another night. He said he would stay another night and went out by the back door to confirm his way of access when he returned.

Then he looked for a barber's and found one just a short walk down the street.

A lone hairdresser was cutting a man's hair. The barber acknowledged him as he walked in and he took a seat. There was a newspaper with headlines about the invasion of the Channel Islands by the Germans and further stories about the consequences of the surrender of France. Luca wondered if it would be long before the Germans attacked Britain.

"Ready for you now, sir," called the barber.

Luca asked for a hair wash and cut, and a shave. He had reckoned it was worth investing more of his diminished resources into looking clean and tidy. His clothes were another matter. The barber engaged him in conversation about the war but Luca was only half listening. He was thinking about the Italian consulate and wondering what they would do to help him. After the haircut and shave Luca went back to his hotel and looked up the address of the Italian consulate in the telephone directory. He obtained directions from the kitchen staff who were now clearing away breakfast.

He figured the delegation would not be open for some time so he spent the next hour familiarising himself with the centre of Dublin, in particular looking out for possible places where he might find work. He was never much of a tourist but he was impressed by a stroll along the river and some of the grand buildings, especially the castle and The Custom House; he was beginning to feel he was at the heart of things in his new city. Then at about half past nine he headed to the Italian consulate, asking directions a couple of times on the way.

The Italian delegation was situated in a large, red-brick, semi-detached residence and was instantly recognisable by its flag fluttering in the breeze. He walked in the front door and approached the reception desk. A man with fair hair and glasses obscuring his pale blue eyes looked up from his paperwork.

"Can I help you?" he prompted in English.

Luca spoke in Italian and explained how, less than twenty-four hours before, he had escaped from enforced emigration to Canada and had made his way here. If he had expected a warm welcome he was disappointed. The man took his glasses off and polished them deliberately with his handkerchief in silence while Luca waited. Eventually he reached into a drawer and took out a file.

"What was the name of the ship you were due to embark on?" he asked. His face betrayed no emotion.

"The *Arandora Star*," replied Luca.

The man turned a couple of pages and then looked down a list. "The ship left port yesterday or today, I believe," the man said. "Have you any proof of identity?"

"No – my papers were with my luggage and that went off with the *Arandora Star*."

"That might be seen as convenient. How can I be sure you are who you say you are?"

"I can give you details of where I lived and worked in London. It must be possible to check my records."

"It's rather difficult for me to access London's records at the moment. In any case, they would just tell me that the person you claim to be lived and worked in London, not that you are that person." There was a flicker of a smile on the man's face. He reached in to the drawer again and took out a large pad. "Please give me as much information as you can as to date of birth, family in Italy, facts about you that only your family would know, places you lived and worked in Italy and the same for England."

Luca gave the details as required and tried to give as many idiosyncratic facts as he could that only he and his close relations would know, such as the names of his pets when he was a child and the name he took when he made his confirmation.

The man took the information down as it was dictated to him, pausing only to clarify details or to check a spelling. Then, satisfied that he had all the information he needed to progress matters, he sat back in his chair and tapped his tortoiseshell fountain pen on the pad in front of him.

"Well, Signor Morenelli," he said, sitting back in his chair and stroking his chin while sticking a thumb in his waistcoat pocket, "is there anything else you would like to tell me?" Though obviously a young man, no more than twenty-eight, he spoke with the air and speech pattern of someone much older.

"I don't think so."

"Please take a seat and I shall see if the consul is free." He took his notepad and disappeared through a door to the right.

Luca sat in a chair against the wall. He had not seen anybody else in the ten minutes or quarter of an hour he had been here. He presumed there would be few Irish people seeking visas for Italy, while those Italians living in Ireland would be in no hurry to return home. Was *he* in a hurry to return home? He thought not. The man from reception came back after several minutes.

"The consul will see you now." He made a short phone call and a couple of minutes later a young woman came from the back of the building to escort him to the consul's office.

He was shown into a large office, probably once the drawing room or morning room of the house when it had been a residential property. A large, bald man in an obviously Italian-cut, light-grey suit rose from behind his desk and walked over, extending his hand as he did so. He fixed his gaze firmly on Luca and took his hand in both of his.

"Signor Morenelli," he proclaimed, "how very proud and humbling it is to meet you after your brave escape from enemy captivity. Do come and sit down." He pointed to a pair of small armchairs either side of a round table. "I am the consul here. My name is Rudolfo Di Pasco. Would you like some coffee?" He stood over Luca, beaming at him and clasping his hands behind his back.

"Thank you, sir; I would love some decent coffee," said Luca. "I apologise for my appearance but my clothes took the punishment of my hurried departure from England."

Di Pasco waved his hand to dismiss the apology. "It is of no consequence; you have been through a lot I am sure." He walked over to his desk and rang on his telephone to ask for coffee and cake. He then sat down opposite Luca, crossed his legs and opened the notes taken by his colleague. "It must have been a great ordeal for you. Perhaps you would like to tell me about your internment and how you escaped."

Luca recounted the experiences of internment and escape while Di Pasco nodded and made a few more notes.

"A wonderful story," said Di Pasco when Luca had finished. "You have behaved admirably. Now, how can I be of assistance?"

Despite his benevolent attitude and general bonhomie there was something about Di Pasco that made Luca feel uneasy... but he couldn't put his finger on what it might be. For now, he just carried on answering his questions.

"Well, I obviously cannot go back to England, but in Ireland I have nowhere to live, no money and no work. I would like to work but I don't think it will be easy unless I have references and can look the part at interview."

"You do not wish to return home to Italy?"

"I have lived in England for ten years and I am married to an Englishwoman so I have roots now in England and I would like to go back there someday."

Di Pasco shook his head a little then nodded. "I understand. There is one other factor you may wish to consider. The war is going badly for Britain and an invasion by Germany is very possible. If the British government fears that the invasion could come through Ireland it may well decide to invade Ireland itself to protect its rear. In those circumstances you could be interned by the British again."

Luca shrugged. "You may well be right but I assume there will be time to reconsider if the situation becomes difficult. I want to stay here, at least for now."

"Very well, I take it you want some financial or other assistance

31

while you are staying in Ireland?" Di Pasco hit the sides of his chair with his hands and uncrossed his legs.

"I would be grateful for help of any sort that would help me get on my feet here."

"There are things that might be done if your story is true. The problem for me is that you have no way of proving who you are and of substantiating your statement. You could be an Italian living in Ireland who is seeking something for nothing, or you could be an undercover agent looking to give yourself a credible Italian persona. How am I to know you are even Italian?"

Luca raised a hand, as if in protest, but then put it down again. Di Pasco had a point. He could not prove he was who he said he was. He shook his head.

"I can see why you might have doubts." Then he thought of something. "But the captain of the ship; he helped me escape. Could you not check with him?"

"The captain only knows what you told him. By your own admission there were no soldiers looking for you. Let us assume that there was a Luca Morenelli on the passenger list of the *Arandora Star*. That man may still have left for Canada. How long will it be before we can check what happened to him? In the meantime I have only your word for it that what you say is true."

There was a knock at the door and the same young woman he had seen before brought in a tray with coffee and cakes. This time she smiled at him and he felt even shabbier than before. After pouring coffee she quietly left the room. Di Pasco offered cake to Luca, who politely declined it but savoured the real Italian coffee that brought back nostalgic memories and made his eyes water.

"I don't know what else to say to convince you that my story is true," said Luca after they had sat in silence for a minute or two.

"I believe you," said Di Pasco.

"You do?"

"Yes, I believe you. I could easily check you out if you were an Italian resident here, your story is too absurd to be made up, and anyone working as an agent would have had documentation or at least a better story." Di Pasco had resumed his genial disposition. "Now, as to help I can offer… Because you are an Italian citizen in distress we are able to provide assistance to get you home and to obtain a passport for you but we are limited in what we can do to maintain you while you live in Ireland. I am sure you understand that. I can give you a little money to assist you while you get some work. Where are you staying?"

"The captain who helped me gave me two pounds so I stayed in a pub last night. I was hoping to get a job which included accommodation."

Di Pasco changed his language and began speaking in English, "How well do you speak English? Probably fluently as you lived in England for so long?"

"Yes, I speak it pretty fluently."

"Perhaps you could pass yourself off as English or someone from the British colonies. It would be much less complicated getting work. We have to face the fact that though the Irish government is sympathetic, perhaps even sentimental, towards Italy, many Irish people do not feel the same towards us because we are allies of Germany. Furthermore, Ireland has no shortage of labour so an Italian with no references would not be in the strongest position."

Luca thought that the situation looked more than a little tricky. How could he pass himself off as English with his still quite noticeable Italian accent? And without references the situation would be extremely difficult for him. Di Pasco seemed to sense Luca's doubts.

"You have shown, from your escape, that you can take the initiative, and I am sure you will be able to deal with any situation."

Luca was not so convinced but said nothing.

Di Pasco thought for a moment. "Of course, you could try an Italian restaurant. There's The Unicorn, and there is a smaller French-style one which is run by an Italian." He went to his desk and looked through an address book, then jotted down the name and address of both restaurants and gave the slip of paper to Luca. "I would vouch for you as to your status if they call me." Then he made another internal call. "I will give you the equivalent of your fare back to Italy by ship," he continued, "and a small payment for out-of-pocket expenses. You will have to do the best you can."

The same young woman came in again and gave the consul an envelope before leaving the room. The consul looked in the envelope and pulled out some Irish bank notes. "Here's eight pounds. Use it wisely to get yourself a job and somewhere to live. When you are settled, come again and give us details of your address so that we can get in touch with you if necessary. If all does not go well with you come back and see me again, but please don't ask me to finance you indefinitely." The consul gave the money to Luca and began to walk towards the door.

Luca sensed that the interview was drawing to a close. "I have a brother in Italy but no other close relatives. Would it be possible for you to get him a message that I am safe?"

Di Pasco nodded. "Of course. Write his name and address down on that pad and I will see he is advised of your safety. What of your wife? I am sure there must be some way we could get a message to her."

"I would prefer nobody in England knowing I escaped for now." Luca thought it sensible that the British authorities did not know of his whereabouts. He hadn't yet made up his mind when he would get news to Ellen.

"Well, I have to get back to my other duties," said Di Pasco holding out his hand. As Luca shook hands the consul put his other hand over Luca's. "Italy is proud of your heroic escape from enemy hands. The ambassador is sure to mention this in his report to Rome and it will be an inspiring story for all who hear of it. I am sure you will be willing to serve your country if the opportunity arises."

Luca nodded. "Thank you for your kindness," he said.

The consul opened the door for Luca and he walked out

through the hall and past the young man on reception, who looked up and wished him luck.

Back on the street Luca assessed the situation. His visit to the consulate had confirmed his concerns about his employment prospects and other difficulties, but the affirmation that he was being realistic about his condition he found comforting. In addition, his limited funds had received a welcome boost but now he had to make good use of them. He began a search for less affluent shopping areas and wandered around until he found a second-hand clothing shop. In the window were a couple of tailor's dummies, one male and one female. The female one was wearing a grey dress with an open coat draped over the shoulders, while the male one was wearing a white shirt and a dark suit with a dark-blue tie, his left arm bent in a peculiarly unnatural way.

Luca went through the open door into the shop. Behind the counter was a thin, weasel-faced man of about sixty. Like his dummy he was also dressed in a suit and tie and wore the badge of office of a tape measure around his shoulders. He was writing in a ledger and looked up as Luca approached the counter.

"Good morning. Can I help you?" the tailor asked, looking Luca up and down and removing the tape measure from his shoulders.

"I'm looking for a suit and tie and a white shirt," said Luca, "and perhaps some black shoes," he added, as he noticed that his own brown shoes were both scuffed and not the right colour.

The tailor asked for details of requirements as to suit colour and then measured Luca. He then walked over to a rack of suits and pulled out three of them, two plain black and one charcoal-grey pinstripe. He asked Luca to remove his jacket, then whipped each jacket from the hanger in turn and tried them on him, checking shoulders, underarms and chest for fit.

While the jackets were tried on Luca looked at his changing image in the mirror and moved this way and that to try them for comfort. He chose a black one priced at thirty shillings with what he now noticed was a herringbone pattern and tried the trousers on in a makeshift changing room behind a curtain; they fitted well. He checked the seat of the trousers for shine and there was none. The suit had clearly not been worn many times and he wondered why – but decided he didn't want to know. The label showed a gentlemen's outfitters in Nassau Street.

He took the suit back to the counter and said he would have it. The tailor then fitted him out with a shirt, tie and black brogues for another seventeen shillings and sixpence. He wore his new outfit and the tailor put his other clothes in a bag.

Luca left the shop with his chest out and walked with purpose. He pulled out of his pocket the bits of paper he had retrieved from the reefer jacket and looked at the details of the two jobs he was interested in. Stepping in to a telephone box he picked up the receiver but then replaced it. This was no good; how could he expect to get a job just walking in off the street? He tried to figure out whether the Italian restaurateurs might ask fewer questions. He looked at the addresses he had for The Unicorn and the other one Di Pasco had mentioned: Giraudo's. Perhaps he should try them first.

First, he tried The Unicorn. It was very busy setting up for lunch and, when he finally managed to speak to someone who could be bothered to listen, he was told that the best they could do was invite him to write in with his details and references and they would keep him in mind if something came up.

Disappointed, he then tried Giraudo's, which was a couple of hundred yards from The Unicorn. This restaurant was open but not yet serving lunch, and there were a few customers with coffee and pastries at tables in the window. Luca walked in and asked the waitress behind the counter if he could see the owner. She asked if he was trying to sell anything but he shook his head and said he was looking for a job.

The waitress went off and a couple of moments later a man appeared from the rear of the restaurant, or at least partly appeared, as half of his body hung back behind the doorframe.

Before Luca could speak, the man said, "I'm sorry; I don't have any vacancies at the moment. In any case I can't afford male waiting staff." He was about to disappear again when he was stopped in his tracks by Luca speaking to him in Italian.

"Could I please just have a few minutes of your time?"

The man reversed back into the restaurant and stared for a moment before he beckoned Luca to follow him. They walked down a short passage into a tiny office no more than five foot square. The man held out his hand: "Arturo Giraudo."

"Luca Morenelli."

Motioning for Luca to sit down, Giraudo squeezed through the gap between the desk and the wall to sit down himself. "That was a surprise to hear an Italian voice; I am very pleased to meet you. Which part of the country do you come from?"

"Umbria, but I left there about ten years ago and I've been working in London."

"You were lucky to get out before internment."

"Actually, I was interned, but I managed to escape as I was being moved to board a ship for Canada."

"Really? That's incredible! When was this?"

"Just yesterday."

Giraudo laughed. "How did you find me?"

"I went to see the Italian consul, and when I told him I was looking for a job he gave me your name. You see, I have none of the documentation I might need to get work. I hoped that, as an Italian, you might take a sympathetic view of my circumstances. I know the restaurant trade inside out and could do pretty well any job available."

"You are certainly a resourceful man."

"Do you think you could help me?"

"You know, Morenelli, you certainly have guts and I admire what you did. I would like to help if I can. Tell me more about your work experience."

Luca recounted his experiences in Umbria and in London, both as a waiter and then when he ran his own place. Giraudo asked him if he would mind a little test and Luca was happy to demonstrate his knowledge. Giraudo asked him questions, such as how he would fillet a sea bream at the table or prepare Crêpes Suzette; what the main regional dishes of Italy and southern France were; and what wines he would serve with particular meats.

"I'm impressed," said Giraudo; "I think you could get a far better job than I could ever offer you if you went to a grander restaurant." He thought for a minute. "Look, I have to be honest. I don't need any staff at the moment and am not likely to in the near future; this is a small business and I am not ambitious." He was silent for a minute while he sought for possibilities. "I have an idea. What if I give you a reference? I could say you've worked here for, say, eighteen months, and give you a good recommendation. I could also confirm that I know you've worked for the places in London you mentioned so they might not feel the need to check them. I don't have much contact with the bigger establishments in town so they wouldn't have a clue whether you'd worked here or not. But you will need a good story as to why you threw up your career in England."

Luca was touched by the help being offered by Giraudo. "You would do that for me?"

"Of course! Why not? You are in trouble through no fault of your own. The same thing could have happened to me if I had stayed in London rather than moving to Dublin. This bloody war hasn't done any of us any good. Why couldn't Mussolini keep out of it?" He threw up his arms in resignation before continuing, "Show me the jobs you are interested in and I can tailor the reference accordingly." He looked at the job adverts and nodded but made no comment. "I must get on now but I'll type the reference up after lunch and you can collect it this afternoon. Shall I head the reference 'Luca Morenelli'?" He took a pen and a piece of paper.

"I don't know if an Italian would be very welcome in a French restaurant or even in an Irish one at the present time, and what with having no papers I was thinking of using the name 'Harold Baxter' – try to pass myself off as English, or at least British. What about being registered for tax?"

Giraudo scratched his head. "Well, you don't look very English, but then nor do James Mason or Cary Grant, so I suppose you might be able to get away with it. Perhaps you could say you're from Malta or Palestine or somewhere. As to the matter of tax you probably won't earn enough to pay income tax and tips aren't taxed so that should be no problem. We can discuss that later. Come back after three and your reference will be ready."

At that moment, the waitress looked round the door at them and gave Giraudo a look which combined slight irritation with a plea for help.

Giraudo said, "I'm coming, I'm coming," and, after giving Luca a quick shake of the hand, went back to work.

Luca waved to the waitress as he walked out of the restaurant whistling nothing in particular and found a telephone box to ring the hotel about the waiter position. After some delay he was put through to the staff manager who informed him that the job had gone.

He then tried the restaurant which had advertised for a wine waiter. It was Gillot's, a French restaurant in Nassau Street which, Luca noted, was the same street his suit had originally been sold; a good omen perhaps. He was put through to the *maitre d'* who asked for his name. The position had not yet been filled and he was asked if he could attend for interview that afternoon at four o'clock.

After the call Luca looked at his watch and calculated he had about three hours in which to do some preparation. As it would now be serving lunch he thought it might be a good idea to have a look at the restaurant to get an idea of its style and class. As soon as he mentioned the name of the place the first person he asked had no trouble directing him to it and, a few minutes later, he stood on the pavement and watched the staff serving lunch. He saw immediately that it was a high-class establishment with silver

39

service trained staff. He was tempted to go in himself and act as a customer to get the feel of the place but thought that might be seen as underhand, and anyway he couldn't afford it. Instead he went to the central library to do a bit of research, perhaps some background information on the restaurant and a little revision of his knowledge of wine.

The library staff were very helpful and guided him to the relevant sections of the reference library. There was a trade directory which gave him some background information on Gillot's and a rather elderly encyclopaedia of wines which contained a very useful guide to matching wines to food; it also had a list of good vintage years for Bordeaux that went back before the Great War. Planning his tactics for the interview, he thought he would try to mention an 1899 or 1900 Bordeaux for a discerning customer if he got the opportunity. Looking at the encyclopaedia of wines, Luca was encouraged that the basic knowledge he had picked up from his family and from working with wine waiters had stayed with him despite not having worked as a waiter for years. After an hour and a half he felt he'd done enough to help him navigate his way through a superficial interview, so he took a break to have a cup of tea and a ham roll in a nearby café. After calling in at The Nag's Head to tell the landlord that he would be staying another night he went to see Giraudo who, as he had promised, had a reference waiting for him.

"Good luck. Let me know how you get on. Perhaps you would like to come round for dinner with us soon? Come on Sunday if you can; just let me know so I can tell my wife."

"Thanks, I'd like to. I'll be in touch," said Luca, taking the precious reference and Giraudo's card.

Just before four o'clock Luca went through the back of Gillot's and asked for the *maitre d'* as he had been instructed to do.

The *maitre d'* was a man of about fifty who towered over Luca and had a girth to match. He greeted Luca with a broad smile and shook hands with him.

"Ah, Mr Baxter, thank you for coming. My name is Charpentier."

"Good afternoon. Thank you for seeing me so promptly." Luca spoke in what he hoped might pass as a rather odd English accent.

"Come through to the office. We shall have a discussion about the post with the sommelier."

Luca followed Charpentier through the back of the restaurant to his office, which was not very large but was neat and tidy and devoid of any papers, even on the leather-topped desk. Another man was already seated in one of the chairs but stood up when they came in.

"This is Etienne Roussel, our sommelier and head wine waiter. Etienne, this is Mr Baxter." They nodded at each other, shook hands and sat down.

Charpentier rather elaborately flicked back the tails on his morning coat as he sat down and took a notebook from a manila file and wrote Harold Baxter on the top of the page.

"Let me begin by explaining about this position. We have enough full-time staff but we would like to employ an extra wine waiter to help when the restaurant is very busy and to ensure that each of our wine waiters is able to have some evenings off. Thus the person appointed would normally work an average of eighteen hours a week. The pay would be on an hourly basis at the same rate as a full-time staff member and there will be a share of tips when on duty. Because the number of hours is variable we envisage it being treated as casual work so that it does not attract holiday pay or other benefits. Would those be acceptable conditions to you?"

Luca smiled to himself. Some of the concerns he had had about his legal status and registration had largely disappeared. This would be casual work, a common feature of the hospitality industry all over the world, and employers were far less bothered with the finer details of where people came from.

He replied, "I understand and that would be perfectly satisfactory. Could you give me an idea of the structure of the working week?"

"Essentially, the person appointed would work on Fridays and

Saturdays from five until half past midnight, with a break in the middle of the session, and a similar shift on one other day per week, which would vary according to the needs of the restaurant. You would always be given two weeks' advance notice as to which day it would be."

Luca nodded, "That's fine."

"Good. May I see any references you have to hand?"

Luca handed over the sparkling reference from Giraudo which Charpentier read through then passed to Roussel.

"Tell us about your background in your own words."

Luca began by explaining that his understanding of and interest in wine had originated in his father's work in the wine industry. Then he gave an account of his work in London restaurants and hotels, emphasising the experience most relevant to the job on offer – to some extent exaggerating his wine waiter roles. He said that he had come to Ireland to try to broaden his skills and had stayed when the situation in Europe became more threatening.

"You have a great deal of experience, Mr Baxter, and you come with a glowing reference from Mr Giraudo. Perhaps you will not be happy for long in a junior part-time position?"

"I know this restaurant has a high reputation so I think working here would greatly add to my repertoire, and I am in no hurry to leave."

Charpentier smiled at the use of a French word. "I will now hand over to Mr Roussel, who has a few questions for you."

Luca looked over at the man in the corner who had been silent up till then. He also had a folder and he took from it a single piece of paper which he looked down. He took off his glasses and smiled at Luca, his lined face now producing yet more lines round his eyes.

"What would you say is your favourite wine?" he asked.

Luca had rehearsed this question. "Well, I am very fond of the wines of the Rhone but if I could afford to drink any wine I would go for a wine of the Medoc or Haut Medoc, probably a St Estephe or a St Julien – not that I am a particularly religious person."

Roussel's eyes opened wider when Luca answered but he didn't comment. Charpentier chuckled at the joke.

"What wine would you recommend with halibut?"

"A good dry white such as a Chassagne-Montrachet or a mature Chablis."

Roussel had begun with fairly easy questions; he then continued with more tricky ones but Luca felt he scraped through them, being careful not to recommend Italian wines but sticking to the French.

Roussel put down his notes. "If I might say so, Mr Baxter, you have an unusual accent for an Englishman."

Luca had also rehearsed this question. "Yes, I know," he smiled. "My mother was Italian Swiss and we lived in Switzerland until my late teens. I spoke Italian most of the time and the accent stuck."

Roussel nodded. "One problem we do face is that our stocks of wine are not being replenished because the French market is now controlled by the Germans. Would you be able to recommend Italian and Spanish wines as suitable alternatives?"

"Of course, but there are no circumstances in which I would recommend a German wine."

They all laughed at this comment, but Luca didn't mention the Germans again as neither Frenchman showed any inclination to discuss the war. After going over one or two queries he had about the job, he was asked to wait outside.

After ten minutes a smiling Charpentier asked him back into the office and told him that the job was his, subject to his working for two weeks on probation. Luca gladly accepted. Charpentier went over the more detailed matters such as uniform and preparation for the job. Roussel gave Luca a copy of the wine list so that he could familiarise himself with the wines on offer and gave him a draft suggestion of the hours he would work. It was agreed that he would start the following Wednesday when Roussel would show him the ropes and sort out the uniform. Finally, Charpentier asked Luca to give him an address so that a formal offer could be sent to him. Prepared for this question, Luca explained that he was in the process of changing his address and asked if the letter could be sent care of Giraudo. After a few more pleasantries had been exchanged Charpentier wrapped things up and the interview was at an end.

IV

Luca had a spring in his step as he walked back to The Nag's Head. By nature he had always been decisive, probably impetuous, possibly sometimes hot-headed. He didn't like dithering or indecision, and once he had a made a plan he would stick with it and attempt to put it into effect as soon as possible. For him, when it came to goals there were two types of people: those who, whatever they aim for, never quite make it but can live with failure; and those who meet their goals and then try to go a bit further. Luca saw himself in the second category.

So, when he and Ellen had decided to start their own business he had sorted something out within a matter of weeks, perhaps rather more hastily than Ellen would have wished. Similarly, once he had decided to escape from the ship taking him to Canada, he had known that he would have a go at it however great the odds of succeeding. He liked thinking of himself always as a man of action. Today had gone far better than he had dared hope but it reinforced his belief that any action is better than passivity. The only real bit of luck was that Gillot's was not too fussy about checking out a part-time worker, while his working hours there meant that he would be able to take on other part-time work to supplement his income. He celebrated by going into a chemist's and buying a razor and shaving brush, a comb, soap and a toothbrush and toothpaste;

he then went to a haberdashers to buy a change of underwear and socks.

It was nearly six when he walked into the bar of The Nag's Head. The same two people as yesterday were there: Nancy and the barman. Nancy looked him up and down as he came in.

"You're looking very smart if you don't mind my saying so," she said.

"I've been for an interview for a job," he replied.

"I hope it went all right?"

"Yes: I got the job!"

"Well, that's grand. I am pleased for you."

"Will it be possible for me to have the same room again tonight?" he asked.

"Yes, they have it ready for you. Can I get you something to drink?"

Luca felt hungry more than anything but welcomed the idea of a beer too. "I'll have a pint of mild and bitter, please. Do you serve evening meals here?"

"No, we don't. We just have a few rolls left and crisps and that kind of thing. There are plenty of cafés and restaurants around here though." She passed him his pint. "There's an evening paper if you'd like to read it."

"Thanks," he said, taking the paper and his pint over to a table. As on the previous evening it was quiet with only a few workers finishing off a post-work drink. He sat down and supped his beer while flicking through the paper. The war was the main topic, and the occupation of the Channel Islands was the top story. As he read this, an item about a ship being sunk by a U-boat off the Irish coast caught his eye, and he was horrified to see that, though the ship was not named, it was carrying interned Germans and Italians to Canada. He knew at once that it was the *Arandora Star*. Much to his own surprise he began to cry, quietly but profusely. All the heightened tension and emotion within him surfaced and then overwhelmed him and he just wept.

Nancy noticed. She had glanced at him a couple of times while he read the paper and then saw him visibly crumple. She gasped and stared at him for a moment in case he had been taken ill. There were no customers at the bar so she lifted the counter and walked over to him.

"Come with me," she said, taking his arm in one hand and his pint in the other. He didn't resist; he just did as he was told as she took him out of the saloon bar and into the lounge, which was empty. One or two customers looked up as they walked past but it was all too fast for anyone to notice what was going on. Luca slumped onto a sofa and Nancy sat next to him.

"I thought you would find it more comfortable here," she said. "If you'd rather be alone I'll go, but if I can be of any help…?" Her voice faded away.

Luca wiped his eyes with the handkerchief she had offered him. He resisted the temptation to blow his nose on what was such a small, pretty thing.

"Thank you. I just had rather a shock." He wanted to tell her, or someone, what had happened but was not sure how much he should say. "A ship was sunk early this morning off the Irish coast," he said, framing his sentence carefully. "Many of the people who died were known to me."

"How awful for you; that's a terrible thing. I am sorry," she said softly and put her hand on his forearm. "I ought to get back to the bar but if you need anything or I can be of help just let me know."

"You are very kind. Sorry to have lost control; I shall be all right now."

Nancy smiled, squeezed his arm then left him alone.

Luca regained his composure and thanked God that he hadn't boarded that ship. He did not cry again that evening; he was too numbed by what had happened and so grateful that ever since he'd fled the quay two days before he had led a charmed life. He was not a particularly religious man but he was tempted to believe that somebody or something was looking out for him. When, later, he

47

read the full details of the tragedy he wept again. He didn't feel the guilt of a survivor because he didn't count himself as having had anything to do with the ship once he'd escaped. He wept partly with relief that he hadn't been a victim of the tragedy but also with frustration that all these people had died for nothing: the Italians, who were probably not a threat, hadn't wanted to be on the ship and then had been afraid to leave it when it started to sink; the British captain and his fellow officers, who had walked off the ship and into the sea when they couldn't save any more of their conscripted passengers; the guards, who were not active combatants but just performing an escort role; and, maddest of all, the German prisoners, who were prevented from living out the war in peace by a torpedo fired by their own side.

Of course, he had other emotions – most obviously there was relief. He knew that there was little chance he would now be sought by the British or anyone else. He would be presumed dead and probably entered as such in the records. He also felt concern for Ellen. He mulled over the possibility of getting a message to her, but if she knew he was safe could she keep it secret? For now he would do nothing.

He drank his beer and realised he'd lost his appetite. He couldn't be bothered to go out to dinner and, in any case, he had to be careful with his money. But he realised he ought to eat something as he'd had virtually nothing since breakfast.

He finished his beer and took his glass back to the saloon bar. Nancy was serving a customer but she glanced at him as the saloon door opened. He walked over to the same table as before and picked up the newspaper where he'd left it. Having read through the rest of the item on the *Arandora Star* he went to the bar. Neither he nor Nancy alluded to what had happened. He asked for another drink and for a couple of the cheese rolls that were in a cabinet at the end of the bar. Nancy told him to sit down and she would bring them over.

They were a bit stale and the cheddar cheese was a little dry but the crust was good and Luca enjoyed them. They were what he expected from a cheese roll in a pub, and there was a pleasure in the familiarity they brought with them. It was the right food at the right time.

When he had finished his snack he felt refreshed, but also restless. The day had been both eventful and exhausting, emotionally and mentally. He didn't want to go back to his room and lie there with everything going round in his head. He wanted to feel the freedom he'd gained, to do something without a purpose, without a need to justify himself. He looked around the bar. It was beginning to fill with the evening's customers and he recognised two or three from the previous night. One of them even nodded at him and he smiled in return. He guessed he could make conversation with some of the patrons but they were happy with the company they had and they'd probably ask him lots of questions; he was tired of questions. He looked at Nancy while she was busy with some customers. She was laughing at something one of them said while she poured their drinks, and Luca smiled too. He found her even more attractive than when he had first met her and speculated about her life. He waited until she had no customers, and the barman was dealing with people in the public bar, before walking over.

"Same again, please, Nancy", he said and put down his glass.

She nodded and refilled the glass, intuitively leaving room for the mild as she pulled on the bitter pump.

"You were very kind to me earlier," said Luca, lowering his voice a little. "I'd really like to repay your kindness; perhaps I could buy you a drink after you finish your shift." He thought this suggestion might not appear too forward and that he would soon be able to gauge what she thought by her reply.

Nancy slowed slightly the rate at which she was filling the glass. "Oh, it was nothing," she said, causing Luca to think this was a negative. "In any case, I don't normally drink with customers. I don't think it's good if other customers think you have favourites."

A second negative, and Luca was wondering whether it was time to throw in the towel. "But," she said, smiling at him as she put down his glass, "as you're a stranger here and you've had a bad shock I'll make an exception." A positive, however it was followed by a but. "The trouble is, I don't finish till 10.30 so that's not much good to you." She shrugged – a negative but with room for manoeuvre.

Luca took a sip of his beer. "Well, I have some things to do. I want to try to find lodgings as I can't really afford to stay here indefinitely." He shifted up a gear to see what the reaction would be: "So I could do that now and meet you later."

Nancy hesitated then said, "OK, there's a bar, Delap's, about a hundred yards from here, down Crown Alley. You go out the front of the pub, turn left, take the second road on the left and you'll see it on the right-hand side. They stay open till midnight. I'll meet you there just after half past ten." She said this in a slightly disengaged manner, like someone telling the time to a passing stranger, then she turned away from Luca and went to serve another customer.

Luca took his pint and made his way through to the lounge with the newspaper. For the first time since he'd arrived here the lounge was occupied. A middle-aged man was laying out papers on the large table which had been against the wall when Luca had had his breakfast that morning but was now pulled out so that a dozen or so people could sit round it.

"Good evening," said Luca.

The man looked up and said, "Good evening to you," then carried on with his task.

"May I ask when the meeting will start?"

"Seven o'clock. Are you attending?"

Luca looked at his watch. Still twenty minutes to go. "No, I just want to look at the papers for five minutes. I shan't disturb you."

The man nodded, and Luca stood up while he scanned the newspapers for adverts for lodgings. He made a note of the letting agents listed in the classified advertisements but could find no 'room to let' adverts in any of the papers. He guessed that most lodgings would be advertised in the windows of the premises themselves. He drank his beer, left the glass in the lounge and went out for a walk. It would be light for almost three hours more and there was an opportunity to check where Delap's bar was and also to explore some of the main streets he hadn't yet visited; he wanted to get a map in his mind of the main roads and how they connected the city together.

So, he wandered down Westmoreland Street and Grafton Street, meandering off the main routes if he saw something of interest. Then he turned west towards Christchurch Cathedral, taking a detour to get a closer look at the castle, before crossing O'Donovan Rossa Bridge and walking up Chancery Place and Greek Street then heading east until he got to O'Connell Street where he took his time walking up and down. He knew nothing of the history of Ireland and stopped to look whenever he saw a memorial plaque which gave him a scrap of information or a story worth remembering. Finally, he went back down to the river and crossed the O'Connell Bridge on his way to the pub, checking out Delap's on the way.

It was around half past nine when he got back, so he collected his key and went to his room to freshen up. He had a shave for the second time that day, a very unusual thing for him to do, then took a great deal of trouble cleaning his teeth and combing his hair. "Not bad for fortyish," he said to the mirror. Then he locked his door and headed for Delap's bar.

He arrived at the bar a bit early. It wasn't very large and was a bit dingy, with assorted chairs around a few bare tables and some stools at the bar, all lit by low-wattage lights around which swirled columns of smoke. The place was about half full and the clientele was a varied bunch: one or two couples sharing intimate conversations; a couple of men quietly doing a deal of some sort; a trio of men sitting on the bar stools who were clearly regulars, with a proprietorial attitude to their seats and an easy conviviality with each other. In the corners of the bar were others, alone or in pairs, quietly and seriously going about their drinking; some had been at it all evening and one or two were heading for oblivion. There was also an elderly lady nursing a pint of Guinness for the evening as if she had nowhere else to go.

Luca guessed that Nancy had chosen this bar because it was sure to be open late but couldn't see much else to commend it. He walked over to the bar and ordered a whiskey and ice with a beer chaser from a blank-faced barman and took a table with a view of the door. Apart from the three men on stools, who greeted him when he walked in, none of the other customers paid him any attention. He lit a cigarette and idly counted the money he had in his pocket. There was a newspaper on the table and he looked to see if there were any accommodation adverts. There were none, and he tossed the paper aside just as Nancy walked in.

"Hello, I hope you've not been waiting long." She sat down opposite him at the table and Luca snatched a whiff of her perfume. He could see she'd freshened up her make-up and hair, and she looked great.

"What can I get you to drink?" he asked, rising from his seat.

"A gin and bitter orange, please."

"Thanks for coming. It's a long day for you," said Luca as he returned with her drink.

"Thank you for inviting me. It's not such a long day. I don't start till one o'clock and I have the morning off, so I don't mind a late night sometimes. Cheers," she said and raised her glass.

"Cheers," he said and finished the whiskey. "Have you worked at The Nag's Head for long?"

"Too long really. I started working there six years ago until something else came up, and I'm still there. I don't mind it really. It's not a rough pub so you never get any trouble, and there are lots of organisations and groups who use it for functions and lunches and so on. I meet lots of different people and most of them are pleasant enough. The boss is good to work for and Joe the barman let me get off early when I said I had a date. I don't often go in to pubs when I'm out, otherwise it's like a busman's holiday."

"That's why you chose here?"

"Yes," she leaned over; "not great, is it? But I wanted to be sure it was somewhere that would be open." She laughed and took a sip from her drink.

Luca smiled and reflected on the fact that she had used the word 'date'. He hadn't thought of it quite as that when he'd asked her out, and it was the first time he'd invited a woman out other than Ellen since they'd married.

"It must have been a terrible shock for you today. Did you lose any close friends on the ship that went down…? I'm sorry, perhaps you'd rather not talk about it."

"No, it's all right. The people were just acquaintances; I didn't know them well."

Nancy nodded. "I suppose it was the shock and that you'd only just arrived in Dublin. I think you were very brave to come here without a job or anywhere to live. What made you decide to do that?"

He was silent for a few moments. Too many questions! He wasn't sure how much of the truth, if any, he need tell her. "It was the war that made me want to work on land again. After all, I'm a cook not a sailor."

She nodded. "Is that what you'll be doing in a restaurant?"

"No, a waiter. I've spent a long time working in restaurants so I can do pretty much any job. You said you'd worked in the pub for six years; what did you do before that?" He preferred to talk about her so he could stop having to think before he answered every time he was asked a question.

"I was a seamstress in a dress factory but it closed in '33 and it wasn't easy to find work after that. My mother was not keen on me working in a bar but I convinced her that The Nag's Head was a kind of hotel with a superior type of customer, so she's happy with that now."

The conversation continued with an exchange of fairly basic information. They didn't ask each other about their personal lives or their hopes and ambitions or their fears or failings. She talked about Dublin and how much it had changed since independence, and he told her about Italy and why he'd left there and some of the famous places he'd worked in London. They were merely setting foundations should they wish to take their relationship further. They had another drink and then another, the last of which Nancy insisted on buying, though Luca went to the bar to get them. By the time the barman called last orders Luca didn't feel drunk but could feel it a bit. He'd had a few earlier in the evening and he wasn't used to drinking so much.

Nevertheless, he said, "Shall we have one for the road?"

"Better not; I hate being in a rush to finish my drink. I don't usually drink this much as it is. I bet my cheeks are red; they feel very hot." She touched them with her hands to confirm her suspicions. "In any case, I have to be getting home."

"Sure," said Luca. "I'll walk you home if I may."

"It's not far; I'll be fine."

Luca insisted. They said a general goodnight to the barman and anyone else listening and set off to walk the half a mile or so to Nancy's home. At first they were silent, the cool air bringing with it a feeling of sobriety. They were running out of small talk and Luca was happy to be quiet. He was thinking about his change of identity and felt he ought to tell Nancy, as he wanted to see her again.

Eventually he plucked up the courage: "Nancy, I hope you won't think this strange," he said, "but I'm using the name Harry while I'm over here; it makes it easier to get work."

"Why is that?"

"It's just that some people aren't very keen on the Italians because of the war, and I want to fit in as well as I can."

Nancy nodded. "That's fine by me, *Harry*," she said and laughed.

Eventually, Nancy pointed to a house and said that that was where she lived. It was a two-storey house in a well-kept Victorian terrace off Rutland Street. As they walked the last few steps Nancy thanked Luca and asked if he was sure he'd be able to find his way back to the pub. He assured her he would but she went through the directions just to be on the safe side.

"Thank you very much for this evening," said Nancy.

"Thank you. Perhaps we can do this again some time."

"I'd like that," she said and they shook hands. Nancy walked to her front door and turned to wave as she unlocked it and Luca waved back before heading for the pub.

Luca began his walk back to the hotel and quickly realised he didn't know the way after all, despite all that orienteering earlier in the evening. After a couple of wrong turns he was on a road that led towards the river so he followed that and got his bearings when he reached it and could see the Ha'penny Bridge; he found his tracks from there. He was relieved that the back door was still open as he hadn't thought to ask about it earlier.

He went up to his room and then searched for the bathroom Nancy had talked about. He saw there was a linen cupboard near the bathroom and helped himself to a large towel. The big roll-top bath took a long time to fill and the water was at best tepid but he was glad to get any kind of bath after several days without a chance to wash properly. After he'd dried himself he washed his shirt and underwear in the bath as best he could and returned to his room draped in his towel.

While he hung his wet clothes on hangers and left them to dry, he pondered on the need to get more clothes and considered how difficult it was to start from nothing. Then his thoughts turned to starting a relationship with a woman. He thought he'd like to see Nancy again, at least to give him some sort of social life and maybe sex. He'd never been unfaithful to Ellen and had rarely considered the possibility, except as a fantasy, but he considered his situation now as having changed. Enforced celibacy was not to his taste and, while he didn't know what lay in store, he couldn't see himself waiting till he saw Ellen again, not if the opportunity presented itself. He went to bed and tried to think of something else.

V

There was a sliver of routine creeping into Luca's life. The next morning, he went down to breakfast at about seven and saw the same cook who cooked the same breakfast and gave him the same newspapers as the day before.

When the cook brought in his breakfast he enquired as to whether there was a laundry service in the hotel, as he needed to iron a shirt.

"Oh, I'll be glad to do it for you," she said; "I like to see a man looking smart. Just bring it down after breakfast."

"Thanks very much. I'm going out to search for a room today."

This was the priority today: to find somewhere to live. So, he jotted down the addresses of letting agents who advertised in the newspapers. The cook told him the areas where he might find more salubrious accommodation and advised him on typical charges for a room. When he left the kitchen with his freshly ironed shirt he tipped her a shilling this time.

From a glance in the windows of one or two letting agents Luca could see that they were more likely to be offering unfurnished flats and houses rather than a room with some facilities, which is what he was looking for, at least for now. He traipsed the roads in the areas suggested by the cook and looked for houses with a card in the window. It was a dispiriting process as he knocked on a succession of doors opened by unsmiling, middle-aged women, occasionally men, who showed him shabby furnished rooms on the top floor of their houses. He was given each time a list of conditions, can't dos and must dos, and a take it or leave it attitude. These were people whose hearts had been hardened by years of having to chase for the rent and being let down by lodgers who wanted a place to call home but couldn't behave as if they did in someone else's house. Luca guessed he could make a go of it in some of them but he was minded to try to start well and not have to win the approval of a landlady. He was beginning to think he would have to take whatever came up when he knocked on the navy blue door of a tidy looking house in one of the roads off Grand Canal Street which had a neatly written card in the window offering a furnished room to let. The door was opened by an elderly man with white hair and a military moustache. He was wearing a waistcoat with a large gold pocket watch chain draped across it and his shirt sleeves rolled up.

"Good morning," he said, cheerfully enough.

Luca had half-expected the man to have an English accent. "Good morning. I believe you have a room to let?"

"Yes, we do. Just a moment." He turned and called down the hall behind him: "Clara! There's a gentleman about the room." Then he turned back to Luca, "Nice day, isn't it?"

Before Luca could reply, a short, roundish lady appeared behind the man. She was well-dressed in a style that had been fashionable some years before.

She smiled and said, "Can I help you?"

"Yes. I'm interested in the room you have to let."

"Come in, won't you," she said and led the way into the house. The hall was not as dowdy as the last few he'd visited and there were no cooking smells. The wallpaper in the hall was light and bright, and Luca thought how much better this was than the dark browns and burgundies that had made many of the other houses he'd seen look dingy and forbidding. "I'm Mrs Donovan and this is my husband, Mr…?"

"Baxter, Harry Baxter," said Luca.

"I'll show you the room," said Mrs Donovan. She led the way up the stairs, which were covered in a geometric-patterned brown lino. The upper parts of the walls were painted cream and below the dado rail there was an anaglyptic, moulded wallpaper painted lichen green. The hall looked as if it had been decorated fairly recently and so had the room which he was shown at the top of the stairs. This room was wallpapered in a green willow pattern which, though not particularly to Luca's taste, he could certainly live with. It was a decent size, maybe twelve feet by eleven, and it was furnished with a single bed, wardrobe, chest of drawers and an armchair with a tea table, all the furniture being in different shades of mahogany. In the corner of the room was a small washbasin.

"This is the room," said Mrs Donovan. "As you can see there's a washbasin, and the bathroom is next door. There's a lavatory next to that."

"It's very good to have an indoor lavatory and bathroom," said Luca. He was thinking of his café in London and the flat above and how the toilet was at the back of the house, freezing cold in winter and not updated since the last war at least.

Mrs Donovan smiled, "Yes, the house was built in 1885 and obviously didn't start off like this. We're not getting any younger and our son, who's a builder, was able to do this without too much trouble to give us a little more comfort. It's a big house and we could afford to lose a bit off this bedroom. You're not Irish or English judging by the accent; are you from somewhere in Europe?" There was just a hint of suspicion in her voice.

"Yes, my family lived in Switzerland for a long time and I picked up this accent."

"Switzerland, eh?" said Mr Donovan, who had been hovering in the background. "What do you do for a living, Mr Baxter?"

"I'm a wine waiter. I've recently taken up a new job at Gillot's restaurant."

The Donovans looked at each other and nodded when Luca mentioned the name of the restaurant. Mrs Donovan gave Luca details about the rent, meals and arrangements for access to the bathroom and said that there was a coin-operated telephone in the hall.

"I work shifts at the restaurant so sometimes I won't be back until after midnight. I hope that wouldn't present a problem," said Luca.

"Not at all; you'll have your own door key and we only ask that you let yourself in quietly. There is only one other lodger, a Mr Phillips, and you'll meet him soon enough."

The room was a little more expensive than most of the others he'd looked at but he thought it was all right – better than all right.

"When will the room be available?"

Mr and Mrs Donovan looked at each other. "Well, it's free now."

"Could I move in today? You see, I had to leave my old accommodation when I left the last job."

"Well," said Mr Donovan, looking at his wife, "we do normally like to see a reference."

"Would a reference from my previous employer be satisfactory?" asked Luca. He took out his reference from Giraudo.

"That'll be fine," said Mr Donovan, giving the reference a cursory glance. "Are you able to give us a week's rent in advance to secure the room?"

Luca handed over the rent.

"I shall get you a rent book," said Mr Donovan as they turned to go downstairs.

Luca was furnished with a rent book, the first week's rent already written in and signed off, and a card with the address and telephone number of the house. After they'd exchanged a few pleasantries Luca left to set about finding another job to supplement his pay from Gillot's.

He went to an agency on Grafton Street which had a number of part-time jobs and, after a couple of phone calls, the agency secured him an interview with a firm that hired out catering staff for receptions and other social occasions. He saw the manager of the business after lunchtime and, with his background and reference from Giraudo, was quickly recruited. The manager was particularly interested in the fact that he spoke Italian fluently and French well. No work was guaranteed but he was assured that he could expect to average twelve hours a week. Luca estimated that this would be enough to enable him to manage until something more permanent came along, and he gladly signed up.

He spent the rest of the afternoon getting together his belongings at the pub and checking out. He used the writing paper in the lounge to write a note for Nancy, in which he wrote his address and telephone number. He then phoned Giraudo to inform him of his new address and telephone number and to accept his offer of dinner on Sunday. Then he went into the bar. Nancy was behind the counter, getting ready for the evening session.

She looked up as he came in and smiled, "Hello, how are you?"

"Hello Nancy, I'm well thank you. I hope you don't have to work *every* evening."

"No, it's just your luck that I'm always here whenever you come in! I have every Thursday off, and one week Saturday, the next week Sunday, alternating. So, you have somewhere to stay now and you're leaving us?"

"Yes. Here's my forwarding address in case there's a need." He passed her the envelope with the note in it.

A listener may have presumed this was merely friendly casual chat between barmaid and customer but the tone of voice and the body language indicated the true nature of the exchange; the slightly over-jolly way they spoke, the gratified smile at the other's answers to their questions, the slightly furtive glance as the note was exchanged.

Nancy saw the note was addressed to her and went into the office to read it. As well as his address and phone number, Luca told her how much he'd enjoyed her company and hoped to see her soon. She came back to the bar without commenting on the note but smiled broadly and asked Luca what he wanted to drink. He declined the offer as he didn't want to turn up at the Donovans' with the smell of beer on his breath.

He'd borrowed a rather battered suitcase from the pub to carry his clothes in and give the impression to Mr and Mrs Donovan that he had rather more possessions than was in fact the case. The more he thought about it the more pleased he was with the room. He would be spared the burden of queuing up for one washbasin and of having to trudge outside to go to the toilet. He would also be spared having to eat breakfast at a table with six or seven strangers. The higher rent was unwelcome but, alone in a foreign land with a limited social life, what else would he spend his money on?

When he returned to the Donovans' house with his nearly empty suitcase, he was invited in for a cup of tea, and Mrs Donovan asked him if he would want an evening meal on a regular basis. He said not but they arranged that he would have the odd evening meal if he gave adequate notice. He asked about laundry and whether the Donovans could help in this area, and Mrs Donovan agreed that he could use their laundry service for his shirts and so on and this would be settled when he paid his rent. Then he went to his room and washed some clothes in the basin.

He had barely finished this job when Mrs Donovan knocked on the door to say that there was a phone call for him which he could take in the hall. It was the company that hired out catering staff, and they wondered if he was available for a reception on Tuesday as someone had had to drop out at short notice. He was expected to dress in black trousers and a white shirt; the firm would supply him with a bow tie and waistcoat. He was very pleased by this offer of work as he wouldn't be paid for over a week by the restaurant and would have another week's rent to pay by then; it was going to be a close-run thing.

Luca went to his room and lay on the bed, his arms behind

his head. The pillow smelled clean and fresh and the sun's rays shone into the room, making it simultaneously brighter and more pleasing to the eye as some parts of it were thrown into relief while others stayed in shadow. Luca gazed contentedly around the room. But as he reflected on how well things were going the sense of achievement was clouded by a sudden feeling of deflation. After the excitement of his escape to Ireland and establishing himself here what did he really have? Here he was living in one room and working as a waiter with few prospects, in a land where he hardly knew anyone. He was back to where he'd been when he landed in England ten years before. But it was a passing thought; he would start again and things were already getting decidedly better, he told himself. Kipling might have recognised in Luca a role model for those lines: 'Watch the things you gave your life to, broken, And stoop and build 'em up with worn-out tools.'

He got up and hung his few clothes in the wardrobe. It was a double-doored oak gentleman's wardrobe with over half of it devoted to a rail, enabling clothes to be hung on hangers. The remainder was divided into compartments for clothing and a number of drawers, some shallow, labelled socks, studs, cufflinks, and so on. There was on the inside of one door a rack for ties and on this Luca hung his solitary tie. He put the suitcase on top of the wardrobe, ready to return to The Nag's Head later. Looking at the almost empty wardrobe he knew that Mrs Donovan would probably think it strange he had so few clothes but he couldn't be bothered to worry about it right now. He would get a new set of clothes in due course.

On Sunday he joined Giraudo and his wife Polly for dinner.

"It's very kind of you to invite me into your home," he said when he met Polly in their flat above the restaurant.

"It's nothing. I'm pleased for Arturo that he has a new Italian friend. I think that sometimes he worries that he'll forget how to speak Italian. Take a seat and I'll get you a drink; in this household the husband does the cooking and the wife gets the drinks." She winked at him, walked over to the drinks tray and waited for his order with a quizzical look on her freckled face.

"A beer if you have one, please." As he watched her pour the beer he calculated that Polly was a lot younger than her husband, not a generational gap but certainly more than ten years. "How did you and Arturo meet?" he asked.

"We were both working in London. I was a nurse, and Arturo came to a dance at the hospital. That was eight years ago and here we are."

"Here we are indeed," said Giraudo as his heavy steps reached the top of the stairs and he came in the room carrying a tray laden with antipasto.

"You don't sound very happy, Arturo," said Polly; "is it the seven-year itch?"

"What's the seven-year itch?" asked Luca.

"Don't pay any attention to her," said Giraudo. "She picked this up from some psychiatrist she dated once. People are supposed to get fed up with each other after seven years or so."

"Well, I am fed up with you," said Polly, and she tickled Arturo under the chin so that he nearly dropped the tray.

They sat down to dinner and Giraudo opened a bottle of Chianti.

"You don't have to pretend you prefer French wines when you're with us," he said. "Welcome to Ireland, Luca."

Luca had a very enjoyable evening with Polly and Arturo, complemented by Italian wines and traditional food from Piedmont.

"You're a very good cook, Arturo."

"That's why I married him," said Polly, reaching over and squeezing his hand.

"What made you come to Ireland?" asked Luca.

"It was my fault. I got homesick, and Arturo gave up his job in London for me."

"I didn't mind the change, and then your father helped me get my own place, so we were both happy."

Luca raised his glass. "Here's to the two of you. I'm very happy to have met you."

VI

As the summer weeks wore on Luca settled into his new routine and was more comfortable with his new identity. He still thought of himself as 'Luca Morenelli' but he was happy calling himself 'Harry Baxter' and playing at being an Englishman. The fear he'd had when he first arrived – that he might be detected as an escaped internee – soon went out of his mind. Most people he met weren't bothered about where he'd come from or how he'd got there. They were interested in whether he did a good job, or whether he paid his rent, or whether he acted sociably, and he did all of those things.

There was one colleague, however, who did take an interest in Luca's background. This was Jean-Claude Braid, the deputy head waiter, part English and part French, with a flawless accent in both his mother tongues. They were on duty together on Luca's first Friday and, during their break, Braid asked him about his work in London.

"So, you were at the Criterion for a time?"

"Yes."

"You'll remember Stan Thompson, then. He was there for years."

"Yes, he was one of the wine waiters."

"You were on the waiting side?"

65

"Yes."

"How long were you there?"

"Oh, just a couple of years."

"In the '30s?"

"Yes." Luca could feel himself getting a little hot under the collar. The questions were becoming an interrogation. Just then one of the waiters came in to the restroom to speak to Braid and he went off without resuming the conversation.

The following day it happened again. Braid asked Luca about his time spent in Switzerland.

"Interesting that you lived in Italian Switzerland; people forget that part of Switzerland is Italian-speaking. Where did you live?"

"Ticino is the main Italian-speaking part; there are a few other areas."

"So, you lived in Ticino?"

"Yes, in Lugano."

"I should think it's a lovely area by the lakes. I've never been there."

"Yes. Excuse me but I have to see Mr Roussel about some of the wines that we're running low on."

After that second evening Luca went home and read through his reference and made sure he memorised all the places that he was supposed to have worked in London, whether or not he'd actually done so.

The next morning he went to the library and read everything he could about Ticino and Lugano and the lakes. But though he did all he could to prepare himself for Braid's questions, he dreaded being on duty with him. The following week he avoided going to the restroom and took his break having a cigarette outside the back door.

As the weeks passed the questioning sessions were less frequent but that didn't help Luca feel better because he worried about being caught out when his guard was down. As it was, every time they were on duty together Luca would be uncomfortably aware that Braid was watching him, and he would look up or turn round to catch Braid look away or pretend to be looking past him. He mentioned his discomfort to Giraudo, who told him to ignore him and eventually Braid would get tired of it and the problem would go away. But the matter got under Luca's skin. He found himself obsessing about refining his story and would spend periods at the library deepening his knowledge of Italian Switzerland, even learning the distinctive words and phraseology of Swiss Italian. But always there was the worry that Braid would check out his reference and find out it was false. As soon as Luca relaxed and thought Braid had lost interest, up he would pop again with a question or a throwaway remark like: "You would know that, coming from Switzerland" or "You worked at Coates, didn't you, Harry?" So, Braid's inquisitiveness hung over his head like the sword of Damocles.

Apart from the irritation he endured with Braid, Luca's work at Gillot's settled into a comfortable routine. Each weekend he worked at Gillot's and most Wednesdays. Charpentier would give him a proposed schedule for the month every four weeks so he knew when he'd be wanted for days other than Wednesdays. This gave him a structure around which he could do his other work. Gillot's had a fairly predictable trading pattern and it reminded him of the old days working in London. The restaurant was large, with entrances both on Nassau Street and the road behind. There were private rooms upstairs. The decor was traditional and well-lit and still had a *fin de siècle* feel about it. The clientele was varied but included many of the leading lights in the several branches of Dublin society, from the arts through academia to business and politics. He overheard lots of interesting and entertaining, and sometimes heated, discussions and was often required to serve copious amounts of wine to relatively small numbers of people. His knowledge of wines grew, and he made it his mission to familiarise himself with the provenance of as many of the wines in the cellar there as possible.

He worked most closely with Etienne Roussel, the sommelier and head wine waiter. He was a man nearing retirement with a shock of grey hair over his heavily lined face. He'd worked at the restaurant for over twenty years, having worked in Paris and Biarritz before that. He didn't tell Luca anything about his private life or explain what had brought him to Ireland. He was generally reserved and quiet but could be sparked into animated conversation by the great wines of Bordeaux, especially those of St Estephe, on which he was something of an authority. When Luca sought his advice or knowledge Roussel was always helpful, and he was not the kind of person to try to catch his colleagues out by exposing their lesser understanding – a fault of too many wine waiters whom Luca had known. Roussel felt no need to show off his knowledge; within his own domain he was the master of all he surveyed and neither the head waiter nor the manager nor even Mr Gillot himself would ever challenge his authority.

Luca got to know the other wine waiters, one Irish and one French, as well, but they had their breaks at different times, so there wasn't much social mixing with them. He had only a nodding acquaintance with the rest of the staff even after several weeks, except of course for the ever-watchful Braid. Those who knew him at all in the restaurant thought him friendly and good at his work but reserved and reluctant, so it seemed, to talk about himself. They put it down to a common trait of introversion and lack of communication among wine waiters, as Roussel was the same. Braid, on the other hand, had a different view.

The catering agency used him a lot after that first event because of his highly professional skills, both in waiting at table and in serving drinks. Above all he was reliable and could be trusted to spot potential difficulties and bring these to the head waiter's attention. In addition, his ability to speak other languages was appreciated by customers. So, in all, he worked about thirty-five hours most weeks and sometimes more, as when he was offered overtime he took it.

Having two places of work suited him and he enjoyed the variety it brought.

Luca's work with the catering agency was much more varied than the restaurant, from wedding receptions and private parties to events and dinners for civic society, industry, commerce and awards evenings. He felt he was gaining some insight into Irish society and the Irish in general. He was impressed by their politeness, equal – or perhaps even superior – to that of the English, and he had respect for their ability to hold their drink. However much they consumed at an event, they always seemed to disperse in a quiet and peaceful way afterwards. Unfortunately, he had to turn down work for the agency on Fridays or Saturday evenings, but most business evening events avoided the weekend. Occasionally he worked at lunchtime and then went straight to Gillot's, but he tried to avoid a double booking like this as the timings could be very tight. Most of the agency staff were part-time like himself so he often worked with completely different sets of people from one week to the next. He could be relied upon to guide the less experienced staff and to deal with issues as they arose. After a couple of months he was asked to serve at a reception at the Italian Delegation. He wasn't surprised to be selected for the job as the agency told him that the delegation had asked if they could send people who spoke Italian.

The delegation reception was held on the first Tuesday evening in September and was a drinks party with light buffet for Irish and Italian businesses based in Dublin and surrounding areas who traded or wanted to trade regularly with Italy. The Italian government was desperate to ensure that it kept its trade routes open, as it depended so much on imports to sustain its fragile economy. On the morning of the reception a hand-delivered note from the delegation was delivered to Luca's home address. He was surprised to receive any post, let alone delivered by hand – not to mention the wax seal on the envelope. The note was from the consul and was written in English:

Dear Mr Baxter,

I gather you will be assisting at a reception at the delegation this evening. Would you be so kind as to meet me after your work has finished as I have another job you might be interested in. Ask for me at the reception desk.
I look forward to seeing you.

Yours sincerely,
R Di Pasco, Consul

P.S. Please do not keep this note after receipt.

Luca had sent the consul details of his new name, address and work contacts a few days after he'd got settled, but he'd heard nothing from the delegation since his visit that day after he first arrived in Dublin. He dutifully disposed of the note, then sat back in his chair with a cigarette, wondering what the 'job' might be. He thought it most likely to be assisting with hospitality at the delegation, or some sort of translation role.

The Italian envoy, Vincenzo Berardis, was at the reception, and he gave a short speech of encouragement, setting out out his hopes for the future. He also took the opportunity to remind the Italian businesses in Dublin that he expected them to display a photograph of Mussolini in their windows, a statement greeted with silence and one or two expressions of disbelief.

Luca didn't think any more about why Di Pasco wanted to see him until he'd neared the end of his shift just after ten o'clock. As the other staff dispersed out through the tradesmen's entrance, he went back through the public rooms to the reception desk. The same young man he'd met when he'd first come to the delegation was waiting for him.

"Ah! Mr Baxter, this way, please."

Once again, he found himself in Di Pasco's office, this time with the young man and another man new to him who Di Pasco introduced as Roberto Fanucci of *Servizio Informazione Militari*. He was gaunt to the extent of almost resembling a skeleton with a layer of skin drawn over it, only his short brown hair giving another dimension to his build. As he shook hands with Luca, his bony hand felt like a clamp and his face gave a rictus smile.

Di Pasco spoke in Italian. "Well, Signor Baxter," he said with a conspiratorial wink, "you look much better than when I last saw you. Life in Ireland suits you. Would you like a drink?"

He motioned to a drinks tray and Luca asked for a Campari and soda. Di Pasco poured Luca's drink and then a glass of wine for the young man, before refreshing the drinks of Fanucci and himself. While he performed his duties as host Di Pasco asked Luca how his lodgings were and how he was managing in his employment and so on. When all four were seated round the table Di Pasco got to the point.

"Thank you for coming to see us this evening. As you know, the war continues to go well for us and our allies, and an invasion of Great Britain by Germany cannot be too far away. It is important that our government receives as much information as possible that will assist them in planning future operations against the British, especially if they seek to invade Ireland to cut off that option for us. We know that your work at Gillot's and at social and other events involves seeing and hearing many of the prominent people in all areas of life in Ireland. We believe that you could use your position to gather information that would be of great use to us." He paused and waited for Luca's response.

Luca wasn't sure how true this statement was and was rather taken back by the suggestion that he should work for the Italian authorities. Though he didn't know if he would have the opportunity to garner information of the type that was wanted, he was intrigued by the idea. His own work was not too demanding and it left him free to pursue hobbies and interests if he so wished. The problem was that he had no hobbies or interests to speak of. At the age of forty and a foreigner it wasn't easy to integrate into Dublin society and he had yet to widen his social contacts, so he had a lot of time on his hands. This idea might provide him with an interest that had an edge to it and so spice up his life a little.

"If I can be of help I would be glad to do so," he said after a lengthy pause.

"Well, that is splendid," said Di Pasco, clasping his hands together rather extravagantly. "Please do not be modest about your talents. You've already shown through your escape from captivity that you have initiative and great resourcefulness. We know from your background that you are discreet, can keep secrets and have been able to adopt another identity with ease. All these will help you in doing what we have in mind."

Fanucci now took up the thread: "You see, Luca, it's important that Italy pulls its weight in the gathering of information. Although they would never admit it, the Germans know that the *Servizio Informazione Militari* is superior to German Intelligence in the way we go about our business. Unfortunately, we're much smaller and have limited resources, especially in Ireland. So, it's important that we have undercover operatives who can aid the collection and analysis of intelligence."

Luca nodded, still sceptical as to how helpful he could be.

Di Pasco continued: "Obviously we don't expect you take on this important work without reward. We shall pay you a small retainer to cover your time in producing weekly reports, and of course we will reimburse any out-of-pocket expenses."

"Thank you," replied Luca. "Just one question… How will I know which items of information I pick up will be useful to you?"

Fanucci leaned forward and spoke quietly, as if they might be overheard, "It is better to report things that are of no consequence than to leave out something which on the face of it is unimportant but which may have clues towards something that is significant. The more detail we have about a person the more likely it is that we'll uncover a connection or a weakness that may be of use to us.

Don't worry; we'll be happy to read through everything you come across." His face creased into a smile for a second, then he sat back, his gaze fixed on Luca.

"Very well," said Luca.

Di Pasco turned to the young man who'd been silent up till then. "Bertolini, you will be Luca's contact at the delegation; is there anything you'd like to add now?"

Bertolini nodded. "Ideally, we'd like a report from you each week. Just to avoid anyone becoming aware of your activities, it would be best not to come here to deliver it. I suggest you leave it at the station in a left luggage locker and we'll collect it," said the young man. "If you need to get in touch you can call me anytime." He handed over his business card. "Obviously, this conversation must not go outside this room and anything you learn that you wish to communicate to us must not be revealed to anyone else, including friends or social intimates, such as a girlfriend."

"I understand," said Luca.

Bertolini then produced a document similar in nature to the British Official Secrets Act, asked Luca to sign it and gave him a copy for his own information.

The four men talked for a little while about recent developments on the various war fronts, nothing top secret but events that had been reported in the newspapers. Neither Di Pasco nor Fanucci spoke triumphantly but they appeared quietly satisfied with progress so far. The meeting broke up and Bertolini took Luca to his own office to go through the details of report writing, the use of the station locker and ways and means of contact between the two of them.

"Any questions?" asked Bertolini.

"As I've never done anything quite like this before I'd be grateful for any advice you have."

"It's common sense really, but first of all don't tell anyone else what you're doing and don't keep any notes where someone might come across them. Second, always behave naturally and avoid making people suspicious of you because then your effectiveness would be reduced. Third, don't push it too hard, don't try to engineer situations, always be just the watcher and the listener. You'll soon develop a style that suits you."

"Thanks," said Luca.

"Any problems, just give me a ring on that number. Good luck."

In the first few weeks, evenings away from work were often spent in his room, listening to an old radio he had acquired and reading, or perhaps going to the cinema on his own, or to a pub for a drink or two. About once a week he met up with his new friend Giraudo and had a glass of grappa and sometimes a meal. Often this represented the only meaningful conversation he'd had for days and with Giraudo he could talk about serious subjects, like politics, the war, economic and business matters, in a way he couldn't with anyone else. However, he resisted the temptation to tell his friend when he was recruited by the delegation, not because he didn't trust him but because he took his oath to secrecy seriously.

As it happened, Giraudo had been recruited himself by the delegation as a source of information and for his views on the suitability of a candidate. So, he knew about Luca's appointment and was able to advise the delegation that Luca had passed the test of not telling even his friends what he was doing for the Italian war effort.

Luca spent many of his days off taking little bus trips out into the countryside and going on long walks, but the summer was drawing to its close so he knew he had to seek other ways of passing his time. This was why the chance given to him by the embassy to do something he could get his teeth into was so attractive, especially as he had now moved on from a hand-to-mouth existence and was no longer preoccupied with making sure he had enough money. He was now able to save a bit, even while expanding his wardrobe to a decent level and doing what he wanted in his leisure time.

His lodgings were comfortable and the Donovans were friendly and made him feel at home. It did seem more like a home as there were only two lodgers and he didn't see much of the other one, Mr Phillips. Luca met Mr Phillips at breakfast on the first morning of his stay at the house. He had already sat down to eat breakfast in the dining room, a dowdy place with dark furniture and dark curtains, when Phillips came in. He was a man of about fifty and was dressed in navy blue overalls under a suit jacket.

"Good morning," said Luca.

"Good morning to you," replied Phillips and sat down in the chair opposite Luca. He took a newspaper out of his pocket and opened it to read.

"You are Mr Phillips?" asked Luca. "My name is Harold Baxter."

Phillips looked up reluctantly. "Yes. Look, I'm not one for conversation in the mornings; I like to read the paper." With that he averted his gaze from Luca back to his newspaper.

Luca thought, *Vaffanculo*! but gave his best waiter smile and resumed his breakfast.

Apart from a cursory greeting each morning that was almost the only conversation between Luca and Phillips. When Luca asked about him, Mrs Donovan just smiled and said, "It's just his way, Mr Baxter. He means no harm but likes his own company best, and who can blame him for that? I've never had more than ten words at a time with him. All I know about him is that he works at Varian's Brush Company; I think he's a foreman or something like that. He came to live here after his mother died and his brother took over the family house. He's no trouble and that's all that matters to me, as I'm sure you understand."

Luca did indeed understand and it suited him well enough. He spent most of his working day being friendly and courteous and making polite, often pointless, conversation with the customers, so it was no hardship not to have to do the same thing when outside work.

VII

When Luca booked out of The Nag's Head he was keen to see Nancy again but was in no rush. At first, he was busy settling into his new rooms and getting to grips with his jobs. After a couple of weeks, Luca was ready and thought that taking the suitcase he'd borrowed back to The Nag's Head would be an ideal opportunity to reintroduce himself to her. He remembered that she was off on a Thursday, and as the weekend was impossible for him he decided to call on the Tuesday of the following week.

It was just six o'clock and the saloon bar was fairly quiet, as it always seemed to be at that time. Luca walked in with the suitcase, and Nancy, who was flicking through a newspaper, looked up and smiled when she saw him.

"Hello Nancy," he said. "I've come to return the suitcase."

"I'll take it for you," she said, leaning over the bar so that he could pass it to her. He could smell the same perfume she'd worn when they went out and felt her arm lean on his as she pulled the case over. "How's it going at the new place?"

"It's very good. I have a nice room and there's only one other lodger. The landlady and her husband are friendly and kind so I've got nothing to complain about."

"That's grand, and the job?"

"Early days, but it seems to be going well. I like the place; they do things right. I've been very lucky as I also have some casual work with a catering agency."

"What do you do for them?"

"Waiting, serving drinks; that kind of thing."

"I'm pleased that everything seems to be going well for you."

"No Joe tonight?"

"You've got a good memory for names; no, it's his evening off. Michael's on tonight. He's in the other bar at the moment."

They looked at each her as if it was time to get down to the real business, and Luca looked round to check they could speak privately. The barman was nowhere to be seen and nobody was coming to the bar for a drink.

"I wondered if you were free on Thursday evening?" he asked.

Nancy was expecting this but still flushed a little. "I can be. What did you have in mind?"

Luca guessed she was free on Thursday but didn't want to sound too eager or too limited as to her social options. "I thought perhaps we might go to the pictures and then have a drink afterwards."

"That sounds nice; where and what time?"

"Would you mind choosing? I don't know the cinemas here yet."

"Let's see." Nancy picked up the evening newspaper from behind the counter and opened it at the entertainment page. There was a whole column of cinema listings, as Dublin had undergone a massive programme of cinema building in the 1920s and '30s; there were eight cinemas in the vicinity of O'Connell Street alone. "How about *Rebecca*; it's showing at the Savoy? We could see it at 6.30 and that would leave plenty of time afterwards."

Luca had never been an avid film fan so he was happy to go along with whatever Nancy chose. They agreed to meet at 6.15 outside the cinema and then, not wanting to have a conversation constantly interrupted, as the pub was getting busier, he soon made his farewell.

On Thursday Luca enjoyed his trip to the cinema. Nancy was already waiting when he arrived at 6.15. It was an overcast, slightly cool day and she was wearing a cardigan over her summer dress. She waved as he approached and he thought how pretty she looked. As they went into the cinema she remarked that it might remind him of home, and he soon saw why. The Savoy was designed in the 'Grecian Moderne' style but with a Venetian theme, complete with a painting of the Doge's Palace and decorative Venetian balconies and windows looking down on the audience.

They sat in the circle, and Luca was both amused and pleased as he looked round the theatre. Nancy asked him if he'd ever been to Venice and he replied that he hadn't so he knew it no better than she did.

Rebecca is a long film so it was the only one shown, though they had to sit through some advertisements and trailers for future viewings. They sat close to each other but there was no more intimate physical contact than their shoulders rubbing together. For both of them the cinema had ceased to be a place for the timid holding of hands, the slowly encroaching arm round the shoulder or the furtive reaching out of hand on thigh. They just sat back and watched the film.

Afterwards, they went for a drink in a more salubrious bar than the one on their first evening together. Luca asked Nancy if she wanted anything to eat and she declined, saying she'd had tea before coming out. Luca was rather hungry but made do with eating the crisps and salted peanuts provided in bowls on their table. As they started their first drink Luca asked Nancy what she thought of the film.

"I thought it was great," she replied, her eyes lighting up, "but I thought that Max caused a lot of the wife's, I can't remember her name, problems. She was very young and rather immature but he just let her get on with it and never seemed to think she might need help settling in. Mind you, she was useless, letting that awful Danvers woman walk all over her and hiding the broken china in the drawer like a guilty kid."

Luca thought that he couldn't remember the name of the wife

either. "Yes, unless Max watches out she'll end up in the arms of the estate manager; he seemed much kinder to her and had certainly taken a fancy to her."

Nancy smiled. "He was a nice man but a bit boring, sort of solid and reliable. She'll stick with Max. Just as well; it wouldn't get past the censors here if a married woman had an affair."

"Are they very strict?"

"So I've been told. Anything to do with divorce, or priests behaving badly, or sexual suggestiveness, or even some dancing, is likely to be cut here and there. Because of the cuts we hardly ever see the same version of the film as they'd see in England. I believe they even banned one of the Marx Brothers films here."

Luca laughed. "Do you go to the cinema often?"

"Yes, quite a lot. There are not that many things for a single woman above a certain age to do here. I'm getting too old to go to dances and wait to be asked to dance by some fella who thinks that a dance is the ticket he has to buy for a quick grope later on." She didn't sound bitter, or even wistful, just matter-of-fact. "But I do enjoy the films. I often go with my mother; she likes weepies."

"What do you like?" Luca asked. He liked the way she said 'film' as if it were spelled 'fillum'.

"It's hard to say. I suppose I like dramas but not too sentimental, and I like the women to be independent and stand on their own feet, like Barbara Stanwyck or Bette Davis or Katherine Hepburn. I suppose it comes down to the film. I've enjoyed westerns and historical films too if the story is good and believable."

"Are the films they show just American or are any made in Ireland?"

"A few, mostly musicals, but not enough to keep the cinemas busy. We get English films too and some of those have Irish settings, though the characters are usually the English view of what Irish people are like."

"Same as Italians," said Luca. "In films, actors play the same part all the time so you know what they're going to be like when they turn up; not just comic Irishmen or excitable Italians – everyone in the film."

Nancy laughed. "Do you think it was like that tonight?"

"Yes, to some extent. George Sanders; you knew would be a kind of upper-class crook; the housekeeper looked like a mad woman and she was; the man who played the likeable buffoon always plays that part; and so it goes."

"Next time we go to the pictures I'll show you the actors in it and you can tell me what they'll be like; we'll test you out."

Over the next round of drinks Nancy changed the subject and asked about his family. "It must be difficult for you to keep in touch with your family what with you travelling around so much."

"My parents are dead and I haven't seen my brother in years."

"You're not married?"

Luca knew the question would come up at some point; he smiled at her. "I was married but we're separated. I have no children. How about you?"

"I had my chances but I never met anyone I could think about spending the rest of my life with, at least not anyone who wanted to marry me."

"What about your family?"

"I live with my mother; my father died several years ago. I had two brothers and a sister but my elder brother Pat joined up in the last war and was killed at the Somme in 1916. The other two are married."

"I'm sorry about your brother; it was a terrible war. You haven't thought of getting a place of your own?"

"I get on fine with my mother; we do our own things so we don't get in each other's pockets."

At closing time they drank up and walked to Nancy's house. It was drizzling when they set out but the skies cleared and the two of them cast tall dim shadows on the pavement as they neared her street.

"Would you like to come in?" asked Nancy when they reached the front door.

Luca would have liked to but he felt that Nancy needed time to reflect first on his situation, so he said, "I'd love to but I can't. I have to make an early start tomorrow. I'd like to see you again, though, if you want to."

"I'd love to."

They agreed to go out the following Thursday for a picnic at Killiney. Nancy thanked Luca for a lovely evening and they kissed briefly before Nancy disappeared into the dark house.

That July developed into a cold, wet month after the few hot dry days at the beginning had promised so much and, on the 25th, when Luca and Nancy went to Killiney, it rained on and off like a persistent whinger ruining somebody else's pleasure. Yet they persevered with a walk along the quiet, expansive pebble beach and watched the shouting gulls swoop and sweep over the soft waves. They had a picnic, prepared by Nancy, sitting on a bench on one of their macks, with their food on the other: sandwiches, sausage rolls and buns.

"Very good sausage rolls," said Luca.

"My mam made them. She did it all; I just made the sandwiches."

They had barely finished their food when the rain came slanting into their faces and they retreated for a glass of beer in a local pub. Later, in the afternoon, the weather deteriorated further and they decided to call it a day. As they walked along, hand in hand, Nancy chattering about this and that, Luca reflected that she didn't seem to have any annoying mannerisms or ways of speaking, and he couldn't find any excuse for not seeing her again, especially as he was finding her increasingly more attractive.

They saw each other at first once a week and then twice. Often they went for a drink or to the pictures or for day trips. August was fine and very warm so they went for days out, and Nancy showed him more of the countryside and villages around Dublin.

When they'd been going out for a few weeks Luca took her for a dinner party at Giraudo's home where the other guests were Brian and Eileen Coyle, whom Luca had never met before. As they came to the top of the stairs Brian and Eileen were already there, seated on the sofa.

"Good evening," said Brian. "Excuse me not standing but I'm having terrible trouble with my false leg today."

Luca and Nancy made positive gestures of commiseration and were surprised when Polly burst into laughter, until Eileen turned and pushed Brian.

"Ignore him and his stupid jokes," she said. "I am sorry. What must you think?"

Nancy said she thought it was very funny and certainly an ice-breaker to get the party going.

Brian was some years older than Luca, and in a varied career had worked in construction in Britain before the war. He'd returned home in 1933 because he was worried about the rise of fascism in Britain.

"Not that I need have bothered," he said. "The British fascists never came to much, no more than the Blueshirts here."

"The Blueshirts weren't really fascists, Brian," said Eileen.

Brian harrumphed in response then changed the subject. He and his wife kept up a very amusing double act all evening, and Luca could see why Polly would choose them as dinner companions, especially as she had quite a vivacious personality herself. The three men and Polly exchanged stories about the time they'd spent in England and how they'd got on with the English. Brian was particularly hilarious in his recollections, which he told with a straight face but with an increasingly red hue, until it would disintegrate into peals of laughter and watering eyes when he reached the end. He told them of the time he'd gone into an Irish pub in Kilburn when there was an Irish band playing. He hadn't stood for the playing of the Irish national anthem at the end of the evening, was mistaken for an Englishman being disrespectful and nearly got a punch on the nose before quickly standing to attention.

"I once worked for a foreman who told me he could always

recognise an Irishman by his looks, and he said that all Irishmen could be divided into 'potatoes' and 'weasels' based on the size of their heads and their features. When he gave me a few examples I could kind of see what he meant."

"Which one are you?" asked Nancy, amidst the laughter.

"I think I'm probably a weasel but there's a potato trying to get out," he replied to more laughter.

"I think you've been a full-blown King Edward for years, Brian; you just haven't looked in the mirror," said Eileen.

"I wonder how they classify the Italians," said Giraudo, "but perhaps it would be better not to know."

After dinner Luca helped Polly clear away. She was always very friendly towards him but he thought it right to take nothing for granted.

"I hope you don't find having to put up with me too much of an imposition," he said.

"Not in the least, Luca," she said, touching his arm. "It's good for Arturo to have someone to talk to from his own country. He likes his conversations with you because you understand how he feels about things, and you have a lot in common. You know, he worries about the war and thinks Italy will do very badly out of it, and obviously most of the Irish aren't sympathetic to Italy, whatever the government says."

"Brian and Eileen are great company. How did you meet?"

"Oh, I've known Eileen for years; we used to go to a church youth club together. We went on our first date together with a couple of boys from the club. When I came back to Ireland we picked up where we'd left off; it was as if I'd never been away. Arturo gets on well with Brian so it's nice to have them around. I like Nancy too; you must bring her again."

"Yes, I will."

Subsequently, Luca got to know Brian quite well, as Giraudo often invited him to join them for a few drinks. Apart from the conviviality, Luca was glad to mix more with Irish people. He didn't want to live on the fringe of an expatriate Italian community.

Luca and Nancy did get together occasionally with Giraudo and Polly but mostly their dates were just the two of them. On about the fifth or sixth date, they went out early in the evening to go to the pictures but couldn't get in to see the film they'd had in mind so they walked by the river and had a few drinks. On the way back to Nancy's place it started raining and they were a bit damp by the time they reached her house.

"You'd better come in," said Nancy; "the rain is getting heavier."

Luca had been in the house once before, after a day trip, and he'd met Nancy's mother briefly. She'd been very pleasant to him and didn't make him feel she was sizing him up and judging whether he was good enough for her daughter. She'd made them a pot of tea but then left them in the front room while she got on with what she called "a few chores".

On this occasion Luca thought of refusing the invitation but didn't want to get his recently cleaned and pressed jacket any wetter.

"Thanks," he replied and followed her into the house. It was in darkness except for a light in the hall. They went into the front room and Nancy asked him to sit down.

"Would you like another drink?" she asked. "I've only whiskey and gin."

"Whiskey will be fine," said Luca, who had got a liking for Jameson's since he'd been in Dublin.

Luca took off his jacket and hung it carefully on the back of a chair, while Nancy went over to the drinks tray and poured him a generous measure and offered water with it. She had a gin and bitter lemon. Then she joined him on the sofa. Thus far their physical relations had been limited to a couple of kisses at the end of the evening, and Luca was content to let things progress slowly, partly because he enjoyed her company anyway but also because he didn't want to act as if he assumed anything. On the other hand, his mind was full of conjecture and possibilities.

Nancy smiled at him and took his hand. "You're quiet; what are you thinking about?"

"I couldn't possibly say."

"I wonder if it's the same thing I'm thinking," and she kissed him on the mouth. She felt her cheeks glow and thought perhaps she should have had a cup of tea rather than another gin.

"D'you mind if I smoke?" asked Luca.

"Of course not," said Nancy. "I'll get you an ashtray."

She pushed herself a little awkwardly out of the sofa and brought an ashtray back from the mantelpiece. She had to lean over to place the ashtray on the table near the arm of the sofa and Luca caught a glimpse of her cleavage as she bent over. He felt a *frisson* of excitement as he reached into his pocket for his cigarettes. He offered one to Nancy but she refused, as she always did, and he lit one for himself. He inhaled deeply and sought to think of something other than the possibilities going through his mind. Neither of them spoke, and the silence seemed to go on for a long time. Luca started to rise from the sofa.

"I think I ought to go," he said.

"Don't go," said Nancy. "You haven't finished your drink yet and it's still raining."

He half-sat half-slumped back onto the sofa, bouncing into Nancy, and they both laughed. She didn't move away and he could see her looking at him in what he took to be both a desirous and a desirable way.

Impelled to say something but not sure what, he came up with: "I really enjoy the time we spend together," and leaned over to kiss her. Her arms came up to his shoulders as she reciprocated the movement, and the kiss developed from an initial clinch into something more insistent. Their hands moved over each other's backs and there was a moment when things could have gone further, but they desisted and separated. They sat back and held hands; Luca regretted not going on and thought about the next time.

"Would you like a cup of tea or coffee?" she asked eventually.

Luca could hear the rain still falling. "Yes, please," he said.

So, they relaxed and had tea and cake and talked about mundane things.

Then Nancy said, "Next Sunday my mother's going to her sister's for lunch, so we could have the house to ourselves. Why don't you come round about twelve and I'll get you something to eat."

At noon on Sunday Luca arrived at Nancy's. Her mother had gone to church, would take the bus to her sister's from there and wouldn't be back until about five o'clock.

Nancy had prepared a ham salad and he'd brought some bottles of beer. He quite enjoyed their meal together but his mind was elsewhere. After they had eaten, Luca offered to help clear away but Nancy would have none of it.

"Just relax," she said. "Bring your beer into the front room."

He did as he was told and they went into the front room and sat together on the sofa. She was wearing a sleeveless blouse, a skirt, and sandals, which she kicked off as they sat down. She took his hand and leaned towards him.

"I have been so looking forward to today," she said as he moved over and they kissed. The curtailed passion of the previous date had acted as a spur to both of them, and though Luca took the lead he could sense Nancy willing him on. His hands were inside her blouse and sliding up her skirt and she gasped as his hand reached between her legs. He began to undress her but as he struggled with her underwear she said, "Come on," and took him by the hand up to her room.

As she started to take off her skirt Luca turned his back in case she should feel embarrassed by his watching, and then he undressed. When he turned round she was in the double bed and he climbed in beside her. He lay on his side and ran his hands over her naked body, and she smiled, her eyes closed.

"We won't be able to do everything," he said; "I couldn't get anything at the chemist's."

This was perfectly true, since he'd had a fruitless search the previous day, uncomprehending as to why condoms seemed unavailable in such a large city.

"Don't worry, it'll be all right," she said, pulling him towards her.

As he embraced her he knew that, having waited this long, he wouldn't be able to delay once he started, so he pleasured her first, and when he thought it was right he entered her.

Afterwards they lay contentedly on their backs. Luca was vaguely aware of Nancy squeezing his hand but he was preoccupied with his thoughts. Guilt did not even enter his mind. He'd never been unfaithful to Ellen and when he returned to England he would be faithful again. But this was a separate strand of his life, a different world in which he wasn't a married businessman but a single waiter with no ties. He was like a railway engine on a loop line which had left the main line and would re-join it sometime in the future with no change in the final destination. In the meantime, it was just passing through different scenery.

He hadn't paid any attention to the room when they'd come in earlier but now he stared at the white ceiling with its cracks and slight bulges as the weight of the plaster over time created an upside-down terrain. The walls were papered in a floral print and there were velvet curtains at the window; he guessed this had been Nancy's room for some time and was decorated in her taste.

Luca was jolted from his reverie by a second, more insistent squeeze of the hand, and he turned towards her and kissed her.

"You're lovely," he said and stroked her breasts and arms.

Nancy turned on her side so they could lie face to face with their bodies pressed together, and they held each other's backs. They explored this new intimacy, feeling each other's hands over them and muttering the odd sound of pleasure or word of praise. They kissed and cuddled until Nancy felt him stirring again, and then she took the lead in having him a second time.

After, they lay in each other's arms and half dozed, until Nancy suddenly sat up to look at the time; it was after four. She got up, and Luca was pleased she didn't cover herself as she walked over to her clothes. He admired her body, an hourglass shape with well-proportioned breasts and hips, as it slowly disappeared below the layers of clothing. She smiled at him watching her.

"Come on," she said. "Time to get up."

She brushed her hair and restored her make-up while he got dressed. Then she went back to the bed and looked at the sheets before shrugging and pulling the bedclothes into their proper position.

They went downstairs and Nancy made a cup of tea while Luca washed up, a move he thought nothing of but which impressed her.

"No regrets?" she asked him as they sat with a cup of tea in the kitchen.

"Regrets? No, I've had a lovely day. Why do you ask?"

"Well, you never know; some men think you're the most desirable thing in the world but after they have you they don't see it like that anymore. Then again, you're still married, technically speaking at least."

Luca shook his head. "I haven't gone off you and I don't feel guilty about my wife."

"I'm glad." She paused, then asked him, "Are you religious?"

Luca gave a non-committal maybe/maybe-not gesture with his hands. "I'm a Catholic but I haven't been to church much since I left Italy."

"Ireland is a Catholic country too."

"Yes. It's not that it's been harder for me to get to church in Ireland, or England for that matter, it's just different."

He then thought about religion for the first time in years and his mind went back to his childhood, when he had been captivated by the liturgy of the church and, as an altar server, had loved being part of it. The emotional solemnity of the *missa solemnis*; the processions in honour of Mary and those of the Blessed Sacrament, when girls walked backwards, scattering rose petals in the path of the priest carrying the sacrament. For him, religion had been less about piety or faith or even reasoned understanding; he'd been swept up in the assault on the senses of the beauty and richness of the ceremony, the emotional pull of the music and the perfume of the incense, flowers and candles.

He'd found the dramatic ritual of the Church more restrained in England, where Catholicism was a small minority denomination, where a sensuous liturgy was viewed with suspicion and where street processions were banned. In any event, he'd grown out of love with the more exotic aspects of his Church the older he'd become. This was not the difference he referred to.

"In what way 'different'?" asked Nancy. "The mass is the same everywhere – in Latin."

"It's not the mass; it's that the faith seems to weigh more heavily in Ireland, and in England too. The rules are the same but in Italy you don't feel evil if you break them. Everyone is a sinner and must try to do better but what makes you a Christian is that you believe, not that you're perfect."

"Surely that's the same everywhere."

"Perhaps, but in Ireland the people are afraid of the priests. They tell you how to live and what you must believe without question. You're brought up to feel guilty."

"But you've only been here a little while. How do you know us so well?" she laughed.

"I lived in England for a long time and it's the same there; English Catholicism is like a branch of the Irish Church; so many of the priests and nuns seem to be Irish. On top of that, the English Catholics always have to prove something. They feel they have to show they can be trusted and that they're as English as anyone else. So they take pride in knowing a famous person who happens to be a Catholic, as if that was the most important thing about them, rather than that they're a great artist or scientist or something."

Nancy smiled. "You're probably right but you have to understand that for hundreds of years English Catholics weren't allowed to practise their religion and were barred from the big jobs because of it. They're still trying to catch up. We understand in Ireland because it was even worse here – a Catholic country with a Protestant ruling class. We have the shortest masses in the world because when persecution was at its worst the priests had to be able to say them quickly in a hedgerow or somewhere before they were discovered by the military."

"I suppose I don't know enough about it. Do you go to church?"

"Not every Sunday but I sometimes go with my mother, to please her probably. I don't go along with everything the Church says. I suppose I feel I belong there without really believing it all."

"You asked if I had any regrets, but do you? Do you feel guilty or uncomfortable about what we've done?"

"No, I don't. I know I'm supposed to feel guilty about making love to someone who's married, but I don't think it's so terribly wrong to do what we did."

He admired her spirit. "Nor me. I thought you ought to know I was married before we got this far so that you could decide whether it was all right for you or not."

"Well, I did think about it, and as far as I'm concerned you're married and will never be free to marry anyone else but as long as you're not living with her I don't have a problem. It's a matter for you and *your* conscience, not mine."

Luca nodded. "Perhaps we Irish and Italians aren't so different after all."

She put her cup down and folded her arms. "God, I make myself sound so bloody blasé and sophisticated. It's not that I think sex is nothing. I've not done it enough to think it's not important; perhaps I've been too fussy in the past. All I wanted to say was that I'm glad."

He got up, walked over to her and kissed her. "I'm glad too – my only regret is that I couldn't get any rubbers. I know you said it would be all right but I don't like leaving you to take the risk."

"That's sweet of you but it wasn't your fault. The Church in

Ireland got the government to ban the sale of them because the Pope said it was wrong, and that's the sort of thing that really puts me off the Church. It imposes its will on everyone without thinking about individual cases. But that's beside the point. I'm forty-two and I'll be forty-three in October. Maybe I could have a child but I think it more than unlikely, so it's my own gamble and not for you to worry about." She looked at her watch. "Let's go out for a walk, I don't want to lose this moment. My mam will be home soon and we won't be able to talk."

So, they left the house and went for a walk, arm in arm, not anywhere in particular. Although Nancy had said she didn't expect anything so far as marriage was concerned, Luca found himself wondering if she might look for some sort of commitment later.

"I know you accept that we can't marry, but is this enough for you?"

She looked up at him and smiled. "Don't you think I've been over all this in my mind before today? I know where I stand. All I ask is that you are honest with me. Never lie about your feelings for me and don't make a promise you can't keep, and we'll be just fine."

So they continued their walk until they ended up strolling round Mountjoy Square Park, basking in the lovely light of the early evening and admiring the elegant houses.

VIII

Luca took his role as an 'undercover agent' very seriously. 'Seriously' does not imply that he felt either politically or patriotically committed to working for fascism or even the Italian state. Rather it was a job for which he was paid quite well and which he wanted to do right. On the very next day after his recruitment by Di Pasco he purchased a foolscap notepad, and every evening he recorded anything of note that he had overheard, come to hear about or otherwise discovered during his work that day. Then, once a week, he lodged his report, handwritten, in his locker at the station. Each week a cash payment was waiting for him in the same locker, courtesy of the delegation. He didn't go to the station on the same day each week but varied the day and time. Despite the care with which he undertook his duties, Luca was not naturally attracted to cloak and dagger behaviour; he considered the whole business of espionage and undercover activities slightly absurd and wasn't sure it achieved as much as its practitioners hoped. Nevertheless, he did his best.

As a wine waiter it was not that easy to listen in on people talking, as he could hardly hover at a particular table for several minutes, and he was careful not to push matters, as Bertolini had advised. So he tended to hear snatches of a conversation while serving wine or perhaps hear a more protracted discussion while serving at an adjacent table. Most of the customers were of little or no interest to the secret service of either Italy or Germany, and those who might be of interest, Irish civil servants, British or American diplomats and, in particular, members of the French legation, tended to be tight-lipped and discreet when eating in the restaurant. Sometimes people let their guard down a bit when making use of the private room facilities but then he felt more vulnerable to observation so couldn't hang around. As a consequence, Luca found this part of his work quite frustrating. More than once he considered embellishing his reports with a bit more information than he really had, just to make them more worthwhile, but he resisted the temptation.

As the months wore on, the atmosphere in Gillot's became more complicated and sometimes rather tense. Early in 1941 two of the younger staff, an Irish waiter and a French junior chef, left to join the British Army and the Free French forces respectively. Ireland had recognised the Vichy Government of Marshal Petain since July 1940, and as pretty well all the French staff at Gillot's were on the side of De Gaulle and the Free French they resented some of the pro-Vichy comments they saw in the Irish press.

When Xavier de Laforcade, the French minister in Dublin, booked a table in one of the private function rooms for a dinner party, the sommelier, Roussel, asked Luca if he could have a word. They met in the lobby of the wine cellar.

"Would you mind serving the French delegation party?" he said. "I don't have the stomach for it."

"Of course," said Luca. He'd always avoided discussing the French political situation with his colleagues and now held back from saying anything, waiting for Roussel to go on.

"You know, Harry, I'm so angry." He said this quietly and slowly, which seemed to emphasise every word. "My younger brother was killed at Verdun where Petain went on about '*Ils ne passeront pas*'. But for what? So this same Petain can now let the Boche '*passeront*' right through the country and turn France into a German sodding labour camp. I can't serve these people like nothing's happened. I'll probably end up ramming a bottle of Vichy water up the minister's arse."

Luca laughed at the thought of it and Roussel couldn't help but laugh too. It didn't present a problem for Luca to serve Laforcarde, and he thought he might overhear something of interest to his delegation contacts. None of the other staff refused to serve the party, although he was told that a couple of the chefs did something unspeakable to one of the dishes while it was being prepared, a dish that was especially praised by Laforcade.

Subsequently, Luca always dealt with members of the French legation, and everyone always behaved as if there was no friction at all towards the legation. Most of the information Luca passed on from this quarter was pretty bland: talk of a meeting, or interesting tie-ups between Irish diplomats and those from Britain on the one hand or Germany or Italy on the other. Once, he saw a member of the French legation pass a list of names to his German counterpart, and he realised that sometimes the Germans and French were probably co-operating while excluding the Italians. He found this odd and also annoying; after all, Italy was an ally of Germany whereas France was a puppet state. On another occasion, over a long, bibulous lunch in one of the private rooms, he witnessed a German diplomat give an Irish civil servant information he'd received concerning IRA activities.

Sometimes Luca's reports would lead his contact, Bertolini, to ask for more details, or he'd instruct him to follow up the information by watching the person or persons again, if that were possible. As the months progressed and the threat of a German invasion of Britain receded, and with it the threat of a British invasion of Ireland, he saw more frequent liaisons between Irish and British officials and he didn't always report these to his Italian bosses.

The other difficulty remained Braid, the deputy head waiter. Although Braid didn't bother him as much as before, he still seemed interested in what he got up to, and when he was around Luca tended to be much more circumspect about his undercover activities.

Around this time Roberto Fanucci, Luca's supervisor from the *Servizio Informazione Militari,* asked him to keep him informed of any Irish civil servants or foreign diplomats who used the restaurant to entertain their women friends or mistresses. Like pretty well all secret services, the Italian one was not unwilling to use blackmail or other measures to secure leverage over those they wished to influence and Luca found this made his job a bit easier. For some time he'd been so concerned about the lack of information he garnered at the restaurant that he thought they might tire of him. But this gave him the opportunity to use real information on customers' telephone numbers and other details obtained from restaurant bookings. He wasn't exactly keen on delving into people's private lives but assuaged his conscience by convincing himself that the people concerned could themselves be using these relationships to acquire information or influence.

Snooping, as Luca admitted it was, to himself, was a good deal easier at the receptions, dinners and other events he served at with the catering company. In addition, he and Giraudo were frequently asked to serve drinks, etc. at small receptions given at the delegation or the envoy's home. He could wander around with drinks or be standing behind a table at a banquet without really being noticed. He was able to send a stream of comments about collaboration and friction between members of the different diplomatic staffs, the off-the-cuff remarks by all these groups, as well as members of the Church hierarchy, business leaders and even freemasons. He was also able to identify potential weaknesses among those he watched and overheard, from an over-fondness for drink or gambling, through sexual promiscuity or unusual or illegal sexual practices, to a loose tongue or love of gossip or bragging, just by observing and listening. He found it extraordinary the number of people who would assume they could avoid the prying eyes of people like him just by dodging into the first empty room they found.

If he had the time, and the cloakroom staff were lax in their duties, he sometimes quickly rummaged in the pockets of coats looking for clues. Sometimes he would find business cards or receipts or letters which linked the owner of the coat to someone in one of the delegations or the Irish government, and he would try to tie these links up during his break while they were fresh in his mind. He got into the habit of carrying a small clothes brush with him so that he could appear to be going above and beyond the call of duty. He even received tips from grateful coat wearers for his special care.

He was rarely challenged as to what he was up to but there were two occasions when he was nearly caught out. The first time, a man asked him what he was doing while his hand was in a lady's coat pocket. Fortunately, the coat had a handkerchief in the pocket so he pulled it out and explained that he'd found it on the floor and was merely replacing it; the man just nodded and apologised for the remark.

Subsequently, Luca carried around with him items like a handkerchief and a comb so that he could appear to be returning these back to a coat if he were questioned.

The second occasion was potentially more serious, as he became aware of a woman watching him while he was checking along a row of coats. He thought quickly and moved to a row in full view and went along the rail, making sure that every coat was properly on the hanger and that all the pockets were in and scarves pushed more firmly into pockets. Then he took out his clothes brush and brushed the shoulders of each one. The woman went on her way and Luca assumed she'd been reassured but then she reappeared with the manager of his team just as he'd finished going through the last coat.

"That's the man," she said, pointing at Luca when some thirty feet away.

Luca carried on and put some rubbish in the waste bin.

"Mr Baxter," called the manager, "could we have a word, please?"

Luca nodded, smiling, and came over to them.

"This lady states that she saw you taking things from some of the coats."

"I don't see how that can be. I would never do such a thing."

The manager looked at the woman, aged about forty, who shook her head.

"I definitely saw you looking at a piece of paper you put in your pocket. I watched you for a long time and I saw you fiddling with other things." Her voice quavered a little at the end but she spoke firmly.

"This is a serious accusation," said Luca. "If I've taken anything I must still have it, since I've been here for nearly ten minutes without moving. Perhaps you ought to search me." He opened his arms.

The manager looked a little uncomfortable and the woman shifted on her feet.

"The paper you saw me put in my pocket was a shopping list I had found on the floor, and I put it in my pocket before throwing it in the bin. I also replaced a glove that had fallen out of a pocket into a coat but then realised it was the wrong coat so took it out and put it in the correct one. I am more than happy to let you check I have nothing that doesn't belong to me."

"I'm sure that won't be necessary," said the manager.

"Perhaps you ought to check," said the woman, not giving up without a fight.

Luca moved over to a table and emptied his pockets of a clothes brush, comb, handkerchief, packet of cigarettes, some loose change and a box of matches. Then he pulled the pocket linings out, one by one. "All of these items I came with this evening."

"I trust you are satisfied, madam," said the manager.

The woman opened her mouth but didn't say anything. She turned and walked off.

"I'm sorry about that, Harry. I hope you understand I had to go through the motions."

"Yes," said Luca. "I was just trying to give customers an extra service in a slack moment."

"Yes, thank you. I do appreciate all that you do for us."

The manager went off and Harry retrieved the cards and papers from the wastebasket and put them in his back pocket, secured with a button.

Mindful of Bertolini's guidelines, he afterwards stopped searching the coats left in cloakrooms. On occasion he received some feedback from the delegation as to the usefulness of his information but he was never told to what use it had been put. Between making notes and submitting his report he had to keep his notes in his room. He trusted Mr and Mrs Donovan but there was always a chance that he'd forget and leave his notes out one day or that Mrs Donovan might come across them when cleaning and become suspicious of him. He kept them in his chest of drawers underneath a newspaper, which he changed regularly.

The war was impinging on everyone in Dublin. The government hadn't yet adopted formal rationing, relying to a large extent on prudence and a social conscience. But the contraction of trade with Britain increasingly caused shortages in some foods, notably wheat, tea and sugar, and also fuel. For Gillot's the fall of France and takeover of wine controls by Germany resulted in French wines not being readily available, and the blockade of Italy's ports meant that this market was also closed. However, the management of the restaurant had laid down large cellars of wine and, with some additions from Spain and Portugal, they kept going. Fortunately, beer and stout remained in plentiful supply.

As the war went on, the Italians were soon experiencing one defeat after another. In February Giraudo and he were having a drink together, and Giraudo told him that he'd received a letter from his brother who said that his son was fighting in Greece and that things were not going well there.

"You could see this coming," said Giraudo. "Our economy was in a mess and our military capability overestimated: a recipe for disaster. When the war started I thought Mussolini was playing his cards well – act as honest broker between Hitler and the British and then later on see what he can get out of it. We should have gone into the Great War later than we did and we would still have got what we wanted in the end. We could have done the same again this time but *Il Duce* was frightened of missing out on easy pickings. Now he'll have to hope the Germans win quickly."

"Do you think they *can* win quickly now? I'm not sure. The British won't give in and the Greeks are still fighting. What if the Germans have bitten off more than they can chew?"

Giraudo puffed his cheeks out. "I don't know what to think but *we're* not going to win it, that's for sure. D'you ever wish you could do more, you know, be involved in the war effort?"

Luca was aware that Giraudo knew of his undercover work so he wasn't asking about something of that sort. "You mean fight?"

Giraudo nodded. "As the situation deteriorates I sometimes feel guilty that I'm not there."

Luca shook his head. "I wasn't meant to be a hero. I was too young for the last war, and if I'm considered young enough for this one the war won't be going too well. I had a mad moment of patriotic fervour when I thought of volunteering for D'Annunzio's expedition in 1919 but my father was opposed to the idea, and before I could make my mind up the campaign was over. Now I find the idea of going home to fight for your country strictly for sentimentalists – those who have a tear in their eye when they think of the flag, or past glories. I am not a sentimentalist."

"What about love for one's fatherland?"

Luca nodded slightly. "Maybe, but does my fatherland love me? Did it ask me if I wanted a war against a country that was my home? In any case, when my father's elder brother was born, Umbria wasn't even *in* Italy. Patriotism is an emotion; it doesn't bear much rational consideration. Anyway, I think I'm doing my bit with undercover work. The other week I nearly got caught."

"What happened?"

"A woman saw me rifling through some coat pockets at that civic do I was waiting at, and I had to empty my pockets. Luckily, I'm always careful but I shan't be doing that again for a while."

"No, it's best to err on the side of caution. Do you still get bothered by that Braid at the restaurant?"

"Not so much but I know he would love to catch me out so I have to be very careful when he's on duty."

"You know, the British have released most of the Italian internees now. Have you thought of going home soon and forgetting all this false identity stuff?"

"Not really. The war won't be over for a long time. I'm happy where I am."

Giraudo smiled. "You really are getting settled here."

Although the delegation was still upbeat about the war, Luca noticed a change in tone when he spoke to his contact, Bertolini. He didn't say much but he intimated that Italy's resources were becoming dangerously over-stretched and that all was not well in the Italian military campaigns. Despite his lack of fervent patriotism, Luca was deeply disappointed by the Italian failures because he felt they reflected badly on all Italians. He heard jokes about the Italian army among colleagues in the catering agency, and he was strangely glad that they thought of him as English and could make the comments in his presence without giving offence. French staff at the restaurant were more restrained about Italian military failings but many of the customers made disparaging comments about Italian military prowess and he did find them hard to listen to.

Then, out of the blue, he encountered a personal crisis. In May 1941 Luca was covering for holidays by working at lunchtime. He'd just taken an order from a group of regular customers. As he went towards the bar area he heard a male voice say, "Luca! I didn't expect to see you here."

He stopped in his tracks and froze briefly; he hadn't heard his real name called out by a customer in nearly a year. He looked round and there was a table of four men, one of whom was smiling broadly at him. His face was familiar… or was it? In his career he'd seen thousands of faces and the same type of face dozens of times, so that everyone seemed familiar to a greater or lesser extent. His mind was racing, trying to dredge this person up from his mental archives.

"You don't recognise me?" said the man. "Miles Fenton. I used to go to Quaglino's quite a lot in the early '30s; you were the head waiter then, I think."

Luca smiled. He did remember the man: a regular customer who often lunched with some of the aristocratic set. He tried to look as blank as he could, then spoke in his best English accent.

"I'm sorry, sir, you must be mistaken. My name is Harry Baxter and I've never worked at Quaglino's."

"Oh!" said Fenton. He knew Luca looked different, a bit older and without the big moustache, and he thought he'd done well to recognise him. But the changed accent and the firm denial jolted his confidence. He was not inclined to persevere; it was not as if a long-lost friend had refused to acknowledge him. "Awfully sorry; my mistake," he said and turned back to his companions.

As Luca walked on he heard Fenton say, "I could have sworn I knew that chap," and that was the end of the matter as far as he was concerned.

But not for Braid. He'd heard the exchange and almost skipped towards him when Luca went to the bar.

"I knew it. You have some questions to answer." The lights from the chandelier reflected off his dome-shaped head and the sun illuminated his spectacles; he was transfigured.

They spent the rest of the luncheon session waiting for the conversation to come, two wrestlers pacing round the ring waiting to engage. Braid watched Luca with a leer on his face, counting the seconds to his moment of triumph. As soon as the opportunity presented itself he told Luca to accompany him to Charpentier's office and closed the door behind them.

Braid sat in Charpentier's swivel chair and gently rotated it from side to side.

"So, what have you to say about that incident today?"

"What incident exactly?"

"That man knew you, however much you try to deny it. You're not English at all, are you? What are you – a crook, some sort of agent, or just a charlatan pretending you're something you're not?"

"Don't be ridiculous, the man made a genuine mistake and mistook me for somebody else. Hasn't anyone ever thought they recognised you when they didn't know you?"

"You can try to change the subject but I *will* check out your reference, difficult though it is at the moment; your days here are numbered once I speak to the managers about you again."

"Do what you like; I've got nothing to fear."

With that Luca walked out. He was finished for the day and didn't bother to stay for lunch but instead went home. He walked quickly; he was in a hurry to do something but didn't yet know what. The further away he got from Gillot's the easier it was to think, though not to come to a conclusion. Everything could come out, everything could be lost: his job, the work for the embassy, his home even. Giraudo could be trusted not to reveal anything so that gave him time but it would come out.

When he neared home he saw a phone box and went in. He rang Bertolini on his private number.

The telephone rang eight times and he was about to give up; he gave it one more ring, and then another and then he heard Bertolini's voice, "Hello."

"It's Luca."

"Yes?"

"I have a problem. The deputy head waiter at Gillot's, Braid; I've mentioned him before."

"Yes, the one who is always trying to trip you up?"

"Yes. Well, today a customer recognised me from my time in London. I managed to convince him that he'd mistaken me for someone else but Braid thinks he has me now and he plans to expose me if he can. I thought I ought to let you know as it might cause problems for me and affect the work I've been doing for you."

"D'you think he'll be able to check you out easily?"

"I don't know. Obviously the war is a help, but who knows?"

"Don't worry about it and don't talk to anyone else about this. If someone from the restaurant tries to talk to you just stick to your story. He's probably bluffing anyway. Goodbye."

Luca put the receiver down slowly and stood in the phone box thinking, until someone banged on the door. He went on to his lodgings and up to his room. He took that week's notes from the drawer and put them in his pocket then went out again to make himself harder to contact. He wasn't working again at Gillot's until Wednesday and would try to stay out of the way in the meantime. Braid was working tomorrow and Wednesday so perhaps he wouldn't have time to do anything before then. He telephoned Giraudo from another call box and arranged to see him that evening, then he went for a bus ride just to kill some time.

That evening he called for Giraudo and they went out, ostensibly to visit a pub, but instead they talked as they walked in circles round the streets. Giraudo already knew all about Braid so he wasn't surprised that he'd reacted as he had to Luca's encounter with the customer. He took the same view as Bertolini.

"Just don't worry about it. He's probably already told the manager that he doesn't trust you. It'll blow over. If he does prove you're Italian just tell them that your loyalties are with Britain and that you changed your name because you no longer consider yourself Italian. You can bluff it out. The worst that will happen is that you have to start again. Cork is a fine town, I hear."

Afterwards, they did go to a pub and Giraudo succeeded in getting him to take a more positive perspective on the matter. He didn't sleep well that night but the next day he had a job with the catering company and that took his mind off it.

But Wednesday evening came round and he was filled with foreboding as he approached the restaurant back door. He went to the staffroom, greeting people as he passed them. They acknowledged him but nobody seemed willing to engage with him and there was a downbeat atmosphere. He put on his waistcoat and apron then went to the bar.

"Good evening, Harry," said the barman.

"Good evening, Michel, everything all right?"

"I suppose you haven't heard the news?"

"No. What's that?"

"Jean-Claude Braid was run over by a car last night. He's dead."

"My God – what happened?"

"I don't know the full details but there was a witness. Apparently he was walking home after work and a car came very fast round the corner, lost control and mounted the pavement. He didn't stand a chance. The car didn't even stop."

"Was he killed instantly?"

"I think so."

Luca went on with his work. His shift dragged, especially as it was quiet, and he was beset with questions he couldn't ask of any of his colleagues. Finally the restaurant closed and he could get away. He went straight to Giraudo's. The restaurant was closed but the lights were still on. He knocked on the door and Giraudo opened it.

"Hello, this is a surprise. Come in and I'll get some grappa."

Polly was in the kitchen and waved at him as they went upstairs.

Luca waited while Giraudo brought over two glasses and the bottle.

"Something up?" asked Giraudo.

"You don't know, then: Braid is dead."

"What?!"

"Yes, he was run over and killed last night in a hit-and-run. It's in tonight's paper."

"I haven't looked at the paper." He went downstairs and returned with the evening newspaper, turning over the pages, "Yes, here it is: 'Mr Jean-Claude Braid, Deputy Head Waiter at Gillot's restaurant, was knocked down and killed in a hit-and-run accident in Dublin last night. He leaves a wife and two sons. Police are anxious to interview the driver of the vehicle and any witnesses to the accident which occurred at about 11.30pm in the vicinity of Merrion Square.' Well, I won't drink to it but it's certainly a weight off your mind with him out of the way."

"Do you think it was an accident?"

"What else would it be?"

"Well, it is a coincidence that he was killed in a hit and run just a day after I told Bertolini about it."

Giraudo laughed. "You've been reading too many adventure stories. Just because someone you'd rather see the back of dies conveniently doesn't mean it wasn't an accident. It was probably somebody who'd had too much to drink and didn't stop for fear of the consequences. Let's be glad that Braid won't be around to stir things up all the time."

"I'll drink to that."

Luca went home but didn't sleep. He wanted to feel the way Giraudo did but he kept turning things over in his mind. The facts were just too convenient. The next morning he rang Bertolini again.

"It's Luca. The problem regarding Braid seems to have been solved."

"Yes, I saw it in the newspaper. So, that's that."

"Thank you for acting so promptly."

There was a pause on the other end of the line. "It was just an accident."

"You mean you didn't."

"It was just an accident," and he hung up.

Luca debated with himself over whether to attend Braid's funeral, on the day of which Gillot's was closed. Everyone knew they hadn't got on and Luca felt that Braid had loathed him, a sentiment he reciprocated. If he went, would he be considered a hypocrite or accused of dancing on his grave? If he didn't go, would it seem disrespectful or churlish? In the end he attended the service but didn't go to the wake afterwards.

After what happened, although he knew nothing to make him change his mind, he never felt quite the same about his undercover work. The continued decline of the Italian military situation didn't help matters. He believed the Italians were unlikely to plan any more military campaigns without the participation, and therefore control, of Germany. But to try to give up the role would seem defeatist. So he just carried on, though at a lower level of commitment. But there was something else; he found his loyalties more evenly divided. He liked the people he worked with and felt uncomfortable abusing the trust they placed in him by acting as an agent for their enemy.

Despite his expectations to the contrary Luca soon stopped concerning himself with the circumstances surrounding the death of Braid. If there was any lingering doubt that Braid might have harmed his career at Gillot's, this was dispelled a few weeks later. One of Roussel's team left to join the Free French forces and this created a full-time wine waiter post, which was offered to Luca; he happily took it. This event came at the right time since the number of opportunities he had to work for the catering agency was reduced to some extent by the deprivations caused by the war. He was quite pleased to have a more predictable work routine and to stop having to balance the demands of two employers, and he soon ceased working for the catering company entirely.

In his new post he strove to improve his knowledge of wines and other drinks to help him in his work and found that the more he learned the more he enjoyed learning. In this he was greatly helped by Roussel. Etienne Roussel was a man whose knowledge of his subject was born out of a love for it. He never tired of reading books or other sources of information about wine, especially those which told him what he already knew, as he took a quiet satisfaction in having his compendious knowledge confirmed. When he found an area in which his expertise was lacking or under-developed he was overjoyed in having found a new mine of unexplored treasures. His knowledge was not a matter of pride or self-importance, it was a quest to be as good a guide as he could be to those who appreciated wine. When he drank wine, it was as an analyst and a reviewer. The pleasure he took from a bottle of wine was in knowing and understanding it, not so much in consuming it. In truth, when he opened a great bottle of wine, like a Chateau Margaux 1900, there was always the nagging regret that the precious stock was then further diminished. He never showed off his knowledge nor did he try to catch others out or patronise them. An inspirational and encouraging teacher, he found in Luca a willing disciple.

IX

The next few years seemed to pass quickly. Ireland's neutrality did not spare it entirely from the effects of the war. German aircraft bombed Ireland on several occasions, probably in error, but in May 1941 twenty-eight people were killed when bombs fell on Dublin. This event was much discussed in the Donovan household as Mrs Donovan's cousin was one of those whose home was bombed, though fortunately she was out of the house at the time. Rationing had to be introduced in the same year and Luca was pleasantly surprised that he had very little difficulty in obtaining a ration book.

It was in the early part of 1942 that Luca went to elocution lessons. He loathed the way the Italian accent was often treated in the cinema and in other spheres as humorous, especially since the debacle in the war. He didn't want to be thought of as some kind of Chico Marx character, so he went to lessons with Mrs Spillane, a retired speech and drama teacher. When joining the class he made no secret of his Italian origin, as he realised he would be unlikely to fool an experienced linguist. Once a week he joined other students: a group of young ladies preparing for a secretarial career in prestigious organisations; and professionals, including an actor or two, who wished to polish their speech to develop what Mrs Spillane called "the most highly regarded of all English accents, that of Dublin".

So, Luca learned to master the 'th' sound and to pronounce words beginning with 'wh' as if they were spelt 'hw'. He also managed to dispose of the Italian tendency to add a vowel sound to words ending in a consonant. The class practised their newly refined diction by reading to the group great Irish poets like Yeats, Joyce, Wilde, Goldsmith and Swift. They also attempted, to great merriment and some *schadenfreude*, many of the notorious tongue-twisters of the English language, such as *Peter Piper*, *The thirty-three thieves* and W.S. Gilbert's *To sit in solemn silence in a dull, dark dock*. Luca went to the class for several months and by the end of it Mrs Spillane congratulated him on his progress.

"You won't pass for an Irishman, or even an Englishman, but people will have a job deciding where you are from. Your pronunciation and diction are now better than most of the native English speakers I have come across."

After a secret armistice with the allies in September 1943, Italy dropped out of the war and the Italian delegation ceased to collaborate with the Germans. It was at this time he was told that he was no longer required to operate as an undercover informant, much to Luca's relief. By now he'd had enough and had become increasingly worried that Gillot's might learn of his activities and get rid of him. Then Italy declared war on Germany and supported the allied war effort.

His old friend Di Pasco, the Italian consul, appeared at Gillot's, having lunch with his British counterpart, much to Luca's amusement. Tactfully, he acted as if he didn't know Di Pasco when he served him wine, and he received a generous tip.

Meanwhile, the French legation switched from representing the Vichy government to the Free French government in exile, though still with the same Xavier de Laforcade acting as *chargé d'affaires*. His welcome at Gillot's remained muted.

Then came June 1944 and the D-Day landings and rising excitement at Gillot's as the liberation of France gathered pace. On August 26th free champagne was given to all the customers, as de Gaulle led his triumphant march into Paris. After the lunchtime session Roussel asked Luca to join him for a drink to celebrate Paris's liberation. They sat in the little office off the wine cellar and Luca was pleasantly surprised to see that Roussel had a plate of oysters and some cheese as well as the wine.

"Shall we try this?" he said. "I've been saving it for this day."

It was a bottle of Chateau d'Yquem, the greatest of all the Sauternes, from the 1921 vintage, a particularly good one, and Luca wondered how much it would cost to buy. He knew that Roussel would not have filched it or lost the cost somewhere in his accounts because he was very scrupulous about such things. So, this was a very generous gift. The sommelier poured them both a glass of the deep golden wine. They toasted each other and took in the bouquet before drinking. It was cool but not too chilled and Luca savoured its complex sweetness. While they drank the wine and ate some of the oysters and a little cheese, Roussel regaled him with stories about Chateau d'Yquem: how the estate was once owned by the Plantagenet kings of England; that wine-making there went back over 400 years; and how a good vintage will still be drinkable after a century or more. Luca had heard it all before but stretched out his legs and sat back in his chair and contentedly listened to these re-spun anecdotes while he nodded and enjoyed the refreshments.

Such was his feeling of general bonhomie engendered by Roussel's generosity and sociability that Luca felt an impulse to finally, after many false starts, tell him the truth about his identity and background.

Almost against his will Luca found himself saying, "You know, I've never been totally honest with you about my background."

Roussel sat back in his chair and lit a cigarette. He nodded but said nothing.

Luca now regretted his sudden revelation but, after a brief pause, he carried on anyway, "I'm not really part English and part Swiss. I'm originally from Italy and I settled in England. I was interned by the British and escaped to Dublin, and when I was looking for a job I thought I might have more chance if I assumed an English identity. I didn't think a French restaurant would employ me otherwise."

"I know… well, at least I guessed something of the sort when you came for the interview."

Luca gasped, "You know? And Charpentier too?"

"I'm not sure what he knows. You may remember I asked you about your accent, and I felt that gave him the opportunity to raise the issue when we considered you for the job. He didn't, and I wasn't going to. Once you started work you were a good worker and nobody cared about your background. I chose to think of you as someone with an awkward past who wanted his anonymity, and I could understand that; I think most Frenchmen could. The only person with a problem was Braid."

Luca reached for a cigarette himself as Roussel came to this part of the story. "Braid?"

"Yes. About a month after you started here he spoke to Charpentier and Saqueneville. He asked for your references to be checked to prove that you weren't who you said you were, but they weren't interested."

"Why was that?"

"Charpentier prides himself on being a good judge of character so he wasn't going to have Braid challenge his choice of staff. Anyway, I told him I knew you better than anyone else here and considered you to be totally trustworthy. Saqueneville was happy to go with Charpentier, and he didn't like Braid anyway."

Luca blew softly through pursed lips. "Well, I'm grateful for the trust you had in me but why take the risk?"

Roussel shrugged. "Who knows? As I said, I have some sympathy for people who have to start again. I've had ups and downs in my own life so I know it can be tough when things go against you. Let me tell you what happened to me."

Luca sat forward in his chair. Roussel had never previously told him anything of his past life.

"I worked as a junior wine waiter in Biarritz and Paris when I started and then, in 1911, I was offered a job with the headquarters of a wine merchant in Marseilles. This was a job I was very pleased to get as I was keen to broaden my experience to enable me to learn more about the way the wine industry operated. After a few months I noticed there was a pattern whereby some wine deliveries would arrive one day, disappear almost immediately from the warehouse, then reappear a couple of days later. I checked and saw that they were always particular wines. So, I secretly opened a bottle of one consignment when it came in and another when the consignment returned from its period away. My suspicions were correct: the real wines were being stolen and replaced with wines which were good but not of the class and provenance of the originals. Superficially, the labels and bottles looked authentic and so were sold on as the real thing. I wasn't sure about the precise form the fraud was taking but decided to report the matter to my manager, who thanked me and said he would look into it.

"The following night I was followed from the warehouse by three men who roughed me up a little and told me that if I went any further with my story I wouldn't live to give evidence in court. I was really shaken up by this but felt I would get support from my employers. I was young and very naive. The next day when I went into work my manager called me into his office and advised me to seek work elsewhere then gave me an envelope. It contained an excellent reference and 200 francs. I looked at the money and wanted to throw it in his face and do something heroic. But I didn't. I was afraid of the consequences if I stood my ground, and I was being offered a chance to make a new start with the equivalent of three months' wages. I did as I was advised and left the wine merchant, to become a wine waiter on the liner SS *France*.

"You know, I've never told anybody that story before, not even my father and mother when they were alive. I still feel ashamed that I didn't have the guts to do more."

Luca shook his head. "What could you have done? If you'd

gone above the head of your manager you didn't know how far up the organisation the corruption went. If you'd gone to the police, the crooks would have had time to cover things up. It would have been your word against theirs. I think you did all you could be expected to. Most people just do what they have to do to get by; they shift with the prevailing wind."

Roussel did not look convinced. "Perhaps," he said.

"You know, Etienne, it's now almost impossible to find any French man or woman in Dublin who admits to having supported the Vichy regime. It's strange, isn't it?"

Roussel shook his head. "The worst thing about it is that I'm not in the least surprised. You're right; people's principles can become an inconvenience."

The conversation then turned to business matters, and they discussed the training of a young apprentice they had taken on to train as a wine waiter. By this time, Roussel had such complete faith in Luca's abilities that he delegated the training of new wine waiters to him. Luca was also now a firmly established favourite with the restaurant clientele. The frequent patrons of Gillot's were not there because of the quality and variety of the food; these were givens in a restaurant of this prestige and price, *a sine qua non*. They valued it as a place to meet others, to be at ease, to be known and appreciated and recognised by the staff. In his experience nothing made customers feel at ease more than being known by their names, and he was good at this, knowing the names of every customer he had served more than twice. He had become well-known to the clientele and they liked his style and the weight he gave to the wine prejudices of his customers, as well as to his professional judgement. On occasion, customers would show their appreciation with extra tips in the form of free tickets to the theatre or cinema or a sporting event.

It was later in 1944 that he decided to grow a moustache again and within a week had established one he was happy with. This one was not allowed to develop into the grand specimen of his younger years; this, he decided, was to be the moustache of an Englishman, clipped and tidy but conveying a hint of the dashing hero and a passing resemblance to Errol Flynn, though he told his colleagues that he'd grown it in honour of General de Gaulle.

Away from work, the passing years brought him a fuller social life. He was no longer the solitary stranger of the first few weeks, spending most of his evenings off alone in his room or exchanging small talk with whoever sat next to him in a bar. Apart from Roussel he now knew several of the staff at Gillot's and joined in with all the social functions, sometimes taking Nancy. His closest friends remained Giraudo and Polly and Brian and Eileen, and through them and Nancy he'd built up acquaintanceships with many other people; he now felt reasonably well engaged with life in Dublin.

His relationship with Nancy had now lasted for over four years and in October, on Nancy's birthday, he took her out for dinner, as he had done the previous two birthdays. This time, at her request, he took her to The Unicorn restaurant.

"New suit?" she asked.

"Yes, d'you like it?"

"It looks nice on you; is it navy? It's too dark to see properly in this light." She ran her arm down his sleeve.

"Yes." He stroked her hand then kissed it.

"You've got lots of lovely clothes now. You've come a long way in four years, what with the job and so on."

"Are you a part of the so on? I've come all that way with you." He raised his glass to her.

Nancy smiled and reciprocated the gesture.

He looked at her and thought, *I'm happy with you*. Their affair had not grown stale physically, and their sex life had gained, rather than lost, sparkle through more regular practice. They still enjoyed each other's company so they never suffered the fate of those couples who go out for a meal or a drink and sit in silence, looking at anything other than each other. They had established a pattern of living which had hardly changed over four years, and Luca hadn't asked if Nancy was happy with that since the first time they'd gone to bed together.

He called the waiter over and ordered for both of them at her request. He didn't speak Italian because he didn't want to cut Nancy out of the conversation so he spoke English even when choosing from the menu. They had a good bottle of Barolo and after dinner, as it was her birthday, Luca offered to take her wherever she wanted. She chose to spend the night together and, for the first time, he stayed the whole night in her bed. The only disadvantage was that they had to set the alarm for five-thirty so he could be out of the house before her mother woke. This was one of the behaviours which had not changed over the years. Luca never stayed the night, and whatever Nancy's mother knew of what they did in Nancy's room she never let on. The charade of total propriety was maintained by all.

X

A few days after Nancy's birthday Luca came home from work one afternoon and saw an ambulance parked outside the Donovans' house.

As he was about to go in the front door a man in a suit raised his hand, "Stand back, please, there's a stretcher coming down."

Then Luca saw Mrs Donovan being carried down the stairs by two ambulance men. She appeared to be unconscious. Behind the stretcher came Mr Donovan, carrying some clothes and other things in a bag; he was mopping his brow and reaching out, but not quite catching, his wife's hand. Luca was at a loss for words.

"Can I do anything?" he asked Mr Donovan.

"The doctor thinks she may have had a stroke," was all Mr Donovan said, and he followed his wife into the ambulance.

The man in the suit, whom Luca assumed must be the doctor, nodded and went to his car to follow the ambulance. Luca walked into the house and into the kitchen to make a cup of tea. Already sitting there was Mr Phillips, his hands round a mug of cold tea.

"A bad business," said Phillips.

The uniqueness of the situation had prompted his fellow lodger to actually speak to him without being spoken to and Luca was taken off guard.

"Yes," was all he could say in response.

"She was doing too much; I told her," Phillips continued.

Luca made the tea and sat down at the kitchen table. He was shocked by the news but could tell that Phillips was feeling it on a different level.

"You've known her a long time," he said.

"Nearly fifteen years. She's done a lot for me."

So, the conversation went on, the occasional phrase of empathy and comfort from Luca, not wishing to prattle on in case he got on Phillips' nerves, and the brief, telegrammatic utterances of Phillips by way of response. After a bit, Phillips rose from his chair and, with a nod, went off to his room. Luca did the same, as he was going out that evening with Nancy and had to get ready.

When he returned, later that evening, Luca saw the light on in the kitchen and went there to find Mr Donovan having a cup of tea and a sandwich. He looked up when Luca knocked on the door and entered.

"Hello Mr Baxter," he said.

"How are things with Mrs Donovan?" Luca inquired.

Mr Donovan looked up with a smile. "Well now, she's made quite a recovery. She's able to speak all right and move all her limbs. The left arm is a bit weak and she has no grip in her left hand but they're thinking it was a mild stroke and she should make a good recovery. She needs plenty of rest, and she won't be coming home for a while. I left her sitting up with a cup of tea!"

"Thank God; what a relief," said Luca. "If there's anything I can do anytime just let me know. I think I'll turn in now. Goodnight."

Mr Donovan waved and was left with his thoughts.

The next morning Luca rose earlier than usual. He went down to the kitchen where, as he'd guessed, he found Mr Donovan starting to get breakfast.

"Let me help you," he said. "I'm probably more used to doing this than you are."

Mr Donovan nodded and handed his spatula to Luca, then he

looked after the tea and toast while Luca cooked the breakfast. Phillips arrived a few minutes later and was actually quite warm in his thanks to Luca for helping out. Over the next week or so the three men worked together to keep the house going properly, and together they visited Mrs Donovan in hospital while her recovery continued. During that time the Donovan household came to resemble a gentlemen's club, with convivial dinners cooked by Luca and Donovan. Afterwards there were drinks in the sitting room where Phillips acted as waiter. Then he relaxed with his newspaper while the other two discussed the topics of the day.

The day that Mrs Donovan came home Luca cooked them all a dinner of roast beef, and Phillips brought some Guinness and light ale to drink. Donovan was quiet during the meal and, with Mrs Donovan unable to say much and Phillips unwilling to, most of the meal passed in silence. After they'd cleared away and Mrs Donovan had retired for the evening Mr Donovan asked the two men to join him for a whiskey in the sitting room.

After they'd settled down with their drinks Mr Donovan said, "I want to thank you for being so kind during the wife's illness; you both went beyond what anyone could ask in a difficult time. The thing is, I don't think we can carry on as before, you know, having lodgers, not with Clara having had that stroke. I don't want to risk it, and we're both well over seventy now; it's time for us to retire. I am sorry about this, boys, but you see how it is."

Luca was not surprised and, though disappointed, he fully understood the situation. He glanced over at Phillips who looked down at the carpet.

"I do understand," said Luca. "When would you like us to go?"

"Well, I'll manage for a few weeks but I don't want Clara trying to start up again, so I was thinking about the end of the month."

Luca nodded. "That'll be fine by me," he said.

Phillips said nothing other than, "Thanks for the drink," as he put down his glass and went back to his own room.

The next day, Luca began the process of again finding somewhere to live. It wasn't easy to find somewhere which suited him as well as the Donovans', and in the first week he didn't see anything he liked enough. In the following week he tried a different segment of the city: the Portobello area around Synge Street. At the corner of one road a newsagent had a selection of cards in the window, advertising items for sale and cleaning and other services, and one caught his eye:

ROOM TO LET
COMFORTABLY FURNISHED ROOM TO LET IN
PLEASANT HOUSE
BREAKFAST PROVIDED AND OTHER MEALS BY
ARRANGEMENT
WILL SUIT SINGLE PROFESSIONAL LADY OR
GENTLEMAN
APPLY WITHIN

He walked into the shop and told the young woman behind the counter that he was interested in the room. She asked him to wait while she got the owner. A couple of minutes later a well-dressed man of about Luca's age came out from the back room and asked if he could help him. Luca requested some details about the room to let and the man gave him a few basic details.

"Would you tell me a little about yourself, your occupation and so forth?" asked the man.

Luca was surprised to be interviewed by the newsagent but assumed he must have some good reason for doing so.

"I'm English, from London, and I've worked in Ireland for several years. I'm presently a wine waiter at Gillot's restaurant in the town."

"Why are you seeking a room now? Have your circumstances changed?"

"Yes, my current landlady, with whom I have been for over four years, is retiring due to ill health."

The man nodded. "I hope you don't mind all these questions but I'm the brother of the lady who has the room to let and I agreed to handle some of the process for her. She doesn't want any undesirable types calling on her."

Luca smiled. "I hope I don't come into that category."

The man just looked at him without comment so Luca produced a sparkling reference from Mr Donovan which the man read and returned to him with a nod of validation. They discussed the issue of rent and payment, and the man gave Luca the address and his sister's name, Mrs Cody. Luca thought the rent was a bit high for one room but that he might as well look at it as he liked the area. The newsagent said that it would be a good time to call now because he'd arranged with his sister that she would be available to see prospective lodgers from around eleven to one o'clock each day.

With the address on a piece of paper and directions from the newsagent, Luca set off on the ten-minute walk to Mrs Cody's house. The street was terraced with substantial three-storey houses, including a basement; there were steps up to Mrs Cody's red-painted front door. He rang the doorbell, and after a few moments the door was opened by a young woman of about thirty-five in a floral summer dress. She had dark-brown hair with a pale complexion and blue eyes. Her face and arms still bore the last glimmer of fading summer freckles.

"Good morning," she said, and smiled.

"Good morning. I was sent round by your brother to view the room."

"Ah, yes, he phoned to say you were coming. Mr Baxter?"

"Yes. Is it convenient for me to see the room now?"

"Certainly; come in. I'm Mrs Cody, Veronica Cody." She spoke with a soft Dublin accent and Luca thought that Mrs Spillane, his former elocution teacher, would have approved.

Veronica stood back and he walked into a hall with a bold-patterned William Morris wallpaper and green and cream paintwork. She then took him to a flight of stairs which led down to the basement. Their footsteps were muffled by a runner-type carpet in the centre of the stairs. At the bottom a vestibule led to three doors, and Veronica opened the one in the middle.

It opened into a good-sized room, around fourteen feet by twelve, decorated with an unfussy pale-beige wallpaper. The room was furnished with a wide single bed, a side cabinet, man's wardrobe, chest of drawers with a mirror, a tea table and a couple of armchairs. A large rug with a bold pattern on a muted-pink background covered the centre of the room, laid on plain lino. The bedcover and curtains, in a floral design, seemed more suitable for a lady than a man, in Luca's opinion, but this was of no importance. The room was spacious, clean and tidy, and he liked it. The window looked out onto the front. The supporting wall for the garden obscured the view of the lower part of the window but through the upper half he could see the small garden and the street beyond.

"I like the room," he said.

Veronica's clasped hands gave a little nod and she smiled.

"The room has its own front door," she said and led Luca out of the room to a door which opened onto an open concrete area and to stone steps up to street level. Luca mumbled positively, and Veronica closed the door and turned to the third door in the basement. "There's also a bathroom down here which we use, and you would have access to it at certain times of the day. The toilet is outside, at the back of the house, I'm afraid, but there's a covered walkway to it."

She opened the bathroom door and showed him a room painted pale-blue and partly tiled in white, with a large roll-top bath and substantial rectangular basin. Luca looked around the room again. He had instantly liked the feel of this place and he knew that this would suit him.

"I like the room very much," he said, "and I'd be interested in taking it at the proposed rent."

"May I ask why you're looking for lodgings, Mr Baxter?" asked Veronica.

"As I explained to your brother, my current landlady is retiring, so although I was very happy there I have no choice but to seek a new place."

He produced his reference from Mr Donovan and handed it to her. Veronica read it carefully and gave it back to him.

"That's a very good reference, quite satisfactory," she said. She tapped her front teeth with her thumb nail. "You have no family in Dublin?"

"No. I have family in England but not here."

"Oh?" She tapped her teeth with her nail again.

There was a long pause and it was Luca who ended it: "My wife and I are separated and I have no children."

Veronica nodded. "I see; thank you for being so frank. Could you tell me about your work arrangements, as they might affect your coming and going?"

"Well, my job is mostly afternoons and evenings, and I would be coming in quite late, certainly after midnight on some evenings, but I'll try to be very quiet. I would be out of the house most mornings after ten o'clock."

"I think you said you were happy with the rent. You would have a key to the basement and access to the bathroom. You can go through the hall and back door to the lavatory. Early morning tea and breakfast will be provided and if you would like an evening meal that would be possible with two days' notice, but cost extra. The sheets on the bed will be changed every fortnight and pillowcases every week. The rent must be paid one week in advance starting the day you move in. Any damage to furniture or bedding would be charged for." She recited all this fairly quickly and rather mechanically.

Luca nodded. "That will be fine. My current landlady allowed me to put my personal laundry in with hers, for a fee of course. Would that be possible for you too?"

Veronica put her thumb to her teeth. "Um… laundry? Yes, I think so. I'm sure that won't present a difficulty."

"The conditions are fine, Mrs Cody. When can I move in?"

Mrs Cody stuttered a little: "Well, I… that is… whenever you wish, within reason."

"Would the 29th suit you?"

"The 29th of October?" repeated Veronica and then muttered, "Like it or lump it."

"Pardon?" asked Luca.

"Oh, nothing, I was thinking of something else." She held out her hand to shake on the deal. "Yes. That will be fine."

Luca shook her hand. "Just one other thing. Would I be able to use the telephone? I'd pay for any outgoing calls of course."

"The telephone, oh yes. I'll give you a card with the number on."

She went out of the room for a couple of minutes and came back with a postcard on which she'd written the number and her address in a confident, copperplate script.

"Well, thank you very much, Mrs Cody," said Luca. "I shall see you in a couple of weeks. I'll arrive at about six o'clock if that's all right."

"Yes, that will be fine, Mr Baxter," said Veronica as she opened the front door.

Two weeks later Luca left the Donovans for the last time. He wasn't working that day and Mrs Donovan was well enough to cook lunch, though Luca lent a hand. Over lunch the Donovans told him that they'd considered moving to a bungalow but had decided to stay where they were, for now at least.

"Why is that?" asked Luca.

"It's Jack, Jack Phillips. He has nowhere to go, and he was

heartbroken about leaving here," said Mrs Donovan. "We just didn't have the heart."

"So, we've come to a compromise," continued Mr Donovan. "We've given him until the end of January to make other arrangements, so he has time to get used to the idea."

Luca said his goodbyes later that afternoon and promised to keep in touch, then took his luggage and the few possessions he had accumulated in a taxi to Veronica Cody's house. When he arrived at about six o'clock she took him down to the basement and gave him the keys to his door and one for the door out of the basement. In return he gave her an envelope containing one week's rent.

"Regarding the bathroom, I thought you could have it to yourself for half an hour in the morning and one hour in the evening; I trust that will be acceptable. Please remember to lock the bathroom and toilet doors when using the facilities."

"That sounds perfect."

"Would you like a cup of tea, Mr Baxter?" she asked, as they went back up to the hall.

"Yes, thank you, I would."

She took him into the dining room, a darker room than his bedroom, with heavy walnut furniture and a deep-red wallpaper. If his bedroom was a feminine room this one was definitely masculine. In the window was a small table with two chairs, and she asked him to take a seat while she made the tea. She came back after a few minutes with a tray on which were matching teapot, cups and milk and sugar bowls, with a plate of biscuits.

"What made you come to Ireland, Mr Baxter?" she asked, pouring the tea and then offering him the plate of biscuits.

"Please call me Harry," said Luca. "It's a long story. My wife and I separated some time ago and I fancied travelling a bit since I have no children to worry about. I worked in restaurants and hotels all over the place and finally landed here in Ireland."

"You must have been very worried about your relations in

England with the bombing and so on, but I suppose you can see light at the end of the tunnel now?" She took a biscuit herself and held it in her hand.

"Yes, it was very difficult in the first couple of years, and of course there are still the flying bombs to contend with, but the Germans are definitely on the run. As your brother is helping to look after your interests with regard to letting rooms, I assume your husband is away?" he asked.

"My husband died two years ago last month," she said.

"I *am* sorry. He must have died quite young."

"He was thirty-eight. He died in an accident."

"That's awful. A very sad time for you and with a young family too." He nodded towards a photograph of a young boy and younger girl on the sideboard.

"Yes." She looked down.

"I'm very sorry," he said, "I didn't mean to upset you."

She took a handkerchief from her apron and wiped her eye. "Please don't apologise. I still get upset sometimes at the slightest thing or even for no reason. I'm sorry to be such a wet."

"Now I have to tell *you* not to apologise." He smiled and she smiled back a little. "Good-looking children," he said, glancing once again at the photograph. "How old are they?"

"Reggie, the boy, is six, and Laura is three and a half."

Luca took another biscuit from the plate and finished his tea. Veronica promptly refilled his cup.

"You must have a very busy life, bringing up the children on your own and managing to rent out a room as well. I shall try not to be a nuisance for you."

"I'm sure you won't be a nuisance. Do have another biscuit."

"Thanks. Have you been renting rooms long?" he asked.

Veronica blushed a little and tapped her teeth with her thumb. "Not long. Actually, this is the first time I've ever done it. That's why my brother has been a great help, advertising it and advice and so on. You must bear with me if I don't get things right at first, and do let me know at once if you have cause to complain; I'm learning on the job, as it were."

"Yes, there must be a lot to think about." Luca finished his tea and stood up. "I am sure everything will be just as I would want it. Thank you very much for the tea and biscuits and for welcoming me into your home. I will respect it as if it were my own." He smiled once more and left to go to his room.

The room was every bit as pleasant as he remembered it. Veronica had put a little vase with a few winter pansies in it on his table; a nice touch he thought.

The day Luca moved in to Veronica's house was a Sunday, and as Nancy wasn't working they'd agreed to meet up once he'd settled into his new place. After he'd unpacked his clothes and belongings he went to meet her in Portobello and they had a salt beef sandwich and chocolate gateau in a Jewish restaurant in Little Jerusalem.

"You look especially lovely this evening," he said.

"Oh, I don't know about that but thanks very much anyway," she said. Nancy always gave a little flick of her head when she acknowledged a compliment, which made Luca smile. "How are the new lodgings?"

"I've been very lucky. I didn't think I'd get anything better than last time but this place is a real gem. A fine old house and I have my own entrance to a basement flat. There's also a bathroom in the basement that I share with the family. However, there aren't any other lodgers so it shouldn't be a problem."

"What's the landlady like?"

"She seems very nice. She's a young widow with two small children, and I believe times have got a little hard for her hence the need for a lodger. I am her first ever lodger apparently."

"The separate access gives you more privacy, so that's better than the other place," said Nancy.

Luca nodded and smiled; he knew what Nancy was thinking.

Immediately he found himself contemplating the possibility of sex as a focal point for the evening.

"Would you like to see the room later?" he asked.

"Soon," she said simply.

They picked up a couple of bottles of beer from an off licence and walked arm in arm to his new 'apartment'. It was about nine when they entered the basement area quietly, and Luca wondered if Mrs Cody might be in the bathroom. However, there was no sound from there as they went into the bedroom. He pulled the curtains, turned on the light and took the beer over to the glasses Mrs Cody had thoughtfully left on the table. He unscrewed a bottle top, poured them both a glass and Nancy came over to him.

They'd had barely a sip before Nancy kissed him and said, "Unzip me," and turned her back. He did as she bade him, and she stepped out of her dress and quickly removed the rest of her clothing. "Come on," she said and climbed into the bed. Luca took his clothes off while she watched him.

"You *are* in a hurry," he said.

"Oh, I am," she said. "I've thought of nothing else since you mentioned the private entrance." She laughed and grabbed his body as he got into the bed, pulling him on top of her. After a frenzied few minutes Nancy lay half on top of him and played with the hair on his chest. "That was so bloody good," she said, and smiled at him. "Can I stay the night?"

They had slept together in the literal sense a few times when her mother was away and on holiday, a couple of times when she was in the house, and when they had gone away themselves, but this presented new possibilities.

"Not tonight; not the first night I'm here. You understand, don't you?"

"Yes, of course. It was just an idea." She lay on her back. "I thought it would be nice not to have to get dressed again."

He looked at his watch; it was not even a quarter to ten.

"I'll walk you home and maybe you'll ask me in for a cup of coffee?"

"Maybe," she said, teasing him, as she swung out of the bed.

He watched her get dressed and thought how fortunate he was to have her. He thought her just as beautiful as when they'd first met. Doubtless she could have had other men who might have offered her something more than she had with him: a couple of nights a week plus the occasional trip out or a few days away. Yet she'd accepted this for four years without making any demands or ever even broaching the subject of where the relationship was going. He knew that she'd said she would never make demands but she must have thought about it sometimes. While he was happy with the way things were, he couldn't quite believe that she was too, but he wasn't going to ask.

In the months that followed, life for Luca and Nancy settled into a new pattern. Veronica and Luca had arranged times when he would use the bathroom, and Veronica told him that she didn't object to him entertaining visitors and left it at that.

So, when Nancy visited him or stayed the night, which she did now and again, she was able to use the bathroom too. They were very discreet and generally quiet, and Veronica never commented. Either way, it was good for Nancy and Luca's relationship as at last he had a space that belonged, sort of, to him.

XI

By the time Luca had lodged with Veronica for only a couple of weeks he realised how fortunate he'd been in his choice of landlady, or rather her choice of lodger. She seemed a kind woman who looked after his meals and laundry well and didn't intrude on his personal life. He therefore tried to do all he could not to impose on her generosity, especially because he was a little uncomfortable that a woman clearly from a higher social background should do his cooking and take care of his washing. They had the odd chat, especially after the evening meals he occasionally booked with her, and they found each other pleasant company. He formed the impression she was quite lonely and had largely fallen out of the social circle she'd been in with her husband. Her mother came round occasionally, and her brother and his wife too, but she appeared to go out only rarely. Admittedly, Luca wasn't there all the time and he thought that she might have dates of some sort at the weekend. After dinner one evening she surprised him by inviting him into the drawing room and offering him a nightcap.

"I don't really drink," she said, "and I have a drinks cabinet full of bottles my husband bought or was given as presents."

She gestured to a tray with all the most common spirits and fortified wines on it, with a soda siphon and a bottle of tonic water. She had an amontillado sherry and he a rather fine cognac. They toasted each other and sat in the fading light in the drawing room. It was the first time she'd invited him in there, and he noticed it was furnished well with modern sofas and armchairs and one or two antique pieces. It was lighter and airier than the dining room.

"Have you settled in all right now, Harry?" she asked.

"Yes, thank you, Mrs Cody. I'm very happy here and you've made me most welcome."

"Please call me Veronica," she said. "I feel we know each other well enough now. I'm so pleased you like living here."

"I'm very happy with the arrangements and hope you're not too disappointed with your choice of lodger."

"I think you chose yourself really. I remember after I showed you round you asked a couple of questions and then pretty well said you'd take it, and it seemed rude to wait to see if anyone better came along."

"Sorry, I must have jumped the gun."

She laughed. "It's quite all right. I think I would have found an excuse if I hadn't liked the look of you. Like the previous two potential takers."

"Why, what were they like?"

"I suppose they weren't that bad really but when I began advertising for a lodger I had this fantasy idea of getting a professional lady from my sort of background with an amicable disposition; a carbon copy of me, I suppose. Naturally she didn't appear and instead the first one was a very large man with plastered-down hair who breathed rather heavily and, as he put it, travelled in gentlemen's requisites, whatever that means. The second applicant was very smartly dressed and quite good-looking. He said he was in Dublin for a few months to arrange some contracts for his firm, a carpet company. He seemed on the face of it acceptable but I couldn't help but get the impression that he considered himself something of a ladies' man, and I wasn't absolutely sure I would feel comfortable with him about the place. That sounds awful, and probably I would have accepted either of those eventually if I was forced to lower my expectations – changed circumstances and all that. But you know how it is."

Luca laughed. "So, I was the least worst at that point. You should have waited; the next one might have been better."

"No, I'm quite happy. My brother isn't, however. I promised I wouldn't select anyone for the room until he'd given his approval. I don't think he's forgiven me yet."

"I suppose I was rather pushy, but as soon as I'd seen the room I knew it would suit me very well and I didn't want to risk losing it."

"He'll be all right about it; he just worries."

"I don't mean to pry but I suppose the changed circumstances resulted from the loss of your husband?"

"Yes. When Roger died he left me the house but very little else; just a small widow's pension. I don't come from a wealthy family and my father is dead, so my mother couldn't help much. My father-in-law is very kind; he's set up a trust fund to pay for the children's education, and given me a small allowance, but it's not enough to manage this house without help. With your money I can afford to have my home help come in once or twice a week and keep my head above water. Perhaps when the children are older I might even get a job."

"What did you do before you were married, Veronica?"

"I was a nurse." She rose from her chair. "Would you like another?"

He said he would so she poured them the same again then switched on the table lamps and sat down. She asked him about his life in England and the various places he'd worked, such as Quaglino's and The Dorchester and he gave a potted history of his career in London. "D'you know London well?" he asked.

"I've been to London several times, but not since 1937 when I went with Roger to watch the King's coronation procession. Roger wasn't keen on going as it was a bit of a trek, but I talked him into it and I think he enjoyed it really. We stayed with some friends in

Broxbourne the night before, and the night after so we didn't have to stay in London."

"I remember it well. People were in high spirits and they say the crowds were several deep. The weather wasn't very good though."

Veronica laughed. "We got very wet standing on the pavement but most people didn't seem to mind. Where were you that day?"

"I was on honeymoon. We had married the previous week and were on holiday in Scotland. We listened to the coronation on the wireless."

For the next few weeks Luca kept pretty much to his own space. But it didn't stop him thinking about Veronica. Almost from their very first meeting she'd been very natural with him, treating him more like a guest than a lodger. Always she did these kindnesses self-disparagingly and as if anyone else would do the same, but Luca knew that few landladies would be as hospitable.

Gillot's opened for lunch on Christmas Day and was open all day on St Stephen's Day. Every Christmas Luca had spent at Gillot's he'd worked on both Christmas Day and St Stephen's Day so that staff with families could have more time at home over the festive season. As this Christmas approached Luca decided he would follow the same pattern as before, in case Nancy or Giraudo or anyone else might feel they should try to fit him into their family arrangements. The Christmas lunch was booked up several weeks in advance, and Roussel went through the suggested wine list with Luca so he could get a feel for the process of drawing up an appropriate and balanced selection. After lunch had been served and cleared away the staff were given a glass of vintage champagne by the manager before they headed off to their homes.

As it happened, Nancy spent Christmas Day at her brother's with her mother, and she worked on the following evening. Because Veronica spent the holiday with her in-laws, Luca was left entirely to his own devices. On Christmas Day he took some leftovers from the restaurant home with him and had a meal in the silent kitchen. In the evening he looked in on the Donovans for a drink, as he had done in previous years. He didn't stay too long as Mrs Donovan, though still improving, was obviously tired, and he spent most of the evening in a pub, where he stayed until closing time. The pub was full of people like himself who had no one to spend Christmas with, and others who were on their way to a Christmas party but shared a few drinks with friends beforehand. It made for an enjoyable and high-spirited evening where inhibitions were relaxed and singing to a piano accompaniment was unrestrained.

Luca didn't drink a lot and turned down a couple of invitations to go on to parties as he thought Christmas parties were for family and friends, not strangers. In any case, he had to work the next day.

Veronica returned with the children on the day after St Stephen's Day, and when Luca got home in the afternoon there was a note for him propped up on his chest of drawers. It read:

Dear Harry,

I hope you had an enjoyable Christmas and you didn't feel you rattled around in this big house all on your own. I wonder if you are free to join me for dinner tomorrow evening, at about eight o'clock, to celebrate a little, as it is still the Christmas season!

Yours truly,
Veronica

Luca read it and reread it. He thought it a well-crafted note, friendly and warm but light with no pressure. He thought it best not to read too much into it but felt it was a nice gesture of Veronica's to give him a special dinner over the Christmas period. He knocked on the kitchen door and accepted the invitation, as he wasn't working the following day. Veronica looked very pleased and asked him to join her in the drawing room for a glass of sherry at a quarter to eight.

XII

Veronica's Christmas celebrations had been quite structured and formal, and she hadn't enjoyed them very much. Her in-laws lived in a big house in Monkstown and, as well as Veronica and her children, her sister-in-law Margaret and her husband and their three children were also there. Veronica's father-in-law, Basil Cody, was a semi-retired barrister and still called himself a King's Counsel despite the fact that Ireland was to all intents and purposes a republic. Her sister-in-law's husband, Kenneth, was a banker at Guinness & Mahon. Although both her family and the one she had married into had the same Anglo-Irish origins, the similarities were superficial rather than meaningful. While the Codys were wealthy and in the inner circle of Dublin society, the Halls were generally of a lower pecking order, small business people like Veronica's brother.

When Veronica became engaged to Roger, his parents, particularly his mother, were mildly opposed to the marriage for the very reasons that Roger was attracted to Veronica: she wasn't one of the Dublin social set and she seemed a freer spirit and frankly far more interesting than those girls his parents would have liked him to marry. When he'd had a freak fall and died after breaking his neck rock-climbing in the Wicklow Mountains his parents had been very supportive, and the incident had brought Veronica and Roger's mother closer to some extent. Roger's father had suggested that Veronica and the children move in with him and his wife to "make life easier for you" as he put it. Veronica had declined as kindly as she could; she didn't want to hurt their feelings.

Nothing could convince her more that she'd made the right decision than being with her in-laws at Christmas, which every year was very staid and quiet. On Christmas morning this year they'd all attended a service at St Mary's Church of Ireland parish church, where Basil had read the lesson, followed by a brisk walk along the coast road before returning home for a buffet lunch. After lunch it was presents and playing with the children and then off to change for an early dinner so the children could join in with the festivities. They'd been joined for dinner by Mr Cody's widowed sister, Alice. After dinner Veronica and Margaret had put the children to bed and read them stories. The two sisters-in-law got on well and, as Margaret's children were not much older than Reggie and Laura, the cousins liked spending time together. There was a certain amount of playing and loud whispering among the cousins after lights out before they settled down. After the two women had chatted for a bit while they'd freshened up their make-up, they joined the others for an evening of charades and bridge.

Veronica had hoped to duck out of the bridge but everyone was inveigled into it. She found herself having to make a nerve-wracking, tooth-tapping small slam in Hearts, watched over by her partner, Basil Cody himself, like a benign hawk. Then there were a few drinks before Veronica could retire and read a book for a while.

St Stephen's Day started off more relaxed. Veronica spent the morning taking the children out with Margaret, and as it was windy they took kites with them. She enjoyed running along with Reggie as he launched his kite into the air. After lunch the men went to the races and Margaret took Reggie and her three children to a pantomime: *Puss in Boots*. Veronica helped her mother-in-law, Louise, and the cook get things ready for dinner in the evening and played with Laura. It was then that it became a little less relaxed.

"How are things regarding your lodger?" asked Louise, who was preparing some canapés.

"It's going very well, thank you. He's a very pleasant man who's no trouble at all. One would hardly know he's there most of the time." She hoped to disarm Louise with a couple of upbeat statements, but to no effect.

"I wish you'd not taken a lodger. It doesn't reflect well on the family name that our son's wife has to take in lodgers." Louise spoke quietly but used a lot of energy lacerating an innocuous tomato.

"It's only one lodger. I was in a difficult situation when Roger died. How could I keep the house with the income I have? And it's difficult for me to work with children so young."

They'd had this same conversation several times and she could hear herself saying the same lines she always said, like a script. She knew that if she'd taken a job, that also would "not have reflected well on the family name".

"Had it been a lady it would have been preferable, less worthy of comment." Louise did not elaborate on this last phrase.

"As opposed to a single man in his early forties who is quite good-looking, like a slightly darker version of Laurence Olivier, I suppose."

Louise scowled. "It's no joking matter."

Veronica was growing exasperated and could hear her voice rising. "I hoped to have the sort of lodger you suggest but there were none. The streets of Dublin are full of single or widowed landladies who have male lodgers; it's hardly worth mentioning unless you think it's in some way immoral."

"Not immoral, but infra dig."

"I haven't got the wherewithal to stand on my dignity. If the children and I are making the best of things, the least you could do is be supportive rather than critical."

Louise made a lot of noise scraping some peelings into the waste bin.

"My biggest worry is that we don't know the man; what he's like, whether he's totally trustworthy. Then there are the children to think of."

Both mother and grandmother looked at Laura but she was engrossed in her wooden jigsaw.

"He has lodged with me for nearly three months and has never been anything other than polite and honourable. In any case, he never sees the children as he has his own area. Furthermore, all our bedrooms have locks and I keep their doors locked at night. I don't even know why I'm trying to justify myself and defend Harold like this. I'm not stupid and I'm a good judge of character; after all, I chose your son as my husband."

Louise pursed her lips and the two women resumed their tasks in silence. Veronica wished she didn't have to stay another day and couldn't wait to get back home to normality.

The evening was much the same as Christmas Day except that the party was slightly larger with the arrival of Louise's sister and brother-in-law, Elizabeth and Bertie Armitage. Veronica rather liked Bertie, as he always paid attention to the children for a few minutes when he saw them and gave them some brand new coins which he said he just happened to have in his pocket. In the evening he was always entertaining, with a ready wit and a tendency to drink never too much but always enough to give her the hope that something extraordinary could happen – though it never did.

Bertie got the others to play more light-hearted card games like gin rummy and canasta, as well as bridge, and livened up the charades with getting everybody to do impersonations of their favourite film stars. He had a decent tenor voice and could always be persuaded, after some faux resistance, to sing a couple of sentimental Irish ballads while Elizabeth accompanied him on the piano.

It was during a lull in proceedings, while she was sitting with a dry martini and idly flicking through a book in the library, that Veronica had the idea of inviting her lodger to a special Christmas meal. She didn't know if this was a good idea or not but wanted to do it anyway. She wasn't tempted to share the idea with any of her in-laws.

And so it was that, even before she got home that Friday, she was composing a suitable invitation to place in Luca's room. She was very pleased when he accepted and endeavoured to make it special by dressing for dinner and getting out the best crockery and glassware. She prepared everything in advance as best she could and only changed into her dress a few minutes before going down for drinks. When she walked into the drawing room Luca was waiting for her, and she was surprised and flattered that he'd taken as much trouble as she had to make the evening special. He was wearing a dinner suit and bow tie and carried with him a box of chocolate liqueurs and a bottle of wine.

"Sorry I kept you waiting," she said.

"I only arrived a minute ago."

"Would you like a sherry?" she asked him.

"A dry one if you have one, please."

She was wearing a deep-blue satin dress, cocktail length, with a pearl necklace and earrings. The dress was slightly off her shoulders and, if not exactly a plunging neckline, it was cut away enough to catch his eye. Luca watched her as she walked over to the drinks table and returned with the glasses of sherry, an amontillado for her and a Tio Pepe for him. Then he presented her with his gifts. She thanked him graciously and looked at the label on the wine.

"Shall we have this with dinner?" she asked, pointing to the bottle.

"Yes, why not? I'm sure it'll be a good accompaniment to dinner."

Veronica smiled and nodded. She looked at Luca and was glad that he'd worn a dinner suit as she'd been worried about being over-dressed. She offered him a cigarette and took one herself.

"Dinner should be about twenty minutes," she said, looking at her watch.

Luca noticed it was a rather fine watch in platinum or white gold with diamonds.

"That's a lovely watch," he said. "It reminds me of one that belongs to my aunt."

Veronica looked down at it. "Yes, it was a present from my husband on my thirtieth birthday." She wound it a little and stared at it.

Then they talked about Christmas and how each of them had spent it.

"It's quite a responsibility to get everything right for Christmas in a restaurant," said Veronica. "How did you learn so much about wine?"

"Well, it started because my father worked in a vineyard, so I learned a lot of the basics from him, and then I picked the rest up through my work experience and some study. Etienne Roussel, the head waiter, is very knowledgeable and he's been a great help to me since I came to Ireland. It was Etienne who selected the wine I brought. He thought you might appreciate it, partly because the owners of the vineyard are Anglo-Irish, the Leoville Barton estate. It's a very good St Julien."

Intrigued, Veronica went back to the table and looked at the label and smiled.

"Barton," she said.

"You know of it?" asked Luca.

"I'm smiling because my father-in-law would have apoplexy if he knew we were drinking this wine."

"Oh!" replied Luca.

"You see, one of the Barton family who owns this vineyard was a prominent republican and didn't want to compromise with the British. My father-in-law is very anti-republican and thought Barton was betraying his own class and heritage. So, he wouldn't be so keen on it."

"I am sorry; I didn't realise."

Veronica laughed. "Don't be silly. It doesn't matter to me.

I'm sure the Bartons making the wine had enough on their plates without getting involved in the politics over here."

"I don't know much about Irish politics, I'm afraid."

"It's so complicated it would make your head spin. I sometimes think we have more political opinions than politicians, and everyone is a politician. Let's not talk about it over dinner."

She refreshed his drink and asked him to excuse her while she went to prepare the first course. She served him smoked fish terrine, lamb cutlets and apricot pie, with a cheese board to follow. With the cheese she served a bottle of port she'd bought for the occasion. She'd cooked for Luca before, several times, when he had requested an evening meal, so she wasn't worried about cooking for him, but she wanted this to go well.

As the dinner progressed Veronica became more relaxed. She was pleased with the food, and the wine was a perfect accompaniment. Luca seemed to be enjoying it and he was charming company, not just interested in talking about himself but sensitive to which areas of conversation she was comfortable with. Tonight she was happy to talk about pretty much anything: her life; her upbringing in Portobello and education at a private school; her father's business as a newspaper and publication wholesaler, which had failed in the early '30s; and her career as a nurse.

"Did you enjoy nursing?" asked Luca.

"Oh yes, I always wanted to be a nurse. I suppose it was a vocation for me because I had no illusions about it; I knew there would be downs as well as ups but it never put me off. From my very first day it was as if I'd always been there; I never had any doubts."

"But you gave it up when you married?"

"Yes, Roger was my second vocation, I guess. In any case, I would have had to leave nursing once I was married; that's the way it is here."

"How did you meet Roger?"

"There was a dance at the hospital and he came with a friend. We got chatting and it turned out that we had common acquaintances because his sister had gone to my school, although we didn't know each other to speak to at the time. Then it went from there. We got married in '31 and I had to give up nursing then. Fortunately, it was before my father's business got into trouble so he was able to pay for the wedding. He would have been heartbroken if he wasn't able to do that." Her eyes moistened a little.

"You must miss your husband very much."

She nodded. "Roger's family thought he could have done better, and probably they're right, but he didn't care about that. He was a good husband and father. Unfortunately, he couldn't leave me as well provided for as he'd hoped because there was no insurance to cover his accident and he hadn't built up much of a pension."

"Why was there no insurance?"

"He fell on a rock-climbing holiday. He'd never had insurance as it didn't seem necessary; it was a freak accident."

Veronica didn't seem bitter or angry about this; she had long ago come to terms with the vagaries of life.

"I think you've done very well to pick up the pieces and carry on. It can't have been very easy."

Veronica could feel emotions welling up within her; she said nothing but sipped her wine. Luca was still speaking about the hardships of being a widow but she could hardly hear his voice as she reflected on how much she'd missed Roger when he died. It had taken a long time to be like it was now: missing him but not always thinking about it. She'd found that the Christina Rossetti poem, *When I am dead, my dearest*, had relieved any guilt she'd had about the pain of loss fading. *And if thou wilt, remember, And if thou wilt, forget.* The second verse seemed to say that the departed one may forget too, and this chimed with Veronica's belief that Roger would not be missing her at all.

"Either he's in heaven and can't therefore be hurt by anything that happens on earth, or he's ceased to exist," she told herself when she thought about it.

141

She suddenly heard Luca more clearly again: "I don't wish to appear impertinent, but I do appreciate how good you've been to me since I came to live here, and if I can be of service in any way do ask and I'll be only too pleased to help."

She smiled. "What did you have in mind?"

"Well, I'm not sure really – any little problem around the house that I could help with, or babysitting as the children grow older – whatever crops up."

"That's very kind of you, Harry, and I do appreciate it. I'm managing quite well now in balancing the household budget, and the help from my father-in-law is most welcome. So, I can afford to get people in to do jobs if I need to, but I'll keep your offer in mind."

She took the dessert plates away to the kitchen. As she stood she felt the effects of the two glasses of wine and resolved not to have any more. After all, things seemed to be going well and she didn't want to mess it up. She returned from the kitchen with the cheeseboard and biscuits and brought the bottle of port over from the drinks table.

Meanwhile, Luca topped up her wine glass and poured the rest of the St Julien into his own glass. He accepted the offer of some cheese and let her cut him a little cheddar.

"This has been a very fine meal, Veronica. I'm enjoying it very much."

"I'm glad. It's always a little bit terrifying cooking for someone who's in the profession. You must have some wonderful food at the restaurant."

"Yes, but sometimes it can be too much. Often, after a shift, I can't always face rich food and am quite happy just having something simple like egg on toast. But this was very good."

The evening meandered on as the conversation flitted from one thing to another. Luca insisted on helping to clear away the dinner things and he dried while she washed the dishes. Afterwards, Veronica made some coffee and they sat in the drawing room where she insisted on giving Luca a small brandy. They talked about nothing in particular and Veronica wondered if Luca was too polite to wind up the evening.

"Are you working tomorrow?" she asked, noticing the clock showed twenty to eleven.

"No, I have tomorrow and Saturday off this week, in lieu of Christmas," replied Luca, draining the brandy in his glass.

"Poor old you, working while everyone else is having a nice time. Still, as you have a nice long weekend I shall top up your glass."

"Please, but only if you have something too."

Veronica smiled and looked at what she could have that was convivial without tipping her over the edge. She saw she had a bottle of De Kuyper cherry brandy and poured a drop in a small glass before bringing the bottle over to Luca.

"Cheers," she said, raising the glass and sipping the sweet liqueur.

Veronica was thinking about what time the children would wake and how long they had before she must go to bed. She went over to the gramophone and put on a Joe Loss record, making sure the volume wasn't too high.

"D'you think you'll go back to England after the war, Harry?"

"I haven't decided yet," he said. "I have a job here that I like and good friends, but I don't really have any roots so I shall have to see."

"Yes, I know what you mean. I know something of how you feel, as I've become a little cut off from my past life since I married. It sometimes seems as if I'm in no-man's-land."

"But you still have your family, and your children are your new roots surely?"

"Yes, of course; things will straighten themselves out, I'm sure."

She felt suddenly rather churlish to compare herself to him, a man who spent even Christmas without any members of his family.

After they had chatted for a little while Luca looked at his watch.

"I really ought to be going. Thank you for this evening. I've enjoyed it very much."

"Me too," replied Veronica. "We must do it again," she added, not meaning to.

They rose to say goodnight and Veronica offered her hand. Luca reverted to his Italian customs and kissed her hand. She spontaneously kissed him chastely on the cheek.

Veronica took the glasses out to the kitchen, lamenting her gesture at the end of the evening in case he thought her foolish. But she had enjoyed his company and hoped it wouldn't be too long before she had another excuse to entertain him. Indeed, every time they had a chat or a drink or a meal she liked it very much. She was aware that he had a 'lady friend' and that he brought her back to his room, but that was fine. Why would she be interested, even in the vaguest way, in a man whom no other woman cared about? All she wanted anyway was just a bit of company from time to time.

She took her make-up off in her bedroom to allow Luca to use the bathroom. After she thought he must have gone to bed she crept down to the bathroom to have a wash and to clean her teeth. She remembered how she used to worry about bumping into him when she went to the bathroom and now she could almost wish it might happen. Afterwards she climbed the two flights of stairs to her bedroom, looking in on the children on the way, tucking them in and giving each of them a kiss.

XIII

After Christmas, Luca and Veronica continued their cordial relationship, spending the occasional time together over meals, cups of coffee and chatting about the place, but that was all. They didn't replicate their special dinner at Christmas nor did they spend an evening together; it was as if that evening was an aberration, and they reverted to the norm for a landlady and her lodger.

Soon after the Christmas season ended, Veronica's mother came round for coffee. A woman in her late fifties, she looked like an older version of Veronica, her dark hair flecked with grey and another stone in weight, but still clearly her daughter's mother. As they sat talking, she broached with Veronica the prickly idea that she should get out more often and accept some of the invitations that came her way, especially from men.

"You know, darling, you are thirty-five and, lovely though you are, you haven't that many years before eligible bachelors will be harder to find."

Veronica bristled a little at her mother's suggestion, especially the way it was framed.

"I can't think there are many eligible bachelors who want to start married life with two young children."

"All the same, it would do you good to get out more and enjoy some adult company from time to time. I'd be delighted to babysit or even have the children overnight sometimes."

Veronica did think it was a good idea really. Much as she loved her children, conversation with them was limited to topics that concerned them. She did sometimes think that her brain might go soft if she didn't spend more time in adult company. After the first few months of widowhood she'd received steadily fewer invitations or callers, and she was alone, sometimes lonely, in the evenings once the children were in bed. Most of the men she knew were married and had dropped out of her social sphere once she no longer had a husband. She'd made up her mind not to marry again as she didn't want to impose a stepfather on her children. This prejudice arose from her having had a friend who'd been cruelly treated by her stepfather, even though he'd seemed pleasant enough when he'd first married her mother. So, she tended to dissuade single men to call on her.

Except when her female friends or relatives visited, she spent most evenings reading and listening to the wireless or the gramophone, and she really did miss adult conversation. She also thought that after being pretty much out of the social circuit for so long she might enjoy more socialising, perhaps even meeting somebody interesting.

So, over the next few months she did go on several dates, mostly foursomes from her old social set. She also had a few solo dates with well-mannered, very pleasant men, none of whom she particularly wanted to see again, except for Maurice Sturridge. He was a very good-looking bachelor of about forty, tall and dark with a particularly elegant nose and a self-confident but not smug manner. She'd known him for some years and had met him at parties a few times; he had a good sense of humour and was never a bore. He had asked her out more than once but she'd always turned him down; she wasn't sure why nobody had snapped him up if he was such a good catch. But after a foursome he asked her out again and this time she relented and was pleased to go. He took her out to dinner one evening and it went well, so she agreed to go to the Gaiety Theatre with him the following week and have supper afterwards. Her mother willingly had the children for the night so she could be back late if she wished.

After a very pleasant evening he drove her home and she was happy enough to invite him in for coffee and a nightcap. She didn't object when he sat next to her on the sofa, nor when he put his arm round her and kissed her; she was happy to try it out again after such a long time. Nor did she worry when his hand touched her breast through her dress; although a little rusty, she'd handled this situation many times in the past and knew when to call a halt. She put her imagined whistle to her lips as his hand moved under her dress and touched her thigh, and then she clasped the hand and moved it away. Often that did the trick and, if not, a sharp, "Stop, Maurice!" could be expected to do so as she moved his hand away a second time.

But it didn't, and Maurice was becoming insistent now as he pulled her dress up and used his weight to lean on her and trap her where she was. After a couple of declarations of admiration and longing had failed to move her, his tone turned harder: "Come on, Veronica, don't tell me you don't want to; you know you do," he said, in an attempt to coax and challenge at the same time.

She struggled to push him off but it was impossible. His hand was pulling at her pants and she could feel the heat of his palm on her belly. She kept her legs tightly closed as much as she was able.

"Please, Maurice, I don't want this," she said as firmly as she could while grasping at the hand that was trying to pull down her pants. She could feel his hardness against her and in that moment several thoughts were going through her mind simultaneously: *How can I get him off me? How much longer can I resist this onslaught? When do I have to start damage limitation so it won't be too painful for me?* The last thought made her renew her determination to try and put a stop to it and, as she felt the elastic go in her pants and his hand go inside

147

them, she managed to push her other hand between his body and hers and reach for his genitals.

Maurice relaxed his force slightly as he thought she might have changed her mind, then realised her hand had bypassed his penis and was squeezing his testicles as hard as she could. With a yelp he raised his hand to slap her face when the door, which had been ajar, suddenly opened wide and a voice said, "Can I be of assistance, madam?"

His ardour now doubly quenched, Maurice's head swung round to see a man in a dinner suit bearing down on him.

"Who the hell are you?" he said, his grip relaxing on Veronica's arm.

"I am the butler, sir," said Luca.

Maurice looked astonished. "The butler?!"

Veronica used this moment of bewilderment to push Maurice away and extricate herself from under him. She stood up and deftly pulled down her dress.

"Mr Sturridge was just leaving," she said.

Luca picked up Maurice's hat, which had been tossed on a chair.

"Your hat, sir," he said, giving it to Maurice and placing himself between Maurice and Veronica.

"Good night, Maurice," Veronica said, and turned her back on him.

Maurice opened his mouth to speak but was left dumbfounded. He walked slowly out into the hall with Luca shepherding him from behind, and then Luca pushed past him to open the front door.

"Goodnight, sir," said Luca, giving him a gentle push and closing the door after him.

Luca went back into the drawing room. Veronica was trying to light a cigarette but her hands were shaking so Luca lit it for her.

"Are you all right?" he said.

"Yes. Thank God you came in, though; I was struggling to keep him off. You were brilliant."

"You need a drink," he said and fetched her a glass of brandy.

She sat down on the sofa and sipped a little of the brandy, which she didn't like very much but it gave a comforting warmth as it slid down her throat.

"Would you like me to call anyone?" asked Luca.

"No, thank you."

"I can sit with you if you like. Or would you rather be alone?"

"No, stay. It'll go round and round in my head if I'm on my own."

Luca sat opposite her and lit a cigarette. They sat in silence for a few moments.

"How did you know to come in?" she asked.

"I must have got home sometime after you. I was smoking a cigarette and looking something up in a book when I heard a raised voice; it was yours. Luckily, the drawing room door was open a little. I wasn't sure at first whether you two were just playing around but then I heard you shout again. I crept up the stairs and then I heard the commotion and I knew something was wrong."

Veronica smiled. "What on earth made you say you were the butler? Maurice knows I haven't got a butler."

"Well, to begin with I thought that in this outfit I could pass as a butler and also, if I'd got the wrong end of the stick and there wasn't a problem between you, a butler would be less likely to cause embarrassment than a lodger. On top of that, a butler commands authority and respect whereas a lodger doesn't. I didn't stop to think how unlikely it all was."

She was amazed to find herself laughing but knew it wasn't hysteria: it was the elated relief that she'd come through relatively unscathed and that Luca had turned up trumps. "It certainly stopped him in his tracks," she said.

Then Veronica fell silent as she looked down and reflected on the events of the last half hour. *It's not happened to me before. I've always been able to deal with the situation. Or was it that I was never in this exact situation before? It doesn't matter either way; it was awful but he hasn't been able to defile me. Soon, I shall look back and it'll be just an extreme case of someone getting a bit too fresh: very unpleasant but no lasting damage.* She willed it to be so.

Luca sat quietly too but when Veronica looked up he said something that lifted her spirits. "I know it was horrible for you but the way you dealt with it after I came in gave you back control of the situation. He was the one who was humiliated, not you. I'm not putting it very well but I hope that makes sense."

"It does, and it's kind of you to say so, but I think you're understating what you did. Had you not intervened it would probably have turned into something I'd rather not think about. Anyway, it's over now and I do thank you from the bottom of my heart. Won't you have a drink and I can pretend I spent the evening with you and the rest was just a bad dream?"

"If you'd like me to," said Luca and went over to the drinks tray.

"I'll be back in a minute," said Veronica.

She could feel that her pants were barely staying up so needed to change them. Also, she wanted to wash Maurice away from her face and where he'd touched her body. She went upstairs and changed her underwear. In doing so she noticed there was a ladder in her stockings and cursed Maurice, as stockings were so hard to get. She had a washbasin in her bedroom so she washed her face and decided to have a bath before going to bed. Then she repaired her make-up to a 'that'll do' standard before rejoining Luca.

"I'm sorry I was so long," she said. "Could you pour me another drink, please, and put some soda in this one?" she added, holding out her glass.

They sat in silence for a while, Veronica turning over in her mind what had happened in the last hour or so. She was feeling better now and wondered whether Maurice would have taken rejection in his stride and think nothing of it, or whether he now felt foolish or embarrassed. She thought how ironic it was that her mother-in-law had worried about her having a male lodger whereas the man who had attacked her was the sort of man her mother-in-law thought she should consort with.

"I can't believe what happened, really," she said eventually. "I've known Maurice for years; I never dreamed he would behave like that."

"Perhaps he misunderstood the situation and then got carried away. It's a common fault in us men."

But not in you, thought Veronica. "Perhaps he's like that with every woman but has just never tried it on with me before," she said.

"Yes. He may think the word 'no' is just a slow 'yes'."

"Thanks for sitting with me, Harry," Veronica said. "I think I'll have a bath and go to bed." She finished her drink and walked over to Luca. "You were wonderful tonight, thank you." She embraced him and kissed him on the cheek. "Help yourself to another drink," she said.

Luca kissed her hand. "Goodnight, Veronica, I hope you sleep well."

Veronica went up to her room to collect her dressing gown and toiletries and then went to the basement to run her bath. She threw the stockings away and put the dress aside to be cleaned. Then she waited patiently for the bath to fill enough for her to climb into it, though the night was cold and she could feel herself getting goose bumps. Finally, she climbed into the bath and lay full-length. She closed her eyes and could have fallen asleep as the tension in her body slowly subsided.

The next morning Veronica slept late. She'd forgotten to set the alarm and was surprised to see the clock said half past eight. She leapt out of bed and had to decide whether to dress and look presentable, and be even later, or to go down and get Luca's breakfast. She thought it best to go down in her dressing gown and to hell with appearances. She opened her door and saw a note on the floor:

Good morning, Veronica. Please don't worry about me; I shall get my own breakfast.

Harry

She smiled and went back inside her room, then dressed before going down to the kitchen. When she opened the door Luca was sitting at the table, eating eggs and bacon.

He looked up. "Good morning. I hope you slept well?"

"Yes, I did actually, once I got off, thank you. I'm so sorry but I forgot to set the alarm. It was kind of you to get breakfast yourself, but it's a bit much."

"It's fine. Let me get you something."

"Don't be silly, you must have things to do, what with work and so on."

"Please, I insist."

"Well, just a cup of tea and a piece of toast is all I really want."

Veronica was a little surprised that she didn't feel uncomfortable with the situation but she was glad it was like this. After last night, how could she regard Harry as anything other than a friend, lodger or not?

Luca made another pot of tea and put a couple of pieces of bread in the toaster. They chatted over breakfast. Veronica assured Luca that she was absolutely fine this morning and that the whole episode was behind her.

At about half past nine there was a ring at the door and Veronica came back into the kitchen with a large bouquet of flowers. She read the card aloud:

Dear Veronica,

So awfully sorry about my behaviour last night. I hope we can still be friends. Yours,

Maurice

"Well, aren't they *lovely*? What a kind gesture!" she said. Luca looked up and gave a non-committal nod. "Not really," she said and threw the flowers in the bin, and they laughed. "I hope he does feel bad but I don't trust his motives anymore," Veronica said. "I certainly don't want to see him again."

She'd decided she wouldn't mention what had happened the previous night to anyone; it was all best forgotten, along with Maurice.

XIV

A couple of weeks later, around the middle of April, Luca was given a pair of complimentary tickets for the theatre by a customer at Gillot's.

As Luca poured drinks at his table the customer, who knew Luca well, said, "Here you are, Harry, I'm sure you'll enjoy this as you're mentioned all the way through it," and handed him the tickets for a play called *Uncle Harry*. The other people at the table grinned as he took the tickets, and Luca laughed as he looked at the title of the play.

"I hope I don't have to stand up every time my name is spoken," he said, "but thanks very much."

Despite the humour in it, Luca knew it was a genuine gesture of appreciation. Over the years he'd become very popular with the regular customers, who thought him charming. Luca did not effect to be charming. In his professional role, he'd developed over years of experience an ability to say the right thing in pretty much any situation and this had made him likeable to customers, especially as his demeanour was always polite but never obsequious, friendly but never impertinent, and helpful but never smothering. He'd become almost as much a fixture as Roussel and it was rare now for someone to ask specifically for the sommelier when seeking advice on wine.

When he got back to his lodgings in the early evening, he knocked on the kitchen door where Veronica was preparing supper for the children.

"Sorry to interrupt you, Veronica, but perhaps I could speak to you when you have a free moment."

"Yes, of course. Have you eaten?"

"I had lunch so I'll have a snack later."

"I've more than enough for myself. Won't you join me and share it? I haven't really thanked you properly for that business the other week," she said, conscious of Reggie and Laura listening in the background.

"That would be nice, thank you. See you at eight o'clock, then. Hello Reggie and Laura," he added and the children waved.

Later, over a light supper, Veronica asked Luca what he wanted to talk to her about.

"A customer gave me two tickets to a play at the Gate Theatre next week." He produced an envelope from his pocket, took out the two tickets and laid them on the table.

Veronica looked at them and smiled. "*Uncle Harry* – how appropriate," she said.

"Yes, it was a bit of a joke really. I'm not much of a theatregoer and wondered if you'd like to go with a friend?"

"Why can't I go with you? You're a friend."

Luca was genuinely surprised. He'd meant the offer to be for Veronica and hadn't even considered going to the theatre himself or he would have asked Nancy.

"I've never been to the theatre in England or Ireland, except when I went to the opera in London a couple of times, but a play…" He shook his head. "I don't think it's my kind of thing. I'm not a very well-educated person."

"Don't be silly. Not all plays are Greek tragedies or Shakespeare. Anyway, it's the Abbey Theatre that has the most high-brow stuff. I'm sure it'll be fine. Do come with me. I promise I'll explain it all to you afterwards," she said and grinned.

Luca smiled and nodded. "I'd very much like to go with you but would you be comfortable being seen out together?"

"Why shouldn't I be?"

"Well, I'm just a waiter, and your lodger. I don't care about me but I don't want people to talk about you or be unpleasant to you for going out with me."

Veronica shrugged. "People can be such snobs but we mustn't worry about it. It'll be all right; we're only going to the theatre after all."

So, about a week later Luca and Veronica went to see *Uncle Harry* at the Gate Theatre. Veronica thought it best not to ask her mother to babysit, in case she asked a lot of questions, and instead was able to ask Carmel, a girl of about fifteen who lived five doors along from her. The children knew Carmel and she read them a story while Veronica and Luca went out to a waiting taxi. The babysitter had brought a book with her, a romantic novel, and Veronica had left her a box of chocolates and some soft drinks by way of treats.

The evening was very enjoyable. They had good seats and the acting was excellent as the actors avoided hamming up the black comedy moments and played them as if it were a straight drama. *Uncle Harry* is a play by Thomas Job about a man who plans to murder one of his sisters and frame the other one for it, with unpredictable consequences. Luca enjoyed the play, as Veronica had said he would, and she didn't need to explain it for him, as Luca pointed out with a wink.

They were chatting about it in the interval over a drink when they heard a voice say, "Veronica, how are you?"

They turned to see an elegant blonde woman of about forty in a black dress, with a cigarette in one hand and a drink in the other. She was accompanied by a thick-set man, about ten years older, who had a good-humoured expression and thinning hair smartly combed with the help of Brylcreem. He was smoking a cigar and clutching a scotch and soda.

"Marcia, how lovely to see you; I'm fine, thank you," said Veronica. "Harry, these are two old friends of mine, Marcia and Charles McIntyre. Harry Baxter."

Harry stood up and shook Charles's hand. "How do you do."

"How do you do," said Charles.

"Not so much of the 'old', Veronica," said Marcia, flashing a smile as she shook hands with Harry. "Where has she been hiding you?"

Harry smiled. "How do you do. I'm very pleased to meet you."

"So nice to find you out and about," continued Marcia. "Haven't seen you for ages. How are the children? Reggie must be quite grown up now."

"What do you do, Harry?" asked Charles.

Harry thought that this could be the tricky situation he'd worried about when she'd insisted on him coming to the theatre with her. However, he'd never seen Charles at Gillot's and thought it unlikely that he ever frequented the place.

"I'm in the wine business," he replied.

"Ah! It must have been a tough time for you over the last few years?"

"Yes, it was in the early part of the war – French supplies dried up – but things have eased up a lot, especially with the fall of Italy and France. But it'll take time to get back to normal. How about you?"

"I work in the stock market," said Charles.

The bell for the end of the interval rang before he could elaborate.

"Oh, what a shame," said Marcia. "Must catch up soon, Veronica. Very pleased to have met you, Mr Baxter."

Charles shrugged, "Hope to get to know you better next time Harry," he said. He and his wife finished their drinks and hurried off in the opposite direction to Veronica and Harry.

After the theatre they got a taxi home. Luca told Veronica how much he'd enjoyed the play and thanked her for pushing him into seeing it. They arrived home at about 10.15 and Carmel reported that she'd heard nothing from the children once they'd settled down. Veronica gave Carmel a couple of shillings and asked if she would like to be walked home. Carmel looked slightly insulted and said it was only a few yards up the road, but Veronica watched from the front door until she saw Carmel disappear up her steps.

"Coffee and a brandy?" she asked Luca as she opened the door for him into the drawing room.

"That would be just right," said Luca, and while Veronica made the coffee he took the opportunity to look at the books in the large bookcase which took up much of one wall. He surmised that most of the books had belonged to Roger, especially some of the adventure novels associated with boyhood reading, such as *Ivanhoe, Treasure Island* and *Huckleberry Finn,* and many others he'd never come across. There were also lots of books on English and Irish history and one of them, a three-volume set by Froude, *The English in Ireland*, particularly interested him and he thought he might like to read it. He was gratified, too, to see that there were translations of well-known Italian works: the *Autobiography of Benvenuto Cellini*, Dante's *Divine Comedy* and Machiavelli's *The Prince*, among others.

It was a warm evening in the latter part of April and there was no need for heating in the room. His attention was drawn to the empty grate in the fireplace, neatly prepared with newspaper, kindle and coal for the next fire, whenever that should be. He lit a cigarette and daydreamed about living in this part of the house, with its paraphernalia of family life. There was Laura's toy dog, apparently asleep in the corner of the room, and Veronica's sewing basket set on a small table by her chair. The books, military prints and well-stocked drinks cabinet were an evocative presence of a paterfamilias any man would have to usurp to be a part of this. How contrasting was his own room which bore hardly a fingerprint of his own personality: just his clothes, a few reference works on wines, one or two other books he'd acquired since he'd arrived in Dublin, and his wireless. Without possessions he had no discernible persona, and without a persona he had no substance. If he disappeared tomorrow it would be as if the ground had swallowed him up and there'd be scarcely a trace to show that he'd really existed.

He was roused from his reverie by Veronica backing into the room with a tray on which were the coffee things and a plate of shortbread biscuits. She smiled at him and put the tray on a table between their two chairs. Then she went to the drinks tray and poured him a large brandy and a cherry brandy for herself.

"Here's to you, *Uncle Harry*," she said, and raised her glass. "I've had a lovely evening. Thanks for inviting me to the theatre."

"I very much enjoyed it too. How do you know Marcia and Charles?"

"Oh, Marcia used to live near Roger's parents and knew the family well, so when I married Roger we started doing lots of things together. I haven't seen her for a while. Charles is a stockbroker and sometimes has dealings with my brother-in-law, so we keep in touch. I think they're a very genuine couple; there's no side to them at all."

"They did seem very friendly. I hope I didn't let you down when we met them."

"*Harry*," she said with a reproach in her voice, "how can you say that? I'm sure they both thought you charming, especially Marcia."

"I don't know about that, but I'm glad you think so."

Veronica poured the coffee and took a cigarette from the box on the table.

"I saw in the paper that they're making a film of *Uncle Harry*; perhaps we could go and see it, if it ever makes it to Dublin?"

She held her cigarette to her mouth, and as Luca lit it she held his hand steady. Luca went back to his chair and thought for a while.

"Yes, that would be good," he replied eventually.

"Is everything all right, Harry?" Veronica asked.

"Yes, sorry… I'm a bit tired. Think I'll go to bed." He rose from his chair and took her hand. "Thank you for persuading me to go to the theatre. Goodnight." He thought of kissing her but didn't.

"Goodnight, Harry," replied Veronica. She squeezed his hand.

XV

Shortly after the trip to the theatre, the war in Europe came to what seemed like an abrupt end with the collapse of Germany. Although the staff at Gillot's had looked forward to the inevitable victory of the allies, it was difficult for them to relish the countdown towards victory because of the muted attention given to the event by the Irish press. The government, as part of its strict policy on neutrality, censored the newspapers against taking a position on one side or the other, so there was a very bland response to the succession of surrenders by the German forces. However, on VE Day, the 8th of May, the *Irish Times* evaded censorship by delaying going to print until the last minute and producing a big 'V for Victory' headline, with photographs of the allied leaders.

This seemed to open the floodgates for those in Ireland who wished to celebrate the allied victory, and Mr Gillot bought several copies of the *Irish Times* and displayed them in the windows of the restaurant. Later that day around fifty students of the predominantly protestant Trinity College raised the flags of the allies on the roof of the college. Somebody complained that the Irish tricolour was missing, so this flag was added to the bottom of the flagpole. Somebody else complained that the Irish flag should have been more prominently displayed, so it was taken off the flagpole and set on fire. The students sang *God Save the King* and *Rule Britannia*, and they were cheered by the waiters as they marched past Gillot's on their way to Grafton Street. The mood in the restaurant was becoming increasingly excited and Charpentier had to calm things down a little because: "Not all the customers think the way we do."

As the afternoon wore on tempers became a little frayed when the students of the National University tried to hoist the Irish tricolour on Trinity College and, when thwarted, burnt the Union Jack. A near riot followed, and in the disturbances a brick was thrown through the window of Gillot's. There was no other damage and nobody was injured but Mr Gillot instructed the restaurant management to close for the evening.

As Luca was helping to clear away at the end of this truncated session, Charpentier handed him a card from Mr Gillot inviting him to a celebration dinner for the senior staff to mark the end of the war in Europe.

"But I'm not a senior staff member," he said.

"No, but you and John Foster are both invited because Mr Gillot thought it a pity that English people can't celebrate the victory in their home country; so, you are both special today."

At seven o'clock Luca and eight other members of staff joined Mr and Mrs Gillot at their home for the celebration dinner. Gillot had been given advance notice of the imminent German surrender and had already arranged for outside caterers to come in to serve dinner and champagne, the latter from his own cellar.

Gillot was the grandson of the founder of the restaurant and had been born in Ireland but educated in England. A man of about Luca's age, he was very tall and rather thin, with a head of receding dark hair and a neatly trimmed moustache. After everyone had been served champagne he gave a short speech in which he said that, as a Frenchman by blood, he was overjoyed that the allies had won the war, but also, though an Irishman by birth and loyalty, he very much supported the British victory in this war. He knew this was a view shared by many Irish people who'd gone to England to fight or to help in other ways, including some of Gillot's own staff.

There were toasts to King George VI, Generals de Gaulle and Leclerc, Winston Churchill and to the Gillot staff who had volunteered for military service, all of whom had been promised a job if they wanted one when they returned. Some very good wine was drunk.

Luca knew Gillot from his appearances in the restaurant, usually as a diner. He took very little part in the direction of the restaurant as most of it was delegated to the restaurant manager, Frederic Saqueneville. So, although he knew all the people at the dinner by name and sight, Gillot spoke to them after the meal more as a visiting dignitary than a boss. He circled the room slowly and deliberately, making sure he spoke to everybody. He told Luca that he'd heard very good things about him and hoped he would stay with the restaurant in peacetime. Luca nodded and said how much he enjoyed working at Gillot's, and he sang the praises of Roussel.

Something about the end of the European war jolted Luca into a sense of restlessness. Content though he was with life, there now seemed more choices and he wasn't sure how many of the choices he'd made over the last five years had really been his own. Then there were these questions which kept surfacing in his mind: What had happened to Ellen and his business?; Had they both survived the war?; Had Ellen met somebody else?; Had his old life effectively disintegrated? He sometimes thought of going back, as much to find some answers as to take up again what was left of his old life.

Yet Dublin still seemed the right place to be. He enjoyed his work and he'd rediscovered the camaraderie that he used to have when he'd worked in hotels and restaurants in London. He had a good circle of friends and social acquaintances, and his lodgings were more than just somewhere to live; he liked being there. Above all, there was Nancy: the first person to befriend him when he'd arrived in Dublin and his friend and lover for five years. How did he feel about treating her as an object to be discarded when other choices beckoned? When he put his curiosity to one side and thought what going to London would really mean, it was not nearly so attractive. He would have to explain everything to Ellen and to others, try to pick up the pieces he had long before left, maybe sort out legal issues; he wasn't sure.

The early August Bank Holiday was a damp affair but Luca and Nancy had agreed to go out for the day. They'd got used to spending their summer days off on a trip to the seaside or a ride out to the country but this summer Nancy had often been too busy. Luca put this down to changing work patterns and was pleased when Nancy took up his offer to go out for the day. When the day came round the weather forecast wasn't great but she still seemed keen to take a chance and go for it. They went to Malahide and began with a walk around the castle grounds. It wasn't raining but the air was damp and they stayed on the paths, stepping round and over the puddles.

Luca seemed to be doing all the talking. He would start on a subject and she'd just agree or make no comment. After a few minutes, silence fell on them like a dead weight and Luca felt unable to lift it.

Eventually, Nancy led them over to a bench and they sat down, their macks bearing the brunt of the residual damp on the seat.

"There's something I need to talk to you about," said Nancy.

Luca smiled. "Sounds serious."

He watched as two sparrows, oblivious to the clouds gathering above them, scurried tamely around, hoping for some crumbs to come their way.

"I'm not sure." She looked at him silently for a moment or two, then went on. "We've been going out together for five years and I don't know where we're going. I mean, is this it? Are we going to carry on like this for another five years?"

"I thought we were happy with things as they are."

"It's the war being over that's changed everything. I knew there was nothing permanent about us because one day the war would end and you would go; I didn't expect it to last this long. But now the war is over, are you going to stay here or will you go back home to England?"

"What would you like me to do?"

Nancy was about to answer when a couple approached their bench and glanced at them. Nancy paused as they went past.

"I'd like you to stay, of course, but what would that mean for us? Would we go on as before?"

"I've been thinking about what I'll do but I haven't any definite plans. You have to be part of any decision I take."

"Yes, but what does that mean? I suppose we're both trying to make up our minds. You see, we've never really talked about 'us', about plans or whether we have a future. I've been happy with that but things are different now. I need to know where I'm going. I don't know how you *feel* about anything really; I don't think I know what you're like inside any more than when we first went out together. You're never angry or rude or excited or full of joy. You're always cold and steady and polite, like nothing really matters."

"It's not just you; I'm like that with everyone. It's just my way."

"But I'm not everyone: I'm your woman. You've been inside me but you never let me inside you." Her voice rose and quivered a little. She looked away.

Luca lit a cigarette and mulled over what she'd said but didn't answer; he was trying to answer the unanswerable himself. Was he really the same all the way down to his core or did he keep hidden his true feelings and personality even from himself? He'd played his adopted part for so long, even before he'd come to Ireland, that it was second nature to him.

Nancy sounded calmer now: "I know we can't marry as you've never spoken about divorcing your wife, so I assume you have no interest in living with me, let alone marrying me?"

"I understand your questions. I have decisions to make; it's only fair to you."

She let pass his non-answer. "The thing is, Luca," said Nancy,

"I've met someone else and he's asked me to marry him." She hadn't called him Luca for a long time.

So, this conversation wasn't about him; it was about somebody else. This was why Nancy's attitude to sex had changed; he hadn't imagined it.

"Are you going to marry him?" he asked.

"I don't know."

"Are you in love with him?"

"I'm very fond of him. I'm not sure whether I care for him enough but he is kind and he's a widower so I wouldn't have to break him in, if you know what I mean. He has children but they're grown up so I wouldn't have to be a hands-on stepmother."

Luca smiled at her matter-of-factness. "If you think you'll be happy with him then why not?" he answered.

Nancy took a handkerchief from her pocket and blew her nose. "It's not about being happy; it's about avoiding being unhappy. I'm forty-seven, nearly forty-eight, and I won't get many more chances. If I don't settle down soon I'll end up living on my own in rented accommodation. I don't think I'm going to get a better offer." She spoke without rancour.

Oddly, what she said reminded him of the play he'd seen with Veronica. The heroine, Deborah, unable to get Uncle Harry to leave the house he shares with his sisters to marry her, decides to marry someone else. This was not the same. He returned to the matter at hand.

"I don't want to lose you; you're one of the reasons I've stayed."

"But not the main reason; are you saying you feel the same about me as I do about you?"

"Perhaps."

"Perhaps isn't enough. I can't wait for you to make your mind up."

"Is he a good man?"

Nancy audibly exhaled and sat back in her seat. She closed her eyes and rubbed her forehead.

Eventually she answered, "I think he is. I've met his children and they're very fond of him and want him to marry again for his sake. He lost his wife eight years ago; I think he's a bit lonely. He's in his fifties so I suppose he's thinking of what's left of the future, just like me. He said as much when he proposed. He's quite a gentleman and hasn't tried anything on with me; I'm not sure if he's so interested in that side of things." She managed a smile. "I shall miss you in that regard."

"He might be altogether different once you're married," said Luca.

"It's not so important. I've had you and I'll always have that to look back on."

Luca smiled. "What about your mother? I know you've been worried about her."

"She can come to live with us or stay where she is, and I'll be close enough to see she's all right. My brother doesn't live far so he'll also be able to do things for her. She's happy about it, I think." She took his hand. "Tell me it's all right."

Luca put his hand over hers. He thought she had to think of her future and was just being practical. "Of course it's all right; I'm sure he'll make you a good husband. I do care for you but you can't depend on me. Deep down I suppose I'll want to go home to England; there's so much for me to sort out."

Nancy nodded. "I know. I just wanted to know, to be sure that there was no other possibility."

They rose and continued their walk arm in arm without saying much. The weather had worsened again and it was drizzling as the path led them away from the castle. Luca knew that the funeral rites of their relationship were taking place. He was glad she'd taken the step to end it and not trust him to make the right decision for her. He suddenly felt very close to her now they were preparing to go their separate ways.

"Could you eat something?" asked Luca.

"Yes, but I could do with a drink more."

They went for a drink and a sandwich in Gibney's pub. The bar was packed and they had to share a table with a couple of elderly men poring over the racing tips in the newspaper, differing as to the selections and trying to decide whether to go for an accumulator or a full 'Yankee'. Luca and Nancy smiled at the distraction and just enjoyed being together in this strange, quiet twilight of their relationship. They'd never really rowed or fought, and Luca was glad that it wasn't ending in bitterness, for both their sakes. They talked of inconsequential things and then walked a bit more before catching the bus back to town.

"Come home with me," Nancy said, as they got off the bus. So, they walked to her house, which was empty because Nancy's mother was spending the long weekend with her other daughter in Meath. They had a pleasant, languid afternoon, drinking tea, reminiscing about the times they'd spent together and going to bed, to "end on a high note", as Nancy put it. Luca asked her if she would like to have dinner that evening but she thought it was not a time to celebrate, just a time for "a gentle farewell," she said, as they lay in each other's arms.

"I have never slept with anyone else since I met you," she said.

"Nor have I. 'I have been faithful to thee, Cynara! In my fashion'."

"Where does that come from?"

"I don't know, just a line of poetry I picked up. Maybe it was in a film."

"I bet you use it with all the girls," she said, pinching him, though it sounded hollow.

They lay in silence as the sun began to drop lower in the sky and bathed them in a kindly light. "I shall miss you," she said.

"I know. I shall miss you too." He wished he had more to say to make her realise how much he'd cared for her but he couldn't find any words.

Then they got up and toasted each other with a drink and promised to let each other know how the future went for them.

They parted at the door, and when Luca looked back Nancy had already disappeared from view.

As he walked home Luca suddenly knew he was going back to England. Nancy had been the only compelling reason that had held him back and now she had released him from any commitment he'd felt towards her. He found himself making plans as he strolled along. He would become his own master again, building his own business with his wife in their own home. He was confident that she, Ellen, would want that too. He would also be able to renew his links with his extended family in Italy; he would try to see his brother again and restore his aunt's wealth to her.

But Nancy wasn't the only person he would miss. He harboured fond memories of his time spent at the restaurant. He'd always been treated well and he wanted to be sure that he repaid their fairness to him in full. So, he was particularly worried about leaving Roussel in the lurch. The next day he would talk things over with him and find a way to make his departure as painless for the restaurant as possible.

The two senior wine waiters were rarely on duty on the same evening but, due to holidays, they were both working on this particular Tuesday. Luca asked Roussel if they could have a drink at the end of the shift as he wanted to talk about something. They met up in the sommelier's office and poured a couple of glasses of Armagnac.

"What's up, Harry?" asked Roussel.

"Well, it's been on my mind for a long time that I have unfinished business in England and I'd like to go back."

"You mean for good?"

"I guess so. As you know, I've a business there and a wife."

Roussel said, "I would have thought that those were two good reasons *not* to go back."

Luca smiled. "Maybe, but I have to do it."

"I know, I understand." He clicked his tongue. "You won't

mind my being disappointed for the restaurant and for you. You know that you're everyone's first choice to be the next sommelier, and I've been thinking I would retire in the next few months to let you take over."

Luca was not expecting this. He had vaguely considered that there was a possibility he would be offered the job at some time in the future – if he stayed. But not now of all times, when he'd made up his mind to go.

"What about Pat? He's been here longer than me," he said, referring to the third experienced member of the team.

Roussel shook his head. "Pat doesn't want it; he's not interested. I spoke to him about the possibility and whether he would want to go for it but he said he's happy as he is."

Luca had encountered rivalry for internal promotions many times in his career and the opportunity to get the job without the wrangling and bitterness which often accompanied this situation did seem too good to pass up. He blew out his cheeks.

"It's a very tempting offer and you know I'd love the chance, but I can't; I've made my mind up."

"That's a shame. You see, the job's about to become more varied and I think more enjoyable. Before the war I used to get the chance to go to wine fairs and visit producers to select the wines I wanted. It meant a bit of negotiating as well, in order to get the best deals. Now that things are getting back to normal, that part of the job will start again. I was looking forward to us doing it together during the handover phase and they say that this year will be a very good vintage. Now you'll miss all that and I was looking forward to it too. If you turn the job down now I don't think the opportunity will come again, should you change your mind. Are you definitely sure that you want to go back to England permanently?"

"Not definitely, but I think so; of course I don't know what I'll find when I get there. When I first thought about going back it crossed my mind that the café could have been bombed and Ellen might be dead. Then again, she might have given me up for dead and remarried. Any number of things could have happened to stop me taking up where I left off. So, I'm not sure about anything; I just feel I have to find out for myself."

Roussel poured them another drink. "Yes, similar thoughts went through my mind as to what might have happened. The fact is London endured such a terrible time in the war you don't know if your business even survived. Somebody I know had a furniture warehouse in London and it was wiped out in one night of the Blitz, and his business with it. Look, I've spoken to Mr Gillot and Saqueneville; the job is as good as yours, if you want it… If only we could find a way of holding it open for you until you know the situation at home." He tapped on the desk with his pencil and stared at the wall. "I know," he said, "what if we arrange for you to replace me but I hold the fort while you go home to sort things out? If you decide not to come back I'll carry on until they find a replacement. You've got nothing to lose."

Luca rubbed his chin. "I don't know. It's very kind of you but I don't like the idea of messing you about or causing you to change your plans."

Roussel raised his eyebrows. "What plans? I have no intention of going back to France; it'll take a long time to clean up the filth of the last five years. I shan't move when I retire; I'll just live in the same house and find ways of keeping myself amused until I rot. I was going to retire at the end of the year, maybe in the new year, so that gives you plenty of time to do what you have to do in London and come back if you want to."

"Well, if you're sure," said Luca, "I think it's a great idea."

The following week Luca had a meeting with the senior management of the restaurant – even Mr Gillot attended, along with Saqueneville, Roussel and Charpentier. Although it was nominally a formal interview, it was more like a coronation. Everyone praised Luca's work and his contribution to the business and said how much they would like him to take the job.

In a discussion about the practicalities, Saqueneville said that

Luca had earned the right to be treated specially because of his willingness to accommodate the needs of the restaurant whenever he could. Since he'd rarely taken any holidays, Luca was given six weeks' leave with pay and then leave without pay for as long as he needed it. Everyone agreed that this would present no difficulties, as Roussel wouldn't retire until the end of the Christmas period at least. Only Roussel knew that there was a possibility that Luca might not return.

Luca told them he would leave for England at the end of September, to give the restaurant time to find cover for him while he was away. It was one of those rare meetings when everybody had the same view as to what had been agreed and was perfectly content with the outcome.

XVI

The next day Luca considered speaking to Veronica about giving his notice and telling her about his future plans, but he didn't... and he didn't the next day either. Finally, on the third day, he raised the subject over breakfast.

"Veronica, I've decided to go back to England."

Veronica put down her knife and fork. "Oh," she said.

"Yes, I'm sad to be leaving but there are things I have to sort out in England; my business interests for one thing, and also my marriage has to be resolved." He could hear himself sounding cold and formal which wasn't what he'd intended.

"Oh Harry, I'm so sorry that you're going; I shall miss you very much," she said. "I know you talked about it as a possibility once the war ended but somehow I never thought it would ever really happen."

"I wasn't sure I would go myself until the other day."

"Was the need to 'resolve' your marriage the deciding factor?"

"Not totally, but it's partly that and partly other things that've happened."

She pushed away her plate and lit a cigarette. "You're definitely going for good?"

"Not definitely; the restaurant has given me a leave of absence. To be absolutely honest with you, I can't see myself coming back; I intend to stay in England and try to pick up the threads of my old life, insofar as they still exist."

Veronica stubbed out her cigarette. "Well, I guessed it would probably happen one day, and I hope everything goes well for you when you get home," she said, clearing the table and taking the breakfast dishes to the sink.

"I'm still needed at the restaurant until the first week in October so can I give you my notice up to that date?"

"Of course, and if you need to leave earlier I won't hold you to it."

She didn't turn round from the sink but continued to wash the plates, slowly and mechanically.

"I'll miss you too, Veronica," said Luca as he slipped out the door.

The next seven weeks sped by. Luca had little to do to prepare himself to leave Dublin, other than buy a couple of rather smart leather suitcases to accommodate the decent wardrobe of clothes he'd accumulated. Of his other possessions he left the wine books and reference works with Roussel, to hold on for him in case he returned and to keep if he didn't, and he gave the radio to Veronica to give to Reggie when he was a bit older.

Although he methodically went through the process of getting ready to leave Dublin there was a small part of him that wasn't absolutely sure he would go, and this would surface when he had a good session at the restaurant and sometimes when he looked at Veronica. He didn't write to Ellen to tell her he was coming home.

A few friends whom he'd made through Nancy took him out for a farewell drink but Nancy didn't come. He did hear from Nancy, however, when she wrote to tell him she was getting married in the third week in September. She said it was to be a very small wedding with only immediate family and a couple of old friends but she didn't think he would expect to come anyway. He wrote back to wish her lots of luck and best wishes for the future and said that he was happy for her. He sent a bottle of vintage champagne to Nancy's mother's house as a present to the couple.

He saw Giraudo and Brian a few more times and he had a dinner with Giraudo and Polly, Brian and Eileen. Giraudo supplied the food and Luca the wine, and Brian gave a humorous and heartfelt farewell speech in an evening full of sad farewells. Giraudo asked him to come back one more time on the night before he left to say goodbye to him and Polly.

There was no big send off at Gillot's as most of the staff expected Luca to come back in due course. Roussel and he had a meal and few drinks together away from the restaurant as a goodbye, or perhaps an *au revoir*. They were invited to the club of one of the regular customers, who signed them in and bought them a first round of drinks before leaving them to their own devices.

He called round to the Donovans for a last drink and to say his goodbyes. Mrs Donovan had continued to recover her health and they were planning a move to the bungalow they'd long wished for. They'd sold their house to a couple who wanted to have lodgers and it had been agreed that Mr Phillips would stay on with these new owners.

The last parting was that from Veronica. With his departure inevitable they had no future to talk about, and in the present their interactions were low key as the hourglass slowly emptied. Luca busied himself with tying up things at the restaurant and making arrangements for his return, while Veronica threw herself into household matters and the difficult process of finding a new lodger, which she kept putting off. As the time for his departure grew closer they relaxed into discussing their separate paths and shared hopes for the future. At breakfast a week or so before he was due to leave they were chatting about this and that when Luca suddenly asked her to have dinner with him at Gillot's, to thank her for all the good meals she'd given him.

Veronica was caught off guard and stuttered a little over her reply. "Luca, that is kind of you but there's no need. It's been a pleasure having you here and I've enjoyed our times together."

"You've always made me feel this was my home, and we've become friends. I would like to celebrate our friendship as I've done with the other friends I've made since I came to Ireland."

"Well, I would love to," she said. "When did you have in mind? I'll need to arrange a babysitter."

"I thought a couple of days before I leave."

So, it was agreed, and Luca arranged to have dinner with Veronica on the day after his final day at work.

On that last day the farewells at the restaurant were muted because of the official position that he was going on a long holiday. But some did wonder if he would ever come back and many of the handshakes were warmer than he'd expected. When he booked a table, Luca asked if he could have one of the private rooms at Gillot's to avoid any possible awkwardness for him or the customers from his being in the main saloon. Perhaps it wouldn't have mattered to anyone else but he didn't want to be the centre of attention and perhaps be interrupted by well-wishers while he was trying to enjoy some time with Veronica.

They'd dressed for dinner, Luca in his dinner suit, which he thought he'd rarely wear again, if ever, and Veronica in a deep-green dress with her pearls. Luca thought she looked beautiful when he called for her, and Carmel, the babysitter, said as much. They went out to the waiting taxi and drove the ten minutes or so to the restaurant. When they arrived they were shown to the smallest of the private rooms, no bigger than a dining room in a private house, with a table for six people in the middle. A chandelier hung over the table but this was switched off and the room was subtly lit by table lamps. The furniture and decor was Regency, with striped wallpaper and bergère dining chairs; the overall look and feel was heavy enough for a masculine taste but not too oppressive for female customers – with the possible exception of the large wine cooler against one wall, its sarcophagus shape symbolising its now defunct role.

175

Veronica had dined at the restaurant before but not for several years, and none of the staff appeared to recognise her. It was actually the first time that Luca had eaten as a customer in the restaurant and when they arrived they were given a champagne cocktail 'compliments of the manager'.

Veronica asked Luca to choose for her and they both had *Filet de Barbue Waleska* followed by *Mignon de Veau Orlof.* Luca insisted that the young wine waiter on duty choose the wines to accompany the dishes. This wine waiter had been trained by Luca and, despite seeming a little nervous at first, was pleased to be asked, especially as Luca assured him that he wasn't being tested, just trusted. He proposed a Chablis and an old Medoc, which Luca said were exactly the ones he himself would have chosen, and they both had a glass of each wine. Throughout the meal the staff were solicitous, and the chef also made an appearance to check all was well.

"They must think a lot of you," said Veronica when they were alone again. "Everyone's being very kind and it's more than good service: they care about you."

"Perhaps they're trying to help me impress this very attractive lady I brought here this evening." Luca hadn't told his colleagues who Veronica was, only that she was a friend he wished to entertain one more time before he left Ireland.

Veronica gave him a sceptical look. "You're being too modest. I can see that that young wine waiter has liked working with you, and the others too."

"That's kind of you to say and I hope it's true as I've been very happy here."

"I can't eat another thing," said Veronica, after they'd finished their main course, so Luca ordered some coffee and petit fours, with a brandy for him and a Tia Maria for Veronica. These drinks were also served with the compliments of the manager. He lit their cigarettes and they chatted about the meal and the restaurant while they drank their coffee. Then they fell silent. The longer the pause went on the harder it became to say anything worthwhile, so they just smiled at each other and finished their drinks. When Luca went to pay the bill he was told that the staff on duty would be attending to it. Luca could only give a generous tip.

It was about ten when they got back to the house. They had a brief chat with Carmel before she went home, then Veronica made some coffee and poured them both a drink.

"It was a wonderful evening, thank you, Harry," she said.

"I'm glad we could do it. That's the only time I've had dinner in the restaurant and there's no one else I'd rather have shared it with."

Veronica didn't answer at first; she stared for a moment or two and then murmured, "That's a lovely thing to say, thank you."

"I mean it. I wish things were different, that the circumstances were not as they are, but they are what they are."

"I know," she said. "I wish you would change your mind but nothing I say can alter anything." She looked at him for a moment. "I will miss you terribly," she said finally.

"Me too," he said.

They had more coffee and more drinks, neither finding the will nor the energy to end the evening, but eventually Veronica rose to go to bed. Luca kissed her on the cheek and she held his hand for a moment before she left the room. Luca watched her go and listened to her footsteps as she went upstairs, then he took the lonely walk to his own room.

Two days later he was ready to set off for the ferry to Liverpool as he retraced his steps from five years before. Veronica had made him some sandwiches and a cake to take with him. They stood in the hall and said their goodbyes. The previous night Veronica had lain in bed rehearsing all the things she'd say. There would be no pleading with him to stay but she wanted him to know how she felt. But now, as they stood there, she knew there was no need. He knew, and he was going, and there was nothing to be said.

"Goodbye Harry. Safe home and be happy," she said simply.

"Goodbye Veronica. I'll never forget you," he replied, and then he embraced her and kissed her once again on the cheek.

When they parted he pretended not to notice the tears in her eyes as he walked out the front door. She watched him walk up the street until he turned and waved and then disappeared.

XVII

The ferry departed at about eleven and Luca had to find things to do to fill the hours on the long journey. He read a paperback copy of Graham Greene's novel, *Ministry of Fear*, which Veronica had given him, and also a newspaper which he bought at the shop in the ferry terminal. He ate his lunch in the lounge and got into conversation with a commercial traveller from Newton-le-Willows who'd been on one of his regular trips to Dublin. Luca asked the man how Liverpool had fared in the war and the man told him that the Liverpool blitz was reckoned to have been second only to London as to the damage inflicted. They chatted about the war and how it had affected them. The man assumed that Luca was Irish as he'd been resident in Dublin for the duration, and Luca didn't bother to tell him otherwise.

After a time, Luca tired of small talk and went up on deck. On the leeward side of the ship it felt quite pleasant, as the temperature was unseasonably high for early October; in fact, it felt more like late summer. He put his mack over his arm and paced the decks for a while and then had a drink in the bar. When he came back on deck he stood against the rail and stared at the sea.

Gradually, the coast of Anglesey, then of the Welsh mainland, then of England, came into view, and he watched with dismay as finally the scenes of the devastation of Liverpool were displayed before him. The rubble had been cleared but the ruins of the Customs House and the Albert Dock and all the other areas of damage he found quite shocking. He disembarked as it was getting dark and went through customs but had nothing to declare. As no identification papers were required when travelling between Ireland and England nobody asked who he was or the purpose of his journey.

After he left the customs hall he made his way to the dock where he'd been due to embark for Canada those five long years before and, to his surprise and pleasure, the small building into which he'd first taken refuge was still there. He opened one of his suitcases and took out the reefer jacket he had 'borrowed' on the day of his escape and tried the door handle. The door opened and inside the room the stored equipment and other paraphernalia were not very different from those in 1940. The coat hooks were still there and he hung the reefer jacket on the same hook from which he had taken it.

Luca spent the night in a small hotel near Lime Street Station and the next morning took the train to London. He'd hardly been on a train since he'd left England and he felt at once reassuringly at home when he sat in his third-class compartment with its leather straps to open the windows, the rather elderly photographs of St Helens and Southport, and the cloud of dust and coal soot which rose like a miasma from the seat when he banged his suitcase rather heavily on it. Having checked that it was a smoking compartment he put his luggage up on the rack and settled down for the journey.

It was a corridor train due to the length of the route, and he was the permanent fixture as the door to the compartment slid open to enable a variety of travellers to join or leave the train. Neither he nor his fellow passengers sought or engaged in social interaction other than the offer of a light for a cigarette or when he helped an elderly lady with her luggage on her journey between Lichfield and Tamworth.

He was surprised at how many people he saw in military uniform, both in Liverpool and on the train, and when, towards the end of his journey, he was in the compartment alone with one soldier they did get into conversation. The soldier, a corporal, was on his way back to London after a few days' leave at his family home near Rugby and he was due to be demobbed in a few weeks. He'd served with the Eighth Army in Italy and said that his last experience of action had been after the war in the middle of May. Some Yugoslav partisan forces had tried to take over a fuel installation being guarded by his company. Both sides had exchanged fire for a couple of hours but amazingly there'd been no casualties on either side and the partisans had eventually moved on.

"I don't think I'll get a campaign medal for that particular expedition."

"The bombing must have been terrible in London," said Luca. "It was bad enough in Liverpool."

"The Blitz was very bad. Places like the East End and the docks were hit hard, as you'd expect, and the City of course. My brother joined the fire brigade; it was bloody murder most nights. Then things calmed down a bit after '41 before we got the flying bombs. But by then people knew the Jerries were on the run so they stuck it out." He leant over to take the cigarette offered by Luca. "How about you? Where were you in the war?"

Luca smiled. "I was lucky; I was too old to be called up and I was working in Dublin throughout the war. We only had a few bombing raids in the first couple of years and that was it."

"I came across a lot of Irish blokes in the war; you've got to admire them, volunteering like they did. I don't think I'd have volunteered for another country if we'd been neutral, but you never know I suppose."

Luca bought the soldier a drink in the station buffet when they got to Euston and offered him another but the corporal said he had to be getting home and they went their separate ways.

Alone, Luca thought about the final stage of his journey, home to Ellen. He found he was experiencing cold feet; he hadn't been in touch with her for five years and now not having written to her to say he was coming home seemed like a very bad decision. Perhaps he was leaving his options open, he thought, so he could still change his mind up to the last minute. There was no doubt that part of him was having second thoughts now in case what he came home to was very different to what he was expecting.

So, he prevaricated for a day and acclimatised himself to being back in London. In the late afternoon he lounged around the West End and sauntered past some of the places he'd worked as a waiter. Fortunately, they all seemed to be pretty much intact, though the scars of the war were to be seen everywhere he looked, most obviously in the empty spaces where once buildings had stood. The structures that remained seemed dispirited, with their temporary repairs blocking out their true appearance. Others looked as if they were in the wrong place, with wooden buttresses shoring up those that had lost their neighbours or a conjoined twin excised in bombing raids. Pervading everything was a sense of drabness and hardship that endured even though hostilities had ended; the lack of bright lights in Piccadilly Circus, the reminders of rationing in many of the shops and the evidence everywhere to a visitor that things were still tough. *And these people won the war*, thought Luca.

After dinner in an Italian restaurant in Soho, Luca spent a second night in a hotel, a seedy one near Russell Square, and the next morning resolved to 'go home', confident that his misgivings were just nerves and sure to prove groundless. Fortified by a breakfast which contained probably the worst sausage he'd ever eaten, he hopped on a bus at Holborn Kingsway heading to Liverpool Street. From the top deck of the bus he saw at first hand the devastation to many parts of the City, most notably the area around St Paul's, where the cathedral stood in a wasteland of the vestiges of buildings that had once surrounded it, much of the land already being reclaimed by weeds, grasses and the ever-resilient buddleias. From Liverpool Street he walked round the corner to pick up a bus which took him to Clapton where he could take another bus home. He found the bus travel rehabilitating, like a familiarisation chamber between the alternative life he'd lived for the past five years and the one he was about to resume. By the time he was seated on the single-decker at Clapton Pond he felt ready.

XVIII

Luca had told Ellen his story. He didn't tell her everything. He told her about his escape from Liverpool on a ship to Dublin and how he'd got a job as a wine waiter at a very good restaurant and how he'd lodged in Dublin for the last five years with the Donovans and Veronica. He didn't tell her about Nancy or his friendship with Veronica or the undercover work for the Italian delegation or his social life with the people he'd met in Dublin.

Ellen listened to his story patiently but kept waiting for an answer to the only question she really cared about at this moment, and the answer never came. When he'd finished she asked him, "Why didn't you tell me you were alive and safe?"

This was the question he'd been waiting for and had prepared for, and yet he had no real answer to give her. "I wanted to but the Italian delegation told me that they wouldn't be able to get a message to you, and I was worried the Irish police might intern me if I was known to be in Ireland."

Ellen wondered why we told futile lies, the sort of lies we wouldn't believe if someone told them to us. She knew that the internment of Italians was brought to an end, by and large, in 1941, so why was he coming out with this rubbish?

"Surely you could have got word to me when internment ended? You could have come home years ago." She felt the tension in her rising and the pulse in her head throbbing as her frustration mounted. "Why didn't you come home before? Why have you come back now?"

"I thought my brother would get a message to you. I asked the Italian delegation to send him word that I'd escaped."

"Well, he didn't. And it doesn't matter about your brother, you should have got word to me. Irish mail wouldn't be stopped from coming in; Mrs Quinn in the laundry was always getting letters from her mother in Cork."

Luca's futile lie was laid bare. He moved on and turned to her other question.

"I was afraid to come back by sea while the war was going on because of the U-boats but I started things in motion to come back as soon as the war was over. I had a contract with the restaurant which meant I had to give three months' notice."

Ellen thought these were more lies but at least they had some plausibility.

"All you had to do was let me know. I grieved over you for a long time and, just as I get over you, up you pop again." She realised it sounded as if she would rather he were dead and a part of her did think that, at least at this moment.

"I am truly sorry," said Luca.

Ellen needed time to think. "Let's have a cup of tea," she said, and went out to the kitchen to put the kettle on. She didn't return to her seat to wait for the kettle but stayed in the kitchen and busied herself getting the cups and saucers ready because being busy was easier than thinking and she didn't want to think. She made the tea and put some cakes on a plate as she thought it unlikely the café would open again today and they would all go to waste. She waited for the tea to brew and was aware of Luca watching her but she pretended not to see him. She had just poured out the tea when the back door opened and the young woman returned from her trip to the shops.

"Hello Jean," said Ellen. "Just put the meat in the fridge and leave everything else to me. I don't think we'll open again today so you can go now; I won't dock your wages."

"Are you sure, Mrs Morenelli?" said Jean, a reluctance to make everything she'd done this morning merely a waste of time evident in her voice.

Ellen nodded and Jean did as she'd been told. Then, with one last passing glance at Luca, she went out the way she'd just entered.

Ellen took the tray to Luca and he helped himself to a cake, colloquially referred to as a 'cheesecake', though it was a puff pastry, with shredded coconut on top. Ellen didn't take a cake as she felt quite sick.

"Why did you come back?" Ellen asked.

"Because this is my home and I wanted to be with you."

"Is that true? It's not because you were in some kind of trouble in Ireland and had to get away?"

He shook his head. "That's an unkind thing to say. I could have stayed in Ireland if I'd wanted to; there was no pressure. I had reached the point where there was nothing holding me in Ireland and I felt a strong pull to come back." He changed the subject: "How have you been?"

Ellen sipped her tea while she thought back over the past five years. It was hard to concentrate with all that was going on now swirling around in her head, but she took her mind back to those first few weeks and months after Luca had left for internment.

"It was tough at first. I got your letter to say that you'd be going to Canada and then I received an official notification that you were reported missing, presumed lost at sea. After that they started finding bodies washed up and I kept expecting one would be you while I wanted it not to be you and for there to have been some mistake. As time passed and there was no news, I gradually accepted that you were dead. Oh God, if only you'd told me." She looked at Luca and he averted his eyes.

"Anyway, the café still had to be run so it gave me something to concentrate on. People were very kind; my mother came and stayed for a few weeks. The customers were loyal and I had help from Cyril and Gwen, so things carried on. At first rationing wasn't a problem, then after 1942 restaurants were affected as well, but we managed."

Again, she thought back to those first few weeks after Luca was interned and how she'd worried about the reaction of people. There'd been nationwide anti-Italian riots on 11th June 1940 and quite a lot of ill feeling towards Italy, but Luca had been liked by most of his customers and they were sorry to see him interned. Those who felt otherwise stopped using the café for a bit but most gradually came round, as convenience trumped sentiment.

"You did well to keep it going. Was there much bombing around here?"

"St Barnabas Church was hit and one or two buildings near there. The Wick was bombed too and the Catholic church took one; I think they were aiming for the railway lines. It was no worse than anywhere else. One of my cousins, Billy, was killed in North Africa. I don't think you ever met him?"

Luca shook his head. "I'm sorry to hear that."

"He was a nice boy; my aunt was devastated, as you'd expect. I suppose you didn't see much of the war in Ireland?"

"Dublin was bombed and we had rationing but nothing like here. A lot of Irish people joined up though." He changed the subject back to her again: "I guess you didn't remarry?"

It occurred to Ellen that they'd spent more of their married life apart than together and their marriage did seem like a past event, especially as she'd believed she was a widow. At first she'd been treated with sympathetic respect, a woman widowed through tragic events. Then, after about a year, she'd been perceived as being 'back in play'. The occasional over-friendly customer would lean on the counter when paying his bill and hint about taking an interest in satisfying her physical needs without quite saying as much. In the face of her cold reaction none of them ever pursued the matter. Over the next couple of years she had a few dates, none of which led anywhere. Once, she slept with a man she'd met at a party; they'd taken no precautions as she thought she couldn't get pregnant. Then she suddenly realised, a couple of days later, that perhaps it was Luca rather than she who had had the problem so she spent the next couple of weeks on tenterhooks. This was followed by relief when she found she had nothing to worry about. She hadn't very much enjoyed that sexual encounter and hadn't been tempted to repeat it.

Then, just before the war ended, she'd been asked out by someone she'd known for a couple of years from their time together as volunteers in the Royal Observer Corps. They began seeing each other, sporadically at first but then more regularly, and a romance was slowly developing. It had become sufficiently serious for her to investigate the possibilities of remarriage but she discovered that it usually took seven years before a missing person could be declared dead. So, she'd put thoughts of that possibility to one side.

"The subject never arose," she replied, and found herself regretting somewhat that this was now an academic question. She wondered if he'd had other women in his time away. She had seen the Pathé newsreels with the returning servicemen being welcomed by their wives with beaming smiles and fond embraces. But this wasn't like that; she thought he'd come home not when he could but when it had suited his own ends, and she'd probably not entered into his calculations.

"You were too tied up in the business?" he asked, smiling.

It was the business he came back for, thought Ellen. She said nothing.

"I hope the bank didn't present any problems with me being absent?" he continued.

"No, the only instructions requiring both our signatures concerned the closure of the account and obviously I didn't need to do that." She felt more comfortable talking about the business. "Considering the war and the shortages the café didn't too badly."

"Probably because I wasn't here."

Ellen was getting a little irritated by his stupid jokes but she forced a smile anyway.

There was a knock at the front door of the café and Ellen rose to see who it was. She peeked through the side of the blind and saw that it was the long sallow face of Cyril Johnson from the chemist's shop. Cyril, whose dour physiognomy belied his outgoing, cheerful nature, had seen Luca off when he'd been sent away to internment and he looked keen to greet his old friend. Ellen hesitated and then opened the door.

"Hello Cyril," she said.

"Hello Ellen; I'm sure I'm intruding but I just had to welcome Lazarus. Luca, good to see you and don't you look well." He strode past Ellen and grabbed Luca's hand in both of his. "You must be over the moon, Ellen," he continued, looking over his shoulder at the blank-faced woman behind him. He didn't wait for an answer but ploughed on, "What the hell happened to you, Luca?"

Luca was genuinely very happy to see his closest friend on the High Street from before the war. He hadn't changed much: the hair a little greyer and less auburn but as robust as ever, the build a little lighter if anything.

"It's so good to see you, Cyril," said Luca, clasping him by both shoulders. He didn't feel ready to give much detail of his adventures but gave a very brief account of his escape and subsequent five years in Dublin. An account which was interspersed with "Ooh" and "Aah" and 'Well, blow me" from Cyril.

"Look, I can't leave the shop, Gwen's shopping and there's just the junior in there at the moment. How about a welcome home drink this evening?"

"Well," said Luca, looking at Ellen.

"That would be nice," said Ellen, glad of the chance to dilute the tension in what would be a less intense evening than if they sat and looked at each other in the flat.

"Excellent. Gwen and I will pick you up at eight o'clock? We'll go to the Fountain. If we go over the road you'll spend the whole evening having to tell the same story to everyone who comes in."

"That's a good idea," said Luca.

"Great to have you home, old man!" said Cyril, grabbing Luca's hand again.

Then he took his leave and left them alone again. It was lunchtime and one or two people rattled the door handle, not noticing the 'CLOSED' sign hanging on the door. Ellen still felt quite numb and wished she hadn't sent Jean off. Having the café open would have restored a degree of normality to her day.

"I think I'll go out for a bit. There are some things I have to do."

"Would you like me to come with you?" asked Luca.

"No, it's all right. Get yourself some lunch. There's ham, sausages and lamb chops in the fridge, and I think everything else is pretty much as you left it."

Then she took off her apron and put on a coat. She left by the back door so she could go down the alley and come out at the end of the row of shops without meeting anyone. She'd taken her handbag with her but nothing else because she just needed to be alone to think. She walked down the hill and took a path across the fields towards the old watercress beds and sat on a bench to have a cigarette. She suddenly realised she was supposed to be going out with her friend Charlie that evening, and he wasn't on the phone so how could she tell him? She'd have to go round to his flat to tell him and she dreaded it. She finished her cigarette and folded her arms against the wind. It wasn't a cold day but where she was sitting there was nothing to hold back the force of the breeze. She watched the stalks of the longer grass bend in unison as the wind played with them. Her thoughts were a mixture of outrage and guilt. Outrage that her husband had given hardly a thought for her and had now turned up out of the blue to disturb the new life she'd been hoping for; guilt that she felt outrage and not a single tender thought towards him.

Eventually she roused herself from her feelings of tired self-pity and trudged along the canal footpath until she mounted the steps onto Lea Bridge Road. She stood on the bridge to get her breath back, watching a lighter move down the canal and some boys lark around on the bank, trying to push each other nearer the water. Then she walked towards the road in which Charlie lived with his mother.

They lived in a large old building divided into flats, and as she went up the stairs she could feel her heart pounding. When she knocked on Charlie's door it was opened by his mother.

"Hello love, what are you doing here?" she said cheerfully, apparently pleased to see her.

Mrs Ethel Howard was a lady in her early seventies of stout appearance who always wore a hairnet over the back part of her hair, which was pulled up off her neck in a creation of some sort. She didn't know Ellen very well but Charlie had brought her round a few times and she'd always been pleasant enough, though they had never really had anything other than a superficial conversation. Ellen had been unable to make up her mind whether Charlie's bachelor status at the age of forty-three was due to his natural shyness, whether his mother had put emotional pressure on him to stay at home, or a mixture of the two. She'd grown fond of Charlie but their romance had proceeded at a snail's pace and he seemed content with that. As yet, he hadn't shown much interest in the physical side of things and she wondered if she ought to give him a push in that direction to gauge his thoughts on the matter. However, the omnipresence of Ethel in the flat didn't exactly make this straightforward.

"Hello Ethel, is Charlie in?" asked Ellen.

"No dear, he's gone out for a pint with his friends before the match. Of course, there isn't a match at the moment because it won't start properly till next year but he still goes for the drink anyway. He does miss the football but he won't go to the Arsenal or West Ham because he thinks it's disloyal. Come in for a cup of tea?" she asked. She led the way into the living room and turned round. "Aren't you seeing him tonight anyway? Is something the matter that couldn't wait?"

Ellen could hardly refuse to answer and now she was in a quandary as to whether she should tell Ethel the news or wait until Charlie came back from the pub. Before she could answer, Ethel went off to the kitchen to put the kettle on and returned while waiting for it to boil.

"What's the time?" Ethel said rhetorically as she glanced at the clock on the mantelpiece. "Oh, it's gone a quarter past two so he'll be back before long."

Ellen was relieved she'd only have to pad the conversation out for a few minutes without getting into the purpose of her visit. She hadn't been there for a while and, as Ethel busied herself in the kitchen, she looked around the room, refreshing her memories of it. The gilded clock in the centre of the mantelpiece and the matching vases under a glass dome at each end she remembered well and quite liked. She liked not so much the antimacassar-covered deep-green, floral-patterned moquette armchairs and sofa which made her legs itch when she sat on them. There was an oak gate-leg dining table with chairs against one wall and a matching sideboard against another wall, with a bowl of wax fruit standing on it. Overlooking this scene was a reproduction of Landseer's *Monarch of the Glen*, which gazed down from its lofty position on the chimney breast. There was no fire in the grate as it was a mild day, as most days that month had been so far.

"We've had a real Indian summer this year, haven't we?" said Ethel as she came in with two cups of tea, a bowl of sugar and some bourbon biscuits.

"Yes," said Ellen, looking at the clock and thinking, *Less than ten minutes to stall.*

"Are you all right, dear? You look a little flushed."

"Just a bit out of breath," said Ellen. "I should have remembered about his drink with his football mates."

"I'm surprised you're not working this afternoon. Who's looking after the café?"

"I closed early today. Something's come up." She could feel Ethel drawing information out of her in stages like a claw hammer pulling out one nail at a time. "That's why I need to see Charlie."

"Sounds serious," said Ethel, prompting an answer, but none came.

Ellen wondered if Ethel thought she might be pregnant, but that could have waited until the evening. She didn't answer Ethel but instead drank some tea and took a biscuit to eat.

Before either of the two women could say anything else they heard the key in the lock as Charlie came in. Their heads swung round simultaneously and Charlie was momentarily taken off guard by the sight of the two of them staring at him as he walked into the living room.

"Hello Ellen, what a nice surprise seeing you now; everything all right for tonight?"

He threw down his cap and newspaper on the table, took off his gabardine mack and sat down in the armchair opposite her. He looked at her expectantly, a large smile on his round face under his dark, wavy hair and soft-grey eyes.

Charlie had come straight to the point and cut off her hopes of building up slowly to the news.

"No, I can't go out tonight; something's come up."

"Oh, what would that be?" His jovial expression did not change.

She thought of prevaricating but what if he heard it from somebody else first?

She said simply, "Luca has come back." As she spoke she looked at them both. Charlie was open-mouthed but a brief smile played on Ethel's lips before she resumed a neutral pose.

"My God," said Charlie, "how is that possible?"

Ellen related the story of Luca's escape and how he'd lived for five years in Dublin. Charlie and his mother listened in stunned silence as she recounted the key elements of the story.

When she'd finished neither seemed able to speak and, after what seemed like several minutes but was only a few seconds, Ellen said, "So, I won't be able to go out with you anymore, Charlie. I'm sorry." She looked down at her hands and could have wept but refused to give in to tears.

After a moment or two, Ellen composed herself and glanced at Charlie and he was looking down too. Why had she told Charlie in front of the ever-present Ethel? This has nothing to do with her.

"Can we go out for a walk, Charlie?" she asked.

Charlie looked over at his mother; she sat watching them impassively.

"Yes, OK," he said.

He stood up and Ethel said, "Take your scarf in case it's windy."

Charlie took his scarf off the hat stand and tucked it in his mack.

"We won't be long, Mum."

Ellen and Charlie left the flat and went back the way Ellen had come, eventually going down the steps onto the canal path.

"I'm so sorry about this, Charlie," she said, taking his arm. "I had no idea he would ever come back. Perhaps I was too hasty to say I couldn't see you again."

"But you're a married woman."

"I was a married woman when I first went out with you because my husband couldn't be declared dead yet."

"We thought he was dead."

"Don't you want to see me again? We could still be friends."

"I liked going out with you. I thought of you as my girlfriend, and perhaps we might have got married one day. It's all wrecked now."

Ellen stopped by a bench and they sat down. She held his hand.

"It's been a shock for us. I don't know what will happen with Luca and me; he made no attempt to get in touch and I don't know why he's come back now. I don't feel the same about him but I do still feel the same about you. We could still be happy and have a future. Don't give up; we can stay friends for now and then see what happens."

Charlie removed his hand from Ellen's hold.

"I'm sorry, Ellen, it wouldn't seem right; I can't carry on as before. We have to accept things as they are. I wish you well with Luca and hope things turn out for you." He stood up. "I should be getting back now."

Ellen stood up too, her hands at her side, no more appeals left.

"I won't walk back with you, Charlie. I'm sure you have a lot to do."

Charlie nodded and offered to shake hands but she kissed him – what did it matter now?

She sat and watched him go, then stared at nothing for a few minutes. Then she walked to the crossover so she could take a different route, for no particular reason, back along the River Lea. It was getting warmer, not quite as warm as the previous day but still too hot for a coat so she carried it over her arm. In the distance she could hear the sounds of the football matches being played on the marshes and she thought how odd that everything else was perfectly normal: Charlie with his regular Saturday lunchtime drink; the teams playing football; people walking their dogs; and everyone else going about their usual business, all except her, whose world had been turned upside down. She tried to embrace her surroundings and give herself up to the warmth of the sun and the calming changelessness of the slow-flowing water, but despair forced its way through. How she wished Luca had never come back or that now he would go away and let her get on with her life, but he wouldn't; he would stay and she would have to pick up where they'd left off, but it would never be like it was before.

Reluctantly she trudged back up the hill to the café. She slunk down the alley and let herself in via the backdoor. This door that had always stuck a little when pushed open since a bomb had exploded nearby and the shock had slightly adjusted the way the door hung. Today the door stuck more than usual and she had difficulty finding the strength to push it open, let alone go in. She hung her coat up and noticed that carrying it in the crook of her arm had caused creases in her blouse and made that part of her arm sweaty.

Luca was sitting at a table, looking through the accounts. He looked round at her and laid a ruler on the page, to mark the last line he'd read. Then he stood up.

"Everything all right?" he asked. "Manage to get the things done?"

"Yes, thank you." She walked over to the kitchen and put the kettle on.

"Let me make you a drink," said Luca. "Sit down. Would you like tea?"

"Yes, please." She felt tired and there was the beginning of a headache somewhere near the back of her head. She massaged it surreptitiously as he made the tea.

When Luca came over with the tea and cakes, Ellen wondered if a lack of food could be a factor in her headache and she forced herself to eat a cream doughnut, though she had no appetite. Then she lit a cigarette for something to do.

"I'm impressed by the accounts," said Luca. "Profits up in the past two years; you've done well. How did you do it?"

He looked at her with a slight smile and one ear lifted theatrically.

Ellen nodded. "Well, business obviously went down a bit, what with the war and then rationing, but things have eased a bit since last year and I changed one or two suppliers to get better deals. Then the men came back to the factory and they eat and drink more than the girls did during the war."

"Well, I think it's great what you've done."

Ellen smiled. She suddenly felt very tired. "I've got a bit of a headache. Would you mind if I have a lie-down before tea so that I'm all right tonight?"

Luca looked concerned and nodded: "I think you should. Today must have been quite draining for you. Let's not cook this evening;

perhaps I could get fish and chips, or saveloys and pease pudding, or whatever you fancy?"

The thought of food made her feel quite queasy so she merely nodded and said they could decide when she got up. Then she climbed the stairs as if she was wearing deep sea divers' boots, almost fell into the bedroom and slumped on the bed. Her head was pounding like a steam-hammer but it eased after a little while. Though she was tired she knew she wouldn't be able to sleep and she glanced around the room she knew so well. It had been *their* bedroom but had become *her* bedroom and now it was to be theirs again. It hadn't changed much during Luca's absence; during the war redecoration would have been difficult, with a shortage of decorating materials, and would have been pointless in any case with the Blitz and then the V rockets. But she'd made the room very much her own, with chintzy fabrics, ornaments chosen solely by herself and photographs of her family in Devon, including a niece born to her sister just before the war. She wondered if she might have been happier if she'd had a child but she would never know now. Luca hadn't been particularly interested in the decor when they'd moved in but she'd acceded to his request that the room not look "too girly". Now she would keep it as she wanted it. There were too many things to think about and she closed her eyes and drifted into sleep.

When she woke, daylight was streaming through the window. Double British Summertime, introduced in the war, was still in force and now, even in October, the evenings were light until nearly eight o'clock. She looked at her watch, saw it was after six and got up straight away, mindful that she had to get ready for the evening. She combed her hair and went downstairs. Luca had put the account books away and was pottering around in the kitchen.

"Hello," he said. "Hope you feel better now?"

Her headache had faded and was on the cusp of going. She nodded and suddenly felt quite hungry.

"We have loads of bread and some salad in the fridge. Why don't we have some shrimps and other things from the jellied eel stall outside the pub?" she said.

"Yes, I'd forgotten about jellied eels," he said. "I'll go and get some things and some beer from the off licence."

After a meal of various cold fish, cucumber, lettuce and tomatoes, washed down with pale ale, Ellen found herself feeling, if not great, at least more equipped to deal with this insane turn of events in her life. They chatted fairly amicably and Luca told her a little about the restaurant he'd worked in and his life in Dublin. Afterwards, having cleared the food away, she had a bath, made herself up and changed into a navy blue dress.

They were picked up at eight o'clock, as Cyril had promised, and they drove to the Fountain, as arranged. It was a large, Edwardian Baroque-style pub with several bars, and they went through double doors to the lounge bar, which was a single-storey annex to the original building. The room was well-carpeted and decorated in a light-grey wallpaper with steel-blue covered chairs around pale wood tables. There was a Bechstein baby grand piano, which had pragmatically remained in situ throughout the war, despite its unfortunate provenance. The eponymous fountain, which seeped water gently down its centrepiece statue of a water nymph, stood underneath a large, circular stained-glass skylight. At the piano the resident pianist was playing a selection of George Gershwin numbers and smiling and nodding cheerfully at the customers as they came and went.

The two couples found an empty table and Cyril went off to get a round of drinks.

"I still can't get over it; you two together again," said Gwen. "You must be so happy to have him back," she added, giggling slightly as she looked at Ellen.

Ellen smiled non-committally at the rather sheep-faced Gwen.

Unfazed, Gwen turned to Luca: "And you must be glad to be home after such a long time away?"

Luca didn't answer, but before Gwen could continue Cyril arrived back with a tray of drinks.

"Right, gin and tonic for you, Ellen, and a Dubonnet and lemonade for Gwen and two pints of Worthington for us," he said, setting the glasses down before each of them. "Well, here's to you, Luca; welcome home and great to have you back."

He raised his glass and chinked it against Luca's and the others followed suit. A group of people on the next table heard the toast and also raised their glasses to him.

Under Cyril's more open questioning and gentle banter, Luca was able to keep the conversation at a more neutral level as he entertained the rest of them with some anecdotes about his life in Dublin, which even Ellen, despite some initial foreboding, enjoyed hearing. Luca avoided anything controversial and stuck to funny events at the restaurant or some of the characters he'd met. In response to a question from Gwen, he explained how he'd come to have a different moustache and a softer accent.

"Do you ever slip back into your old accent?" she asked.

"No, not really. I can do a more Italian accent but now it feels like an impersonation rather than the real me."

"You seem to have been made welcome in Ireland," said Cyril. "There was a lot of ill-feeling over here towards the Irish government, what with not letting us have access to facilities over there. Then there was that mad business of De Valera signing the condolence book after the death of Hitler, especially as we knew what had been going in the camps by then. Nobody blamed the Irish people; there were so many in the army and the hospitals and so on."

Over the second round of drinks Cyril told a few stories of amusing happenings in the High Street and elsewhere.

"I think the best story concerned Mrs Brown, the newsagent. When the bomb fell on the church it was half past six in the morning. All the other shops in the High Street were closed with the shutters up and she'd just opened up. Anyway, the blast from the bomb blew out the windows and brought half the ceiling down on her. Luckily, she was all right, just a few cuts and bruises. A policeman and some other people helped her out of the rubble, checked her over and cleaned her up at the hospital. Meanwhile the neighbours and the policeman helped to clear up the shop. Then Mrs Brown came back and someone sat her down and made her a cup of tea. While she was sitting there a bloke walked in and said, 'I haven't had my paper yet this morning.' Can you believe it? The copper handed him a broom and told him to help clear up."

"Don't forget the story about the German hymn at the Catholic church, Cyril," said Gwen.

Cyril chuckled. "Ah, yes, the BBC broadcast a service from the local Catholic church and the first hymn was *Glorious Things of Thee Are Spoken* set to the same tune used for the German national anthem. People jammed the BBC switchboard demanding to know why English Catholics were singing the enemy's national anthem. Perhaps it's as well you weren't here, Luca – you might have been lynched!"

These stories lightened the mood and Ellen escaped a little from her inner thoughts. Then, when Luca went to get the third round of drinks, he asked the pianist to play Ellen's favourite song, *You Made Me Love You*, and when it was played, without comment, Ellen was surprised to find herself smiling warmly, if involuntarily, at Luca.

Soon after ten o'clock, Luca said he was feeling rather tired as he'd a long day and would like to round the evening off, especially as it had been a very busy and difficult day for Ellen too. He offered to get a bus home but Cyril would have none of it and he drove them home there and then.

After Cyril and Gwen had said goodnight, Luca and Ellen had a cup of tea and talked briefly about the evening before they went up to bed. Neither of them talked about the sleeping arrangements but as the flat had only one bedroom the options were limited. Ellen went up first and laid Luca's pyjamas out for him. Then she undressed in the bathroom and got ready for bed, climbing in while Luca used the bathroom.

Luca dutifully put the pyjamas on and they lay in the bed side by side.

"I didn't see Aunt Anna's chest when I looked around earlier today," he said. "What happened to it?"

"Oh, it's quite safe. I left it with Eric Runsell so he could keep it in the cellar till the end of the war. I haven't done anything about it yet because I was waiting to hear from your aunt."

"There's no rush; we can sort it out later."

Ellen could feel the warmth of his body, although they weren't touching, and she moved a fraction away. It had been a long time since she'd lain next to someone and she wanted to feel that again but not with him, not now. She took the book she was reading from the top of her bedside cabinet.

"What are you reading?" asked Luca.

"It's just a romantic novel, Daphne du Maurier; I got it from the library."

"Is it good?"

"It's historical fiction so not my usual cup of tea but yes, I am quite enjoying it, and learning something."

While he looked through the newspaper she read her book for a while, without remembering a word of it, then she put her light out and turned onto her side. After he lay down she lay in suspense as he got comfortable. Then she felt his hand on her back for a moment before it moved around her waist towards the front.

"I don't think I'm ready for this," she said. "I need time to get used to having you around again."

"Sorry," he said, "I thought you might like a cuddle."

"Not yet… Did you have other women when you were in Ireland?" She had finally asked the question.

"Did you have other men?" he replied.

"I asked you, but the answer is 'No'." She didn't count that one time, just as she wouldn't count one time by him either.

"Not really; I had a few dates but nothing serious. The Irish are quite strict on such things so it wasn't difficult not to get up to anything."

She didn't really believe him but was glad he'd lied because she could tell herself that there was always the possibility that he'd told the truth. Even if he hadn't told the truth maybe it was just one time, like her, or maybe two or three times because that would still be understandable – he was a man, after all… an Italian man at that. Either way, the fact remained that he'd been in no rush to come home to have *her*. She felt that, on balance, she would rather he'd had a fling or two but come back as soon as he could, rather than this lukewarm return.

"Goodnight," she said.

XIX

The offender became the offended. In the days that followed the distance between Ellen and Luca did not narrow; if anything it became set like a jelly, cold and impossible to grasp. It seemed as if there was nothing that would rekindle their old relationship. Much as he tried, and he believed he did try, Luca was unable to thaw the cold war that existed between them. He understood her resentment at his failure to make contact while he was away and when he thought about it he too found his behaviour inexplicable. When she'd repeatedly asked for an explanation, expecting some extenuating circumstance or lapse of reason or logical thought, he was at a loss to find one – nothing but a shrug of the shoulders, an apology and a banal excuse. So, he did see her point of view, but surely if she had any love for him at all she'd find a way to surmount this hurdle to reconciliation and start to rebuild their relationship.

As the days went on Luca's disappointment turned to frustration then bitterness. He had given up his new life, full of possibilities, in Ireland to come home, but home to what? To a wife who, far from rejoicing at his return or being pleased to see him, seemed to regard his homecoming as an inconvenience. Expecting to be welcomed home triumphantly as an Odysseus, even if not immediately recognised, he'd been received like the Master of Ballantrae, back from the dead but an unwelcome intrusion. His kind words and compliments were accepted begrudgingly, his gifts taken disparagingly and under every conversation was a simmering cynicism. He felt every attempt to show his love and affection was rebuffed. Unsurprisingly his wife did not encourage any physical relationship. They did make love a couple of times but Luca sensed that she was enduring it rather than enjoying it and his own interest waned. He longed for the exuberant love-making of Nancy.

Their domestic disharmony didn't prevent them from working fairly well together and Luca soon settled into his old work routine without interfering with the changes Ellen had made. At first he was pleased with the rapid progress he made in getting back up to speed and there was a brief period when he was comfortable in his work. Most of the customers were friendly enough and some appeared genuinely pleased to see him again, welcoming him back and wishing him well for the future, or acting as if nothing had happened. But Luca noticed that a few customers stopped frequenting the café altogether soon after his return and others that he asked Ellen about always seemed to be in the café when he was out. He questioned Ellen about it but she told him he was imagining it. He supposed that was possible but why was it that none of the shopkeepers, other than Cyril, came into the café to welcome him back? He was particularly surprised not to see ones he'd known quite well, like Eric Runsell in the hardware shop, Ted Silver the butcher, or others to whom he'd given plenty of business over the years. The second week after his return he told Ellen he would pay the baker's, grocer's and butcher's accounts in person that week.

"Why's that?" asked Ellen.

"Just thought I'd show my face to the suppliers."

On Friday he went first to the baker's, Whitlock's. He was greeted cordially by Mavis Whitlock who, when prompted, apologised for her husband Bill's failure to call in.

"Perhaps I could have a word with Bill now?" he said after they'd settled the account.

"It's a bit difficult at the moment. He's in the bake house; there's a problem with one of the ovens. I'll tell him you called," she said with a cheery smile as she turned to serve a customer.

Then he went to see the butcher Ted Silver. As he entered the shop Ted was cutting some loin chops. He looked up and nodded. "Hello Luca. What can I do for you?"

"Hello Ted. I've come to settle the account."

Ted wiped his hands on his apron and came over to take the cash with the invoice. He stamped the invoice PAID and returned it to Luca without saying a word.

"How's business?" asked Luca.

"Busy," said Ted, returning to his block to continue with the loin chops.

"I'll see you around," said Luca and turned to go.

"Yeah," replied Ted and brought the cleaver down on the carcass in front of him.

Luca walked the few doors along to Groombridge's the grocers. Luca had known Ken Groombridge quite well before the war and they'd often had a drink together in the Welsh Harp or the Spread Eagle.

"Hello Ken, how are you?"

Ken was stacking some shelves as the door opened, and he turned, still holding a tin of beef broth in his hand.

"Hello Luca. So, you made it back at last." He put the tin on the counter and both his hands in his brown dustcoat.

Luca noticed that Ken's parting was just a bit lower on his head since he'd last seen him and his coat a little tighter. Ken squinted a little at him through his tortoiseshell glasses.

"You look well, so life must have suited you in Ireland."

"Yes. How are things with you?"

"Not too bad."

"And Ivy?"

"She's fine, thank you very much."

"I've come to settle the account and thought perhaps we might have a drink together like old times."

Ken took the account and the notes Luca handed him and carefully entered the payment on the paper roll protruding from the wooden till before giving Luca his change.

"I'm a bit busy at the moment, Luca; perhaps some other time."

"Maybe next week?"

"Well, I don't know." He turned to put the tin of beef broth on top of the pyramid of identical fellows and carefully ensured the label matched the others.

"Ken, I don't understand. You're not keen on having a drink with me?"

Ken folded his arms. "Look, I think you ought to spend the time with your wife; she hasn't seen you for years and she had a lot to put up with while you were away."

"OK, Ken, I'll see you sometime." Luca turned and closed the door firmly behind him.

Meeting his neighbours did nothing to lessen his disappointment and added to the ennui which was creeping over him. His business provided a living but that wasn't enough. Every time he cooked another all-day breakfast or brewed the umpteenth pot of tea that day he felt like throwing the pan or pot out of the window. He needed greater variety and a sense of purpose in his life and in his work. He had come home expecting something better, or at least some things better if some were worse, but nothing was better and everything was worse. The expectations he'd harboured of coming home he now realised were no more than a fantasy. After the years in Dublin pretending he was Harry Baxter he now felt he was Harry Baxter pretending to be Luca Morenelli.

Since Luca had been away, Ellen had worked longer hours than she would have wished. But she managed through the help of Jean in the kitchen and another woman, Grace, who came in a couple of days a week to serve at tables and wash up. Ellen told Luca she was reluctant to sack either of them because they were both good workers, and Luca was happy to keep them both on so that Ellen would have more time off and he could pass on the mundane tasks. Ellen was relieved, as she'd found her busy schedule increasingly tiring over the last couple of years, so much so that she never seemed to have the energy for anything else.

As the weeks passed Luca and Ellen began to settle into a marriage of polite indifference. Independently of each other they finally initiated the beginning of a thaw between them, if not yet a warming, as they both resolved to make the best of it. Certainly, after about four weeks they were no longer feeling awkward around each other and they enjoyed the odd friendly conversation about something other than the business.

Then Luca received a letter from his aunt Anna, the contessa. He opened it and immediately recognised her neat, small handwriting.

My Dear Nephew,

I do hope this letter finds you and your dear wife safe and well after the terrible war. I am well but your uncle suffered a severe stroke early this year and it has left him paralysed on the left side and unable to walk. He requires a great deal of nursing and I've been fully preoccupied with his health. This is why I've been very slow in writing to you since the war ended. In addition, I've been trying to sort out the house which was requisitioned, first by the Germans and then by the Americans, and left in a terrible state.

Now, at last, I am getting the house back to its former condition and am ready to ask for the return of my chest of valuables. Some of them will decorate our home and many will be used to secure our finances and care for your uncle in our last years.

Thank you for your kindness in looking after these items and I trust you will be able to return them to me in the near future.

With much love,
Anna

Luca was pleased to receive the letter. Here, at last, something rewarding and worthwhile could come out of his return to England. Now he could look forward to reassuring his aunt and uncle that their property was safe. He left the letter in the living room and didn't mention it to Ellen until after the café closed later that day. When they sat down to their evening meal Luca told Ellen what was in the letter.

"It sounds as if they've had it tough during the war. I'm so pleased they're all right," she said. "I'll go and see Eric about the chest tomorrow."

"Are you sure? I don't mind seeing to it."

"I'd like to."

"That would be great. Thanks for making sure the chest was kept safe; you did well."

XX

The next morning Ellen telephoned Eric Runsell's shop. The phone was answered by Eric's wife, Iris, and after a brief exchange of pleasantries Ellen asked to speak to Eric. Iris explained that Eric was at the bank but would be back by eleven, so Ellen arranged to go over to the shop at quarter past.

At 11.15 Ellen went to see Eric about the chest. She opened the shop door, setting off the bell, and saw Iris at the counter, serving a customer with some fuse wire and torch batteries. With the transaction finished and the customer gone, Iris looked at Ellen and smiled.

"Good morning, Ellen, how are you?"

"I'm all right, thank you." Actually, Ellen didn't feel very well at all. She'd felt dizzy that morning and she'd had difficulty getting her breath but she didn't think Iris would wish to know that. There was also a bit of a pain in her chest, which she put down to indigestion, something she had suffered from a lot lately. "How are you?" she asked.

"Oh, I'm fine, thanks. Not looking forward to the shorter evenings but we've been lucky with the weather lately. Eric's back from the bank; perhaps you'd like to go through and see him." She lifted the counter flap and Ellen went from the shop through the lobby to the backroom.

Eric was sitting at a large oak desk with his account books, order forms and other paperwork neatly displayed on top. He took off his glasses and rose from his chair – a reproduction captain's chair in elm with a green leather seat – and shook hands before pulling up a chair for her.

As she sat down Ellen remembered being in this room before, when they'd moved the chest from her café to here, all those years ago. It had hardly changed, with the large desk, the rather nice chair, shelves laden with some stocks and extra supplies and the couple of armchairs with a tea table in the centre of the room. The gas hob for making cups of tea or coffee was still there in the corner. The background to all this was a very large grey stone fireplace, the grate of which had long been superseded by a gas fire. The fireplace, deprived of its status, provided a brooding, claustrophobic presence to those sitting in the armchairs.

"I've come about the chest," Ellen said simply.

Eric stared at her blankly. "What chest?"

"You know, the chest from Italy that I stored for Luca's aunt. We brought it in here in 1940 to protect it from the Blitz." She smiled encouragingly.

"I'm very sorry, Ellen, but I don't know what you're talking about."

"We put it in the cellar," her tone less confident, now puzzled.

"There is no chest in the cellar." Eric shook his head, a lock of brown hair falling over his forehead. "You're welcome to have a look if you wish but I'm absolutely sure that I have nothing of yours here."

"Don't you remember coming to the café with your trolley and bumping the chest down the stairs? We had a terrible job getting it along the alley and I thought you would drop it on the stairs it was so heavy."

"I have no trolley." He smiled. "It was a long time ago; perhaps you took the chest somewhere else?"

Ellen was confused and could feel panic rising in her. "Surely Iris would remember."

"I don't think so; there's nothing to remember." Eric stepped out to the shop and, seeing there were no customers, asked Iris to come into the back room. "Ask Iris, by all means," said Eric.

Ellen could feel herself perspiring and she dabbed her forehead with a handkerchief.

"Do you remember the chest I brought here for safekeeping?"

"A chest? You mean like a large trunk? No, I don't remember one."

"The trunk that I left with Eric at the start of the war. He said he would store it in the cellar for me."

Iris was utterly bemused by Ellen's statement. She'd been in the cellar a few times since the war and she was sure there was no trunk down there.

"I don't understand; there's definitely no trunk or chest in the cellar, either yours or anybody else's; I would have seen it."

"You see, Ellen, there must be some mistake," said Eric. "I'm sorry that I can't help you."

Lacking another line to pursue, Ellen had no choice but to restate her position: "I definitely remember bringing the chest here."

"I'm sorry, Ellen, but you must be mistaken; we have no chest here. You must have taken it somewhere else," said Iris quietly while she fiddled with her necklace.

Eric smiled benignly at Ellen. "I can only assume you're getting me mixed up with somebody else. I've never stored anything for you but you're welcome to see for yourself if it would put your mind at rest."

"Perhaps I ought to have a look, just to check."

"By all means," said Eric and he led the way to the cellar door and took her down the flight of steps into the room-sized cellar. With the light on Ellen could see clearly and she went to look where she thought they'd put the chest. She strained her eyes looking for the sign of a shape in the dust or scrape marks on the floor but there was nothing. After a thorough look everywhere else in the cellar she was satisfied and unsatisfied at the same time and she gave up the search.

Upstairs they went round a circular conversation two or three times more, using slightly different phrases each time, but the result was always the same: Eric didn't have the chest and knew nothing about it.

Ellen took her handkerchief and dabbed her forehead again. The questions were flying round inside her head. Why didn't she check from time to time that the chest was all right? Why would Eric have let her down like this? Should she have chosen someone else? Did she choose someone else? Was she mistaken? How could her mind ever be at rest again? What would she tell Luca? Was she losing her sanity? Her head was pounding, her chest ached. She felt sick and wondered if she might faint.

She looked pleadingly at them both, from one to the other and then back again, but they did not react.

"I can't believe it," she muttered, shaking her head, but then she accepted it and walked out of the shop.

"Poor woman; she looks quite ill. Perhaps I ought to go after her and see if she's all right," said Iris.

"It's been a shock for her. She'll be all right once she remembers what she's done with the chest," Eric replied and he went back to his accounts.

Once outside in the cold, Ellen knew she wasn't going to faint but she could feel, almost hear, her heart racing. She leaned against the shopfront of the doctors' surgery for a moment or two and then walked slowly back to the café. She passed a customer who spoke to her but she didn't hear what he said. She opened the café door and walked in, almost losing her footing as she crossed the threshold. It was late morning and between busy periods so there were no customers. Of the two staff, Grace wasn't working that day and Jean had gone to the butcher's, so Ellen and Luca were on their own. He was in the kitchen smoking a cigarette and looking at the menu for the day; it was the same most days but there was usually one special dish: liver and bacon on a Wednesday, sausage toad on a Thursday, and so on. He looked up when Ellen came in.

"Everything all right?"

"No, they haven't got the chest."

Luca took his cigarette from his mouth and knotted his eyebrows. "What do you mean?"

"They say they never had it… that I must have taken it somewhere else."

"Did you see Eric as well as Iris?"

"Yes, they both said the same."

"Well, what could have happened to it? You would surely remember where you took it."

"I was absolutely sure, but they deny it."

"Perhaps I'd better go round there."

"There's no point. I've been over it with them three or four times. I even looked in the cellar. It's not down there."

"Oh my God, what could have happened to it? Are they lying?"

"I don't know. Why would they lie?"

"That chest is worth a fortune; it must have been tempting."

"Iris is well off; there would be no need for them to take it. Anyway, Eric is a friend of ours."

Luca nodded. "Could you have taken it somewhere else? Perhaps you thought you took it there. Where else could you have taken it? For God's sake, think, woman!"

Ellen slumped into a chair. "I am trying to think. I don't know. I could have sworn I took it there but maybe I'm wrong. I can't think; it doesn't make sense. I can't remember." She held her head at the back, trying to think and stop the throbbing.

"Let's keep calm. Please try to play it back in your mind. I know it was a long time ago but try to think where else you might have taken the chest, if not to Runsell's."

"I have tried to do that but it always comes out the same; I can't understand what could have happened."

"What am I to do? What can I say to my aunt?"

"I'm sorry; I don't know what could have happened."

Luca stared at her. "How could you be so stupid as to have forgotten where the chest is? Can't one thing go right?"

"It's not my fault; everything was left to me. You didn't care when you were in Ireland caring only about yourself. You were and are a totally selfish bastard."

He walked towards her and put his hands round her neck from behind. "Think, think, think! Where is the chest, you stupid cow? Think!" His hands gripped tighter and he shook her and shook her.

Then he relented and relaxed his hold, but Ellen, who hadn't uttered a word or moved a muscle during his attack, merely making gasping noises, did not respond. As he released his hands her head gently subsided and she hung limply forward.

"*Madonna mia*," he murmured as he looked at Ellen's lifeless body. He gently spoke to her and tried to revive her with a pinch to the cheek and a gentle rousing but he knew it was pointless; he had killed his wife and his life was finished.

He stood, frozen, for what seemed an age until slowly his thoughts began to clear. He realised he couldn't leave her here; he couldn't explain anything to anyone at the moment. He gently lifted her up in his arms and took her upstairs to lay her on the bed; she felt so light and small and he wept as he put her down. He looked at her for a while and held her hand and kissed her on the forehead. Then he heard Jean come in. He wiped his eyes and went downstairs.

Somehow, he managed to speak calmly and slowly: "Jean, Mrs Morenelli isn't very well so she's having a lie down. I'll have to get a doctor later, and I don't think we'll manage lunches today. Put the meat in the fridge and take the afternoon off."

"Can I do anything for Mrs Morenelli?" asked Jean, her face creased in concern.

"No, dear, thank you. I'll manage."

Jean did as she was told and left with a wish that Ellen would soon feel better, and Luca locked the back door and turned the

'Open' sign to 'Closed' on the front. He picked up the telephone and dialled 99... and then stopped. He pressed down the receiver and then dialled Cyril's number.

"Hello Cyril. I'm sorry to trouble you but could you spare me a few minutes? It's very important."

Cyril said he would come at once and Luca waited by the door. Two minutes later Cyril entered the café and Luca locked the door behind him.

"What's up, old boy?" asked Cyril.

"Ellen is dead and I killed her."

"Good God," said Cyril, raising his hand to his mouth. "What happened?"

"We had an argument and I lost my temper and put my hands round her throat. There was a moment when I think I wanted to kill her, then it passed, but it was too late; she was already dead."

Cyril considered for a moment and then said, "I think I ought to take a look at her, just to make sure."

Luca was comforted by Cyril's calmness and composure. It was how he would wish to act if the roles were reversed. They went upstairs and Cyril tried for a pulse, held a mirror to Ellen's mouth and put his head to her chest. Then he nodded to Luca.

"I'm sorry, old man, she's dead." He then looked at Ellen's neck and throat. "I can't really see any marks of note. Obviously, I'm not a doctor but I would have thought the marks of strangulation would have been much more apparent. I suppose they might be later."

"I ought to phone the police," said Luca.

Cyril stood up and grasped Luca's arm. "Not yet. If you phone the police first, you're making an admission that Ellen died of unnatural causes, but we don't know that yet. I think we should phone a doctor and let him make the decision."

"But I did kill her."

"Possibly."

"I wanted to kill her and that's as bad."

"You had a passing thought that you wanted to kill her. I'd be hanged several times over if I were charged for murder every time the thought entered my head."

"Yes, but you didn't have your hands round the person's neck."

"That's true. Let's talk it over some more, but not here. I think you could use a drink."

They went into the sitting room and Cyril looked at the drinks tray. He passed on the grappa and the amaretto and poured them both a large glass of Johnny Walker red label. They sat down and faced each other; Luca smoked a cigarette while Cyril lit a small cigar.

"Tell me again exactly what happened."

Luca related the events of that morning: how he'd lost his temper over the disappearance of the chest and then the few moments that ended in Ellen's death.

"Well, the story is pretty much the same so it's the truth, but is it the whole truth? If you relate the events simply and without explanation it seems you killed your wife in a fit of homicidal rage. But the whole truth is that you were angry, you blindly went for your wife and had murderous thoughts, but did you actually intend to kill her? Of course not. If you had planned to kill her you'd be asking me to help you cover it up, not talking about phoning the police. The trouble is that if you go to the police and confess, as you did to me, the law will swing into action to ensure that your admission of guilt sends you to the gallows, or prison at least. What purpose would that serve?"

"But I feel guilty and I deserve whatever I get."

"You feel guilty now. Look, Luca, self-loathing is a very laudable virtue I'm sure but you can have too much of a good thing. If you need to confess, go and see a priest and get it out of your system; isn't that what confession to a priest is for? Then let events take their own course."

"You make it sound so simple; but I'm not so sure."

"I'm very sad about Ellen. She was a good woman and she

deserved better than she got in life, right to the end. But let's be practical. What purpose would be served by you leaping to conclusions based on guilt and remorse? All I'm asking is that you don't rush into anything. Just let's do it my way for now; you can still speak up later if you want to."

Luca shrugged. "All right. Thanks Cyril. You're a good friend and probably the only one I've got round here now. I can't imagine anyone else sticking their neck out for me."

Cyril smiled. "That's because they're all morally superior to me and so can't empathise with someone who doesn't always do the right thing."

"What do you think we should say to the doctor?"

"Keep it simple. Ellen came back from the shop in a state and felt unwell. Suddenly she slumped and you tried to revive her, perhaps shaking her in your panic, but she was already dead."

He went to the telephone and picked up the handset. "Pity Dr Jelley is no longer around; he would have been helpful to us, I'm sure." He rang a doctor up the road who said he'd come in about half an hour.

Waiting for the doctor, Luca and Cyril had another drink and Cyril insisted on rehearsing the story again. Luca did as he was told then they sat and waited. Dr Henderson arrived within the half hour. He was a round, bustling man of about forty-five, unknown to either of them, who introduced himself as a locum for one of the local GPs. He undertook a thorough examination for any sign of life but reluctantly concluded that Cyril had been correct.

"I'm very sorry, Mr Morenelli. It was so sudden I'd guess her heart gave out but there will need to be a post-mortem to confirm what actually happened. The only blessing is that she probably didn't suffer too much." He took out a pad and wrote something on it. "It would be best not to organise the funeral until the necessary investigation has been done but I will arrange for your wife's body to be taken to the mortuary and inform the police; just procedural you understand."

"Would you like a drink, Dr Henderson?" asked Cyril, taking on the duties of host.

"Just a small one, thank you. I have a busy day."

"What is your fee, doctor?" asked Luca.

"Don't worry about that now; I shall send you a bill in due course."

Once the doctor had left, Cyril said, "Well, that's stage one dealt with. I'll go and tell Gwen what's happened and then I'll be back and stay with you until they come for Ellen. You will get through this, don't worry."

XXI

The week that followed was something of a blur for Luca. He kept the café closed and put the boards over the windows, one painted black as a symbol of mourning. He spent each day lamenting what had happened and was filled with a regret which showed no sign of abating. Eventually he decided to visit a priest. He called to make an appointment and a couple of days later went down to the Wick where the church was situated. He hadn't been to the church since 1939 when he'd attended Midnight Mass at Christmas with Ellen. He knew the church had been bombed in the war so he wasn't shocked by the sight that greeted him. The roof had gone and there was extensive damage to some of the walls. The site was boarded up so he was unable to see the condition of the inside of the church. The tower, a local landmark, was still there and seemed unscathed and even defiant.

Luca rang the doorbell of the presbytery and was shown by the housekeeper into a reception room. It was a small room, with a desk and a few upright chairs. On the wall were religious paintings and a crucifix. There was also a large clock. Luca glanced round and presumed it was a room for interviewing and perhaps instructing parishioners, novitiates and others with whom the priests had business to conduct. The house was silent except for the ticking of the clock on the wall. There were the faint smells of a lunch recently consumed, mixed with the cloying fragrance of wax polish.

After a few minutes Luca heard footsteps and then the door opened and a young priest of about thirty appeared. His curly fair hair was fighting hard against the plastered-down hairstyle imposed on it. His handsome, boyish face was set in a friendly smile, though his eyes betrayed a sense of apprehension or timidity. He was wearing a Roman collar but with a black suit rather than a cassock. He held out his hand as Luca rose to greet him.

"Mr Morenelli?" he asked. "I'm Father O'Leary. How can I help you?" He had an English accent.

"Thank you for seeing me so promptly, father. My wife died recently and, although she wasn't Catholic, I'd be grateful if a mass could be said for the repose of her soul."

Father O'Leary asked Luca to take a seat and walked round behind the desk to take some notes. "You're a member of this parish, Mr Morenelli?"

"Yes, father."

The priest looked through a card index and nodded. "Spelt M-O-R-E-N-E-L-L-I? Yes, I have your details here: Luca Morenelli and wife Ellen. There's no mention of any children."

"No, we didn't have any children."

"I see… It makes it harder when you lose your wife and you have no children to bear the loss with you. Do you have any other family?"

"Not in England."

The priest nodded. "I haven't been in the parish very long but I don't think we've met?" He looked at Luca inquiringly but with a slight ambiguity.

Luca shook his head. "I've been in Ireland for five years and have only recently returned home."

O'Leary appeared a little surprised by this statement. "I see; you and your wife were separated?"

"Only because of the war. As an Italian I was forced to seek refuge overseas for the duration."

"Yes, of course. I'm very sorry to hear of the death of your wife. May her soul and the souls of all the faithful departed rest in peace, amen." He crossed himself and Luca automatically did the same.

"So, you would be agreeable to saying a mass for Ellen, father?"

The priest smiled. "Of course; we have faith that as a child of God she will receive his blessing and mercy. Which denomination was your wife?"

"Church of England."

The priest nodded. He took down a few details on a pad designed for the purpose of mass intentions and said that a mass would be said for the repose of her soul on the 3rd of December.

"A mass in Advent is so appropriate for those who have just died since it's a time when we look forward to the world to come," he said, half talking to Luca and half musing on his little homily. "Tell me, if it's not too painful for you, how did Ellen die?"

"I'm not sure. She died very suddenly and the post-mortem report hasn't come out yet; it was probably a heart attack."

"Very sad for you, but surely a blessing for the one who dies without too much suffering. Were you with her when she died?"

Luca nodded.

"That would have been a comfort for her in her last moments."

Luca thought about confessing his assault on Ellen.

"Is there anything else I can do for you, Luca? Would you like us to pray together?"

Luca shook his head, he was still thinking about confession. He could confess and the priest would be bound by the seal of the confessional. Even if he suggested that Luca should go to the police, he couldn't do so himself. But that would be cowardice. If he was going to confess he would tell the police first and a confession to a priest could come later.

"Can I be of help in any other way?"

"No, thank you, father. You've been very kind. I will come to mass on the 3rd, if not before."

They rose and Father O'Leary held out his hand. "Once again, my sincere sympathy. God bless you."

Over the following week Luca's feelings of guilt abated a little as he began to see things more in line with Cyril's view. However, he felt more uncomfortable again when he had to deal with the stream of neighbours who came to pay their respects to the grieving husband; Tom Silver and Ken Groombridge sent their wives to perform this function.

Nine days after the death of Ellen, Luca received a telephone call from a sergeant at Hackney police station to say that he would be calling to see him regarding the death of his wife.

The sergeant arrived with a young constable at 2.30 that afternoon, as arranged. "Good afternoon, sir. Sergeant Spencer, and this is PC Farrell."

The sergeant removed his helmet to reveal his centre-parted, slightly receding grey hair. He had a friendly look about him and Luca wondered whether that was good or bad. The sergeant's large face was rather red and he appeared quite hot when he arrived, fingering his high collar when he was invited to sit down. He had a manila envelope from which he produced a report of some kind and took a pencil from his pocket. The constable, a pale-complexioned slim man, took out a pencil and notebook from one of his top pockets.

"Thank you kindly for taking the time to see us, Mr Morenelli – I hope I'm pronouncing that correctly – it's a very difficult time for you. Please accept my condolences on the death of your wife. I have a report on the post-mortem that was conducted a few days ago and I wondered if I might ask you one or two questions, just to tie up any loose ends for the report."

"Of course; I'll help in any way I can."

"Could we start by you telling me exactly what happened the day that Mrs Morenelli died?"

"Well, the morning began as usual and then my wife went to see Mr Runsell, in the shop a few doors along, regarding a chest she thought she'd stored with him. After about twenty minutes she returned, saying that the chest was not with Mr Runsell. While we were talking she sat down in a chair because she didn't feel well, then she suddenly slumped forward and I realised something was seriously wrong. I couldn't get any response from her so I took her upstairs and lay her on the bed. Then I called Cyril Johnson, the chemist, and he came at once and told me she was dead."

Sergeant Spencer looked over at the constable. "Would you pop down to Mr Runsell's shop and see if he can confirm those details and ask how Mrs Morenelli seemed when she left the shop?" The constable nodded and quietly slipped out the front door.

"May I ask the nature of this chest, sir?"

"It was a family chest which contained some items we were storing for my aunt. We'd planned to ship the chest back to her in a few days."

"Were the items valuable, sir?"

"Yes."

There was silence for a couple of minutes as the sergeant looked down the report. "So, your wife would have been upset or agitated that she couldn't find the chest, Mr Morenelli?"

"Yes, she couldn't understand what had happened and was very upset."

"I see. It must have been quite a shock for you when she collapsed in your presence. Did you know your wife had a weak heart, sir?"

Luca's surprise must have shown on his face because, before he could answer, Sergeant Spencer said, "I gather from your reaction that you didn't?"

"No, I had no idea."

"We can find no medical record for her having been treated for any condition but she must have been in poor health for some time."

"She used to get very tired and sometimes short of breath.

She'd recently reduced the hours she spent in the café because of it."

"I see. Well, the cause of death was quite advanced heart disease and she could have gone at any time apparently. She did have slight bruising on the neck; have you any idea how that may have occurred, sir?" The sergeant looked at him intently and held his pencil poised over the report.

"I can only assume that it happened when she collapsed. I thought she'd gone into a deep faint and I was holding her neck when I shook her to try to revive her. I must have been heavy-handed, I suppose."

"Well, the shaking had no effect on her ability to breathe, if she was still alive at the time, so I shouldn't worry about that, sir – obviously it would be a different matter if someone with a weak heart was shaken violently; it could have an effect, I suppose."

Luca suddenly felt rather hot and hoped he wouldn't blush while the sergeant was watching him intently. "I don't know enough about it but I'm sure you're right, Sergeant."

At that moment the constable returned and both Luca and the sergeant turned to hear his report.

"Mr Runsell is out, Sarge, but I spoke to Mrs Runsell. She confirms Mr Morenelli's statement. She said that Mrs Morenelli had looked quite unwell when she'd left the shop and she'd wondered if she ought to have offered to help her. She says she wishes now she'd done so."

"Well, there it is, Mr Morenelli. There will be no need for an inquest and the coroner's office has released the body of your late wife for burial, so you can begin to make arrangements for the funeral. A very distressing time for you."

The two policemen made their way to the front door.

"Thank you for your help, sir, and once again our sincere condolences. Good day, Mr Morenelli."

"Good day, Sergeant, Constable," said Luca, and he watched

them walk to a waiting police car and remove their helmets before getting in.

Luca had been drinking a little too much over the past few days but he felt he definitely needed one now. He poured himself a large Scotch and sat back in a chair in the café. He hadn't known whether he would make a confession until the sergeant revealed that Ellen had had a weak heart. Now he knew.

He phoned Cyril immediately and asked him to come round that evening, so he could give him the news.

When Cyril arrived, they had a few drinks but it was not a celebration.

"So, how do you feel now about what happened, Luca?" asked Cyril.

Luca shook his head. "Nothing has changed in a way. Ellen is dead and I will never really forgive myself for what happened but it was an accident, or at worst misadventure, and I'll try to cling to that."

Cyril put it succinctly: "If you had known she was ill then it may have been murder, but it might just as easily have happened if someone had burst a balloon behind her back."

XXII

The funeral took place the following week at the Anglican church in the sister parish of the bombed-out church in the High Street. It was near the end of November, that grimmest of months when the watery sun never dries the ground and the air is full of damp and fog. The future offers only more darkness and a need for pagan rituals to raise the spirit. Luca hoped to find some consolation in the funeral rituals of the Church. The service, conducted by a kindly, elderly priest, was in an English that Luca found unfamiliar and sometimes hard to follow. So much of it flowed over him, like a lyrical poem where the reader moves on to the next verse before the listener has had a moment to reflect on its meaning. Some passages leapt out at him, however, and brought tears to his eyes:

"Thou hast set our misdeeds before thee: and our secret sins in the light of thy countenance."

"Man that is born of a woman hath but a short time to live, and is full of misery. He cometh up, and is cut down, like a flower; he fleeth as it were a shadow, and never continueth in one stay."

"Forasmuch as it hath pleased Almighty God of his great mercy to take unto himself the soul of our dear sister here departed: we therefore commit her body to the ground; earth to earth, ashes to ashes, dust to dust; in sure and certain hope of the Resurrection to eternal life..."

The day was unsurprisingly damp but not rainy, and a little sun broke forth as Ellen was laid in her grave. In a moment of hope rather than faith Luca prayed that Ellen was happy now and would forgive him.

At the funeral Luca met Ellen's sister and mother again for the first time in years.

"She had a sad life," said her sister. "She worked hard then had to manage without you; then she has you back for a little while and drops down dead. I wish I'd come up to see her more often. Poor little devil, she's better off now."

Ellen's mother looked old and devastated and filled with the terrible desolation of a parent losing a child. Luca held her in his arms and she sobbed a little and railed against the cruelness of fate that had brought him home to her too late.

Luca was gratified to see so many of the customers and fellow shopkeepers attend, though he knew it was solely for Ellen and nothing to do with him. He gave a buffet lunch afterwards at the Spread Eagle for everyone who wished to come.

Eric and Iris were there and both felt guilty about the last time they'd seen Ellen. They had already given their condolences and Eric felt too frozen by events to be anything other than a silent presence. But Iris again told Luca how sorry she was and how she wished she'd done more for Ellen. Luca told her not to blame herself and thanked her for coming. He didn't blame her or Eric and hadn't thought much about the chest since Ellen had died.

Jean and Grace were also there, and Luca asked Jean who the round-faced man with the dark hair was who'd looked very upset after the service but who didn't come on to the reception. Jean and Grace glanced at each other, before Jean said it was Charlie, a customer who'd been quite friendly with Ellen. Luca didn't probe the subject further but hoped that Ellen had had some friendships, perhaps love, while he was away.

"How will you manage the café now?" asked Cyril's wife Gwen, as the people began drifting away after the reception.

"I don't know yet," said Luca. "I've a lot of thinking to do."

"I know I'm not much use but Cyril will do anything he can to help. He's very fond of you and you know you can rely on him."

Luca was sorry that he hadn't always thought kindly of Gwen and embraced her and thanked her for being a good friend to Ellen and himself.

After the funeral Ellen's mother and sister went back to the flat with him and sorted out anything they wanted: clothes, personal items, pictures, mementos. Luca promised to send them on as soon as he could. They'd arrived the previous day by train and spent the evening reminiscing about Ellen's life and her virtues. Then they'd slept in his bed while he took the sofa. He invited them to stay over again but they preferred to go home and took a train to Devon that afternoon. He saw them off.

With everyone gone, he went back to his rooms over the café and sat staring ahead as the light faded, until he was sitting in the dark. Cyril rang to ask if Luca would like him to come round for company that evening but he preferred to be on his own. He didn't eat that evening and, after several drinks, went to bed. He desperately wanted to sleep but rest wouldn't come; just hour after hour of tossing and turning while he went over the funeral in his mind, and even this sadness was soon superseded by the memory of how Ellen had died.

He must have slept eventually because, although he saw the clock mark the hours of one, two and three, it then jumped to six and he got up. He wanted to make this day a fresh start, practically as well as metaphorically. That morning he got out the lease he had on the café and saw that it had another three months to run, so he wrote to the agents informing them that he would not be renewing it.

During this dreadful period following the death of Ellen he hadn't given his aunt's missing chest any thought but now he did wonder what had happened to it. He owed it to his aunt to try to track it down but where to start? If the chest had been purloined by the Runsells, or by anyone else, how could he prove it and how would he regain possession of it?

In the absence of any other clues he began with the Runsells. He took a piece of paper and wrote down what he knew about them. Eric had his own business, about which Luca knew little, while Iris's father was well off: a landlord with a dozen properties. It was unlikely they needed the money, as Ellen had pointed out. He knew Eric and Iris well enough, as social friends before the war, to conclude that they were not at all likely to have robbed them of the chest. Ellen must have made a mistake as to where she'd left it.

He screwed up the paper and threw it in the wastebasket. Now what? He must be methodical. He took another piece of paper and made a list of the other shops near to the café which had a cellar, as surely Ellen must have been right about that? There was Whitlock's bakery, which definitely had one as the bake house was in the cellar, the Welsh Harp, Ted Silver the butcher, Griffin's motor parts, which had one because it used to be a bakery, and maybe one or two others. He left matters there for a few days; it seemed too early to be delving into this puzzle.

The following Tuesday, mass was said for Ellen and Luca attended the service, as he'd said he would. Mass was celebrated by Father O'Leary and there were about a dozen other worshippers. Most of them were daily churchgoers whom he didn't know but Luca saw Mrs Quinn from the laundry, who had perhaps come specially. She smiled and nodded at him when he noticed her and he wondered if she had a cellar.

The Latin of the mass was more familiar to him than the English liturgy of Ellen's funeral but it was pronounced very differently to that in Italy. He found it more calming than the funeral. He had nothing to do or think too much about; he just followed the pattern of standing, kneeling and sitting, and watched as the priest and the elderly altar server recited all the prayers. There was no sermon and no reference to Ellen, just the silent remembrance by the priest as the appropriate prayer at the centre of the mass was said.

Afterwards, Luca knocked on the sacristy door and Father O'Leary came out, having already removed his purple vestments. Luca gave him an envelope containing a generous donation and thanked him for the service. The priest asked Luca how he was and said he hoped the funeral had gone as well as could be hoped.

"The funeral was attended by quite a few people and I found it a comfort that so many liked Ellen."

"Yes, it's more than a mark of respect when so many strangers come. If there's anything I can do during this difficult period please do get in touch with me at any time. Will I see you at mass again soon?"

"I doubt it. I'm still thinking about my future plans and I'm not sure what I'll be doing in a few weeks' time."

"I'll be sorry not to see you again but I hope the future brings you peace and happiness. Remember me in your prayers, and God bless."

Later that week Luca went round to see each of the shops on the cellar list, using a standard format: "Hello. Just after the war broke out Ellen left a chest for safekeeping with one of the shops which has a cellar. Unfortunately, she couldn't remember which one it was and she died before she had a chance to check with each of the shopkeepers. I wondered if it might have been you that she asked."

In each case he got variations on the same theme: "It wasn't left with me. I don't know anything about a chest. I'm sorry I can't help."

Somebody mentioned other shops with cellars that he didn't

know about but enquiries with them had a similar result. Nobody knew anything about the chest, or if they did they weren't saying. It had been a fruitless day with a succession of dead ends.

That evening Cyril called round to see how he'd got on and they stood in the back room of the café while Luca made a cup of tea.

"I've drawn a complete blank," said Luca. "Nobody knew anything, or at least they all said they knew nothing."

Cyril folded his arms then unfolded them, then rubbed his chin, then finally said, "I know this seems a weird question but are you sure there was a chest? I mean, only you and Ellen seem to have seen it, and of course the person who took it. But it was a long time ago. Could you have sort of imagined it?"

"The delivery firm."

"What?"

"The delivery firm who brought it." Luca walked over to the small filing cabinet where he kept his paperwork and rifled through some of the folders. "Yes, here it is – Albion Motor Deliveries, Lansdowne Road. It was delivered on the 22nd of March 1940."

Cyril nodded. "Right, just thought I'd ask. What do we do now?"

"I thought of going to the police. I know it's a long shot but some of the stuff in the chest might have turned up."

"Have you got an inventory of the contents?"

"No."

Cyril scratched his head. "It *is* rather a long shot but you never know. What about an advertisement in the local paper offering a 'reward for information on', etc.; that kind of thing?"

"Would you mind writing it out for me? I think you'd do a better job than me."

"All right. You visit the police and I'll have a go at the advert and we'll compare notes tomorrow evening."

Because Luca had such low expectations, the visit to the police was fruitless without being dispiriting. A polite station sergeant took details of the missing chest and recorded the dates of when it was delivered and when approximately it was last seen.

"Have you got a list of the items that have gone missing?"

"No, the inventory was in the chest. I can tell you that all the items are antiques: pictures, jewellery, ornaments, cloth and so on. I believe that most of them are over two hundred years old."

The officer recorded the details then placed his pen on the record book.

"I'll get someone to have a look and see if we have any record of such items but I'm sure you'll appreciate that without more information there's not much we can do."

That evening Cyril came round and Luca told him about his visit to the police station.

"Well, we expected as much," said Cyril. "I've had a go at the advert."

He handed Luca his handwritten, blocked-out suggestion:

REWARD OF £50 OFFERED

For information leading to the recovery of a chest from Italy containing decorative and ornamental objects which went missing in the Hackney area between 1940 and 1945. Contact Luca Morenelli, etc.

"I think £50 is about right. I know it's a lot of money but I guess the contents are worth a lot more than that."

Luca read the advert a couple of times. "I'm not sure £50 is enough; perhaps £100."

"£100? Are you sure? That would buy a very decent second-hand car."

"I don't know how much it was all worth but it must have been ten times that. In any case, if I get the chest back I'll be more than happy to pay it."

"OK, £100 it is. I'll put it in for a week to start with. By the way, a couple of people asked me when you're opening the café again."

"I don't know yet. I'd like to deal with this, one way or another, first."

Luca got on with tidying up his affairs. He wrote a long letter to his brother in Italy, expressing the hope that he was safe and well and that he'd been informed by the Italian embassy of Luca's escape to Ireland. He told him of the death of Ellen and said that he fervently wished to be reunited with him at some point in the future.

Having arranged to send Ellen's things to her family, Luca began to sort out her affairs. He found it in a way sad that it was so easy to do. She had no property to dispose of and her money was held in their joint account, while her valuable items of jewellery and so on had gone to her family. It was just a matter of getting rid of her clothing. He asked Gwen, Grace and Jean over to take anything they wanted and he arranged for the rest to go to the Salvation Army. While they were there, he told Jean and Grace of his decision to close the café indefinitely and said he would arrange for both of them to have severance pay of three months' wages. Grace said she thought it was too much but Luca insisted. Then, much to his surprise, he received two responses to the advertisement. The first came when the telephone rang at about eight o'clock in the morning.

"Hello," said Luca.

A male voice, sounding quite young, answered: "Hello, I'm calling about the advertisement regarding the chest of valuables."

Luca pressed the receiver closer to his ear. "Yes, you have some information?"

"Yes, I've seen one like you are talking about in a second-hand furniture shop in Dalston."

"Did you see inside it?"

"Er… no. I think it's empty."

"What did it look like?"

"It was square, about two feet by two, with a round top."

"No, I'm sorry, that's definitely not the one."

"I don't get a reward, then?"

"No, it's not the right one."

The phone went dead and Luca replaced the receiver, disappointed but encouraged that people were reading the advert.

The second call came the following afternoon from a woman who thought she'd seen a chest being dragged into a garage just last week from her flat window and thought it seemed quite suspicious. She couldn't give a clear description but she was sure it was metal. Luca thanked her but said it was not the chest he was searching for.

And that was it. There were no more responses of any kind by the time the week was up: another blank. He'd already given the bad news to Cyril – who'd said he would try to think of other ideas – when he received another call.

"Hello, I'm telephoning about the missing chest of valuables." The voice was that of a young woman.

Luca prepared himself for another call from a chancer or a lunatic. "Yes?" he replied.

"It was pure luck. I don't get the *Hackney Gazette* but I always read it when my fish and chips are wrapped in it, and there it was last night, your advertisement."

Luca was tempted to put the phone down but went through the motions: "Do you have any information?"

"Yes. I know what happened to it. I saw it after your wife left it for safekeeping."

The advert had not mentioned his wife. "Can you describe the chest you saw?"

"Yes, it was wooden with a flat top and about five feet long and three wide, with hinges and a padlock."

"I'd like to hear more and it's difficult to discuss the details on the phone; I think we ought to meet. Would you like to come here?"

"I'd rather meet somewhere public if you don't mind. How about the Spread Eagle? That won't be far for you."

"When?"

"Tonight at seven o'clock?"

"All right. How will I know you?"

She giggled. "It's all right; I won't expect you to wear a pink carnation and carry a copy of *Picture Post*. Let's meet in the private bar; I'm blonde and I'll be wearing a dark-brown overcoat. If anyone else is already there or comes in while we're talking, we can move somewhere else. Don't bring anyone with you. This is just between us."

That evening Luca rang Cyril to tell him the promising news and then went over to the pub at 6.45. It was a very small bar with wood panelling and just one table with six seats round it. As he came in and closed the door, the publican walked along from the saloon. He knew Luca fairly well and had arranged the wake for Ellen.

"Hello Luca, unusual to see you in here, you usually prefer the saloon."

"Hello Jack. I've a small business matter to deal with so I wanted somewhere quiet," said Luca.

The publican nodded and pulled Luca a pint. "I suppose you're still getting over the shock of poor Ellen; it'll take time for your life to get back on an even keel."

Just at that moment the door opened and a young blonde in a brown overcoat came in.

"Good evening, what can I get you?" asked Luca, standing up.

"Hello. A gin and bitter lemon, please," said the woman, and she sat down, taking off her scarf and undoing her coat.

The publican served her drink and winked at Luca. "I'll let you get on with your small business matter," he said and moved back to the saloon bar.

"My name is Luca Morenelli. Can I ask your name?" asked Luca.

"I know who you are – the man who runs the café over the

road," she nodded in that direction. "I'm Pearl". She was in her mid-twenties, pretty, with wide features and large blue eyes which made Luca think of a doll and even a little of Nancy.

"Why did you want to meet here?"

"So that you'd be sure to be seen by someone you knew and would have to behave yourself." She cocked her head on one side and there was a flicker of a smile.

Luca smiled. "I have every intention of behaving myself. Would you like a cigarette?"

"No thanks, I don't smoke."

Luca lit a cigarette. "Well? You have some news for me?"

She sipped her drink. "I know about the chest you're looking for." She stared at him, the smile more evident now and playful.

"I've had a couple of hoax calls and your description could have been a clever guess. How can I be sure you've actually seen it?"

Pearl lifted up the sleeve of her left wrist and showed him her watch. It was his aunt's watch; he had last seen it in the chest.

"Where did you get that?"

"You know where; it was in the chest and I was given it."

"Who gave it to you?"

She waited for a moment and then spoke softly, "Eric Runsell."

"My God," said Luca, unable to keep his voice down. "When was this?"

"About three years ago. He took me out for a bit; I suppose you could call it an affair."

"How did you get to know him?"

"I don't see what that's got to do with it but we were in the same ARP team, fire watching. Anyway, one thing led to another and, as I say, we went out for a bit."

"How did you find out about the chest?"

"So many questions! One day we went back to his shop and I was looking around, and I got him to show me the cellar and there it was under a blanket, this bloody great chest, like something out of a pirate film. He'd never opened it until then, didn't have a clue what was in it. I got him to open it and there was all this gold jewellery and, well… you must know what was in it."

"Would you like another drink?"

"Yes please, same again."

Luca went to get some more drinks, leaning round the pillar to attract the attention of one of the barmen. The pub was filling up now and their conversation wouldn't be heard above the general noise. A couple opened the door to the private bar but closed it again when they saw it was already occupied. Luca returned with the drinks.

"You said you knew what had happened to the chest."

Pearl had removed her coat to reveal a black sweater and grey skirt. She still sat forward in her seat.

"Well, I know what happened after I first saw it, and I can guess what happened after that if Eric hasn't got it now. After all, it was a long time ago."

"Go on," said Luca, lighting another cigarette.

"It all started when he gave me the watch. When we looked at all the things in the chest we were both amazed, and we compared the things we liked and didn't like. I said how much I liked the watch and he gave it to me a few weeks later as a birthday present. He was very sweet on me then and generous, throwing money around all the time. I suppose once he'd taken one thing out of the chest it was easy to take another. I told him that he should leave it alone in case the woman came back for it but he wouldn't listen; if he got a bit short of money he would sell something to raise some cash. You see, nobody else knew about the chest, he hadn't even told his wife, so he thought he'd get away with it." Her voice was softer now than when she'd first arrived.

"Did this go on for long?" He could see why Runsell had been attracted to her. She could have been his type once too.

"I don't know. He dumped me a couple of months later so I can only guess he carried on raiding the piggy bank, especially if no one came back for it. Why didn't you or your wife come to collect it?"

"I was abroad during the war. I don't know why my wife didn't collect it. You know there's been a crime committed here. If I go to the police will you come with me?"

Pearl smiled and shook her head. "Not likely; I'd be an accessory. I'm just giving you a tip-off for the reward. If you go to the police I'll deny everything I told you." She drained her glass.

"Did Runsell give you anything else from the chest?"

"No, I told him I didn't want anything else." She looked at her watch. "Well, if there's nothing else I ought to be going. What about the reward?"

"You have the watch."

"I can't spend that."

"Give me the watch; it might be the only piece I ever recover. I'll give you fifty quid now and another fifty if I get most of the rest of it back."

Pearl didn't look too impressed but slowly and reluctantly removed the watch. "How do I know you'll keep your word?" she asked, dangling the watch in front of his face.

"You don't for sure but if you keep the watch you'll leave here with that and you'll never get anything else out of me."

"I wonder if I can trust you," she said, holding out the watch with that slight smile he couldn't help liking.

Luca smiled too. "That's for you to decide, but at the very least you've managed to offload some stolen property at a good price."

Pearl looked at him for a moment then took a postcard from her handbag and wrote out an address where she could be contacted and passed it to Luca. Then she gave him the watch, took the ten white five-pound notes, thanked him for the drinks and was gone.

Luca left the pub and thought about asking Cyril to drive him over to Runsell's house there and then. Instead he went home and telephoned his friend.

"How did you get on, chum?" asked Cyril.

"She was genuine. She had my aunt's watch."

"Really? That's very interesting. How did she come by it?"

"It was given to her by the man who had the chest and presumably knows what happened to it – Eric Runsell."

"Bloody hell," said Cyril. "Whatever made him deny all knowledge of it?"

"According to this woman he started using the contents to pay for his lifestyle."

"I can hardly believe it; Eric Runsell of all people. What do you want to do next? Go back to the police?"

"I think I ought to talk to Eric first. Depending on how that goes we'll decide whether to get the police involved. Keep it to yourself for now."

"Of course I will. Do you think it's a good idea to see him on your own, without a witness?"

"I want to start off low-key. If he feels under pressure I might not get anywhere and we'll never find out about the chest. Anyway, I don't think he's the sort to become aggressive."

"Fair enough; you can handle him. If you want any help you know where I am."

Luca put the phone down and wondered about phoning Runsell, but he would only have the element of surprise once and he didn't want to waste it. He took out a notepad and wrote out three scenarios, anticipating how Runsell would react to different lines of attack. He played around with these strategies for what started off as a few minutes but became a few hours until eventually he thought any more strategising would be counter-productive. He knew what he was going to do. But still, he didn't sleep much that night.

The next morning Luca rang Eric Runsell at his shop. "Hello Eric, it's Luca."

"Oh, hello Luca."

"I'd like to see you, if you can spare a few minutes."

There was silence for just a second longer than one might expect. "Yes, surely, what about?"

"Nothing much. I'm trying to make some plans for the future and I thought you might be able to give me some advice on selling unwanted electrical and other equipment."

"Well, I'm not an expert but if I can be of any help…"

"Would today be convenient?"

"Yes, come along when I close at lunchtime – say, one o'clock?"

"Thanks, see you then." Luca put down the phone and breathed deeply, wondering if he'd sounded normal. He looked at his watch – only 9.45, and another three hours to kill. He went back to his notes and rehearsed the scenarios again and again like an actor learning his lines.

At one o'clock Luca completed the short journey along the road to Runsell's shop. It was open and he walked in, triggering the bell on the door. He remembered the shop from his rare visits before the war. It had a Spartan feel about it, all plain wood and no decoration, with most things out of sight so that you weren't sure that any transactions actually took place. The overall impression was one of extreme order and tidiness.

A glass-panelled door from the back room of the shop opened and out came Eric Runsell. Luca hadn't really looked at him at the funeral but he hadn't changed much since the war: the mid-brown hair parted neatly on the right, the round horn-rimmed spectacles seated on the long nose, the sallow complexion and the slightly down-turned mouth which made him seem morose.

"Hello Luca, would you like to come through to the back room?" He lifted the counter flap and Luca followed him into the room where five years before he'd agreed to store the chest for Ellen. He walked over to the small gas hob in the corner and lit the kettle. "Would you like a cup of tea? The kettle's nearly boiled."

"Yes please," said Luca.

"Take a seat," said Eric, gesturing to the two armchairs.

Luca sat down and they talked about nothing while Eric made the tea and then brought it over to the table.

"So, you wanted some advice on selling off unwanted equipment," said Eric, sitting back in his armchair and crossing his legs. "Are you planning a revamp of the café?"

"Perhaps; I'm not sure what I want to do now that Ellen is dead. I don't feel the same about the business."

Eric uncrossed his legs and sat a little more upright. "No, I guess not. I'm sorry about Ellen; such a shock for you."

Luca sat silently, waiting to see if Eric could resist asking the question that must be on his mind.

Eric stuck to the matter at hand: "If you decided to sell up I think you'd get more if you sold all the stock and equipment as a going concern rather than piecemeal."

"Yes, I suppose so."

Eric relaxed back into his chair. "I might be able to help you on such a project." He drank his tea and replaced the cup and saucer on the table. "When were you thinking of starting to wind things down?"

"I need to get the business of the chest resolved first," said Luca.

Eric's leg kicked the table as he sat bolt upright. "The chest, yes, quite a mystery as to what became of it." He took off his glasses and polished them excessively with a handkerchief. The colour of his face had faded from sallow to off-white.

"I think you can help me there too," said Luca.

A few beads of sweat glistened on Eric's brow and his handkerchief was put to a different purpose. "How do you mean?" he asked.

"You know what happened to it."

Eric gave a Luca a sickly smile. "I don't know what you're talking about."

"I think you do." Luca reached into his pocket and took out his aunt's watch. "Do you recognise this?"

Eric gave the watch a cursory glance. "I don't think so."

"Pity you've forgotten it already. You gave it as a very nice birthday present to Pearl." Luca could feel his heart thumping as he put the watch on the table.

"It's her word against mine. Why would I lie?"

"Why would she? Look, Eric, she described the chest and its contents perfectly so she must have seen it. She said she saw it here, the place where Ellen claimed she'd stored it. You don't have to be Sherlock Holmes to work it out." He sat back and waited for Eric's response.

There was no spoken response. Eric seemed to shrink as he slumped in his seat with his head down and turned away from Luca.

"I've been to the police, Eric. I've got this watch and Pearl as a witness. They're looking out for items that were in the chest."

Eric looked up, his face ashen. "Have you mentioned me to the police?"

"Not yet."

"Please don't do it, Luca; it wasn't my fault." Eric held his hands out in supplication.

"You know that your lies probably contributed to Ellen's death," said Luca, his voice rising.

Eric began sobbing quietly and his handkerchief was used for a third purpose in five minutes. "I'm so sorry, Luca, I couldn't know that that would happen."

"No, you couldn't. Tell me about the chest."

Eric dried his eyes and pulled himself together. "I did agree to look after the chest, as Ellen said, and I forgot all about it until I met Pearl. We were in the same ARP team, and one night after an evening on duty we went for a drink. One thing led to another and we started seeing each other regularly, and I used to bring her here sometimes; there's a flat above the shop. On one of her visits here she asked to see the cellar and she saw the chest. I had never even opened it before but she insisted on seeing inside. She said she liked the watch and, I had fallen for her a bit I suppose, so I gave it to her as a present. I know it was madness but at the time…"

Luca sat back in his chair and lit a cigarette. "What happened after that?"

"Pearl asked for more things but I didn't want to give them to her because I knew I would have to make good when Ellen came for the chest after the war. Instead I gave in to her on other things, and I took her to expensive clubs and the races and spent more than I could afford. Iris was getting suspicious as to why I had no money so eventually I did rob the chest to get out of debt. A lot of the items would have been unsellable but I sold a miniature painting and a solid-silver candelabra."

"Is that all?"

Eric moved uncomfortably in his chair. "There were some gold coins, twenty lire gold coins; I sold five of them."

"How much did you get for all of these things?"

"It's hard to remember exactly."

"Don't mess me about, Eric, how much?"

"£85."

Eric went over to his desk and produced a bottle of Scotch and two glasses. He poured two doubles and offered one to Luca with his shaking hands. Luca took it and thought it the most expensive Scotch he'd ever been offered.

"What happened to the rest of it?" asked Luca.

"I put the chest into storage after I'd ended it with Pearl. I planned to at least put the value of the goods back and then maybe I could have made some explanation. But the shop wasn't doing that well and after a while I just gave up on that idea and left things as they were. I thought that with you dead, Ellen would never come back for it; stupid I know, but when Ellen did come round I just panicked and lied. I'm so sorry." He shrugged.

"Eric, you did a terrible thing to lie about the chest and I don't forgive your betrayal of my friendship. But I'm not interested in revenge and I don't have any desire to send you to prison. I'm willing to offer you a way out of this."

Eric sat up a little and nodded.

"First, you take me today to the storage location and sign the chest over to me; and second, you pay me £150. I've already incurred expenses in getting back the watch; there will be others, and I don't want my aunt to lose out."

"Where will I get £150 from?" Eric threw up his hands.

Luca shook his head. "All right, £125... and I'm being very generous. Do we have a deal?"

"I should be opening the shop."

Luca rose and stood over the still seated Eric. "You're trying my patience, Eric. Let's get going, and don't try any funny business. I've told someone else where I am this afternoon. Where are the keys to the chest?"

Eric got up slowly from his chair and downed the Scotch. Then he retrieved his car keys and the keys to the chest from the desk. They walked out to the High Street to where his deep-red Austin 14 was waiting.

"I'll just lock up," he said, turning back to the door.

"Nice car," said Luca. "How did you afford that? With some of my aunt's things?"

"Iris bought it for me."

They set off for the storage company premises in Stoke Newington, and the chest was located just a few minutes after they arrived. Eric assigned the chest to Luca and it was safely loaded onto the company's van for delivery that afternoon. Luca had to pay the outstanding bill and the delivery charge, and he added this to Eric's debt.

Eric seemed to have cheered up a little by the time they were back at the shop but Luca couldn't be bothered to ask him why. As he went back to the café to wait for the chest, Luca told Eric he expected the money in cash in forty-eight hours. Though things had gone quite smoothly, Luca still had fifteen minutes of anxious pacing up and down until he saw the van arrive. For a time Luca left the chest unopened, just lying in the kitchen. Finally, he plucked up the courage to open it and checked the contents against the inventory. While he methodically went through his task, Luca's mind was not on the contents, or even on the successful reclamation of his aunt's possessions, he was thinking about the day that Ellen had gone to ask about the chest and he'd been vile to her and shaken her and she had died, and he loathed himself again. And he hated Eric for lying to Ellen and causing all this.

After he'd put everything neatly back in the chest, Luca rang Cyril and told him how the day had gone then invited him and Gwen round for a drink that evening.

XXIII

Cyril and Gwen arrived at eight o'clock and, after he'd got them both a drink, Luca took them to see the chest.

"So, this is the famous chest," said Gwen. "I'm so glad you got it back safe and sound."

"How did it go when you confronted Eric? Was it difficult to wring the truth out of him?" asked Cyril.

"Not really. At first he tried to bluff but when I showed him the watch he soon capitulated. To cut a long story short it seems he took a few things out of it to support his lifestyle through rough patches and then panicked when he couldn't afford to replace them. I went through the items today and nothing else is missing."

"So, Eric's finally come clean, mad story though it was," said Cyril. "What a fool he is. I wish I'd seen his face when you produced the watch. What are you going to do about the police? Are you going to turn him in?"

"No, not as long as he pays me the cash to replace what he took. I can't see the point of sending him to prison. Anyway, forget him. How would you like to see what's inside the chest?"

The eyes of both his guests lit up and they said, "Yes please" in unison.

Luca freed the padlocks and lifted the lid, suppressing a smile as he watched their faces.

Gwen stared open-mouthed and speechless, while Cyril muttered a mild blasphemy.

"I told you to expect a lot of gold," said Luca.

"Is this worth as much as it looks, if you don't mind my asking?" said Gwen eventually.

"Some of the pieces are very expensive but I think it would have been difficult for Eric to sell them even if he'd wanted to as I should think they're quite unusual, at least in England. Apart from their house, I would imagine what's in here accounts for most of my uncle and aunt's wealth."

"What if you hadn't got it back?"

"They would have been ruined, I guess."

Cyril and Gwen looked at some of the items; Cyril was interested in the miniature pictures, and Gwen impressed Luca with her knowledge of the fabrics and the probable period of the main items. When they'd finished browsing, Luca closed the chest and invited them to join him upstairs in the flat.

"I've some other news for you," he said, after they'd made themselves comfortable and he'd topped up their drinks. "I've decided to give up the café and go back to Ireland. I'd be grateful if you would keep this to yourselves as I don't think it's anyone else's business."

Cyril looked quite stunned. "That's a shame. Why are you leaving?" he asked. "Is it because of Ellen?"

"It's lots of things. I just don't seem to fit in here anymore. Ellen was the final straw really; there's nothing here for me now."

"We shall be sorry to lose you again," said Cyril, "but of course we understand how you must feel about things. People haven't been very kind."

"Why do you say that?" asked Luca.

"Oh, just things people have said; you know how vindictive people can be. Not many of them did much to help you."

"Will you have somewhere to go in Ireland, Luca?" asked Gwen, changing the subject.

"Well, there's a job waiting for me if I want it, and I'll soon find somewhere to live."

"You know that if there's anything we can do to tie up any loose ends, we'll be happy to do it."

"Yes, that's very good of you. Don't think I'm not grateful for everything you've done for me since I've been back. I don't want you to feel let down. If I were staying it would be largely due to you two."

A couple of days later, Eric phoned to say that he had the money. He brought it over to the café during his lunch break.

Eric seemed almost to creep into the café when Luca unlocked the door for him.

"Thanks for not getting me into trouble with the police," said Eric; "I would have lost everything."

Luca gave a non-committal grunt. "How did you raise the money?"

"I told Iris I'd lost a lot of money gambling and that I was being put under pressure to clear the debt. She was very good about it. I had to promise not to gamble again."

"It's a shame you didn't think of approaching Iris with your financial problems before. All this trouble could have been avoided."

Eric nodded. "I know. Not that it helps matters but I am truly sorry for what I did."

Luca just nodded, and Eric slunk out of the café.

Life for Luca now became a roster of tasks to complete. True to his word he sent a cheque for £50 to Pearl. Then he arranged to send his aunt's chest home. His first step was to buy five gold twenty lire coins from a bullion dealer to replace those that had been lost. Then he wrote a letter to the contessa in which he outlined his experiences since the outbreak of war and informed her of the death of Ellen. He explained that there had been a lot of upheaval during the war and that the miniature and the silver candelabra had gone missing while being moved around. He said he hoped they weren't of great sentimental value but that he was sending her a money order to replace their monetary value. Then he arranged shipment, and a week or so later watched the chest being taken away by the same delivery firm which had delivered it. He was not sorry to see the last of 'Mussolini's Chest'.

Like Atropos, the Greek Fate, cutting the thread of life, Luca was cutting one by one the threads of his very existence. With the chest disposed of he went to the bank and arranged for an international money order for £75 to be sent to his aunt. He then withdrew the balance in cash without going through the rigmarole of closing the account. This enabled him to pay off Jean and Grace, deal with the few outstanding invoices and to settle his last rent payments in advance. Finally, he cleared the café. He sold off the equipment and furniture that belonged to him for cash to a man with a rasping voice and an eye for a bargain from a commercial clearance firm and then disposed of anything else that had a value with a second-hand shop in the High Street. He worked hard to clean out the café, leaving it as near as possible in a pristine condition. Despite Cyril's protestations he did not attempt to sell the goodwill in the business.

It was now the second week in December and he wrote to Etienne Roussel to tell him that he, 'Harry', would be ready to start work back at Gillot's at the beginning of the New Year.

There remained one thread left of his old life and that was his friendship with Cyril. He'd been well acquainted with many of the other shopkeepers in the area and, in the old days, could go to any pub in the road and know half a dozen people that he could share a drink with, but these people were acquaintances rather than friends and this had been made very apparent by their reaction to him since he'd come home; he owed them nothing. Only Cyril had sought out his company when he'd returned and it was Cyril to whom he had turned when disaster occurred. So, he was pleased to have a farewell dinner with Cyril and Gwen at their home in Wanstead the week before Christmas.

When he'd last been to their house, nearly six years before, they'd shared it with their two teenage daughters but now both were married and the house was theirs alone, a fact they said they still hadn't got used to.

"Not exactly a void," said Cyril, "but you can feel that part of the life, the spirit, has gone out of the place."

"You've spent a lot of time on me since I came back; now you'll be able to put yourselves first. What are your plans for the future?" asked Luca.

Gwen smiled. "Well, I'm going to be a grandmother next year so I shall be enjoying that, especially as I can give the baby back when it's time to go home, but I don't think we have any other big plans, do we, Cyril?" she said, clearing the plates away after a dinner of sirloin of beef.

"No, I'm just wallowing in the pleasures of middle-age and declining responsibilities. The shop pretty well looks after itself but of course there will be changes when the government brings in the National Health Service. I think there will probably be more doctors' prescriptions and less of me doing my own concoctions. Can't afford to retire yet, whatever happens. What about this job in Ireland?"

"The restaurant I was working in has offered me the job of head wine waiter and it's something I would like to do. I have missed that work since I came back."

Cyril nodded. "You know, Luca, with the jobs you had in London I always thought your talents were a bit wasted in a café. I know you were your own boss and all that, but you'll be pretty much in charge of what you do in this job, won't you?"

"I think so."

After the dinner and a few more drinks, Cyril drove Luca back to the eerily empty café and Luca invited him in for a moment.

"Cyril, I owe you a lot and don't think I can ever repay it."

"It was nothing. I was just around and helped you to see things straight when you were going through a tough time. Anyone would have done the same."

"Maybe… All I know is that you did, and that's what matters." He produced a box from his pocket and handed it to Cyril. "Please take this as a sign of my gratitude and affection."

It was a gold watch and chain and the watch was inscribed: 'With grateful thanks to Cyril Johnson from his friend Luca'.

Cyril looked at it and then put it back in the box. "I don't know what to say, Luca. I shall treasure this, thanks very much. I was glad I could be of help to you and I hope we can stay in touch. But it's the future the matters more than the past; mind how you go, old friend." He shook Luca's hand for a longer time than usual then left the café – and the last thread was cut.

The following day a letter arrived from Roussel saying how pleased he was to hear that all was sorted out, and he looked forward to seeing him again, as did all the staff and management of Gillot's. Roussel also offered to put him up at his home until he'd sorted out his living arrangements. The next day Luca packed his clothes in two suitcases and sent them on in advance c/o Roussel at Gillot's.

A couple of days after that he looked round the flat and the café for the last time, seeking affectionate memories, but none came. Then he locked the premises, took a taxi to the agents in Mare Street to hand in the keys and then on to Bethnal Green underground station to carry on with his life. He sat back in the taxi and watched the roads he knew so well come into and go out of view and wondered if he would ever see them again and if he cared.

In the play that is life it is sometimes hard to determine which are the acts and which the interludes.